ce."
River Runs Gold

... transporting and captivating.
I was absolutely hooked."
Polly Ho-Yen, author of _Boy in the Tower_

★

"BOSS level MG dystopia, so vivid!"
Louie Stowell, author of _The Dragon in the Library_

★

"Nicola Penfold makes me want to love our
planet harder, hold it closer."
Rashmi Sirdeshpande, author of _How to Change the World_

★

"I loved Penfold's debut ... and this confirms her as a rising star
of children's fiction, mixing a thrilling evocative adventure with
pertinent themes of the environment and recovery."
Fiona Noble, _The Bookseller_

★

"This is compelling, high-stakes storytelling.
I stayed up late turning the pages and this will be
a favourite that I will return to over and over again."
Nizrana Farook, author of _The Girl Who Stole an Elephant_

BETWEEN
SEA
and
SKY

Nicola Penfold

For Mum, Dad and Emma

STRIPES PUBLISHING LIMITED
An imprint of the Little Tiger Group
1 Coda Studios, 189 Munster Road,
London SW6 6AW

Imported into the EEA by Penguin Random House Ireland, Morrison Chambers, 32 Nassau Street, Dublin D02 YH68

www.littletiger.co.uk

First published in Great Britain by Stripes Publishing Limited in 2021
Text copyright © Nicola Penfold, 2021
Cover image © Kate Forrester, 2021

Quote from *Poems 1955-2005* (Bloodaxe Books, 2005)
Reproduced with permission of Bloodaxe Books
Copyright © Anne Stevenson

ISBN: 978-1-78895-313-9

The right of Nicola Penfold and Kate Forrester to be identified as the author and illustrator of this work respectively has been asserted by them in accordance with the Copyright, Designs and Patents Act, 1988.

Printed and bound in the UK.

The Forest Stewardship Council® (FSC®) is a global, not-for-profit organization dedicated to the promotion of responsible forest management worldwide. FSC defines standards based on agreed principles for responsible forest stewardship that are supported by environmental, social, and economic stakeholders. To learn more, visit www.fsc.org

10 9 8 7 6 5 4 3 2 1

BETWEEN

SEA

and

SKY

Nicola Penfold

LiTTLE TiGER

LONDON

The sea is as near as we come to another world
— Anne Stevenson

ONE
Nat

The dares have started early this year. Normally we wait till summer, but there are still two weeks of school to go and coloured flags are already appearing around the bay. Like everyone got bored at the same time.

It's a trail. You put the flag someplace you shouldn't go. The marshes or shoreline, or ground still saturated with poisons from way back. Mostly it's the solar fields. The fields of silicon panels that have been our playground since we were five, even though they're strictly no access.

The flags are calling cards. Proof you've been where you say you've been. Then you dare someone else to go and get them.

I call on Lucas at 8 a.m. sharp. He's in the apartment next to me and Mum, on the top floor. *The most stairs*, Tally says when we leave her behind on the first floor.

The best view, we retort. *Yeah, of the solar fields*, she'll fling back at us.

"Flag day! Flag day!" I chant through Lucas's letter box. The door swings open into my face.

"Watch it!" he says, stepping out in front of me. "You want my parents to hear?"

"You're joking, aren't you?" I say. "No grown-ups would be awake this time on a Sunday! Mum says her eyes need to be shut for twelve hours straight after a week in the growing tower!"

Lucas smiles good-naturedly. The growing tower is the heart of Edible Uplands, the crop-growing complex where most of the adults in the compound work their shifts. Vegetable and salad plants stacked up in rows in a pink incubating light. Mum says it's like looking into a permanent sunset, especially since Central District upped their quotas again. Sometimes I wonder if they need the extra food at all. Maybe it's stacked in warehouses somewhere, rotting, and all they really want is to show their power over us.

Lucas and I spring down the concrete stairwell. We always take it three steps at a time.

"Tally?" Lucas asks at the first floor.

"She'll be at the bike sheds already," I say, swinging past him and leaping down to the ground floor.

Tally whistles when she sees me. "Nat! Mate! You've not

chickened out then?"

I shake my head, fast. Tally, Lucas and I have flagged together since nursery and today it's my turn to place the flag. A red one. Everyone uses red for their hardest dares. It's meant to be someplace dangerous, that's the point, but we've always left Billy Crier's windmill alone.

"We need to up the stakes. You said it," I say.

"*We've only got two years left, but we're still playing baby games,*" Tally had said at lunch yesterday. I'd known straight away where I'd have to go.

At some point kids stop with the daring. They get pulled into work at Edible Uplands or the desalination plant. Or inland – some assignment will come up at the polytunnels or one of the factories. We've got to make the most of our time together.

"Least there's no wind," Lucas says. I take a gulp of air. It's hot, with the lingering taste of salt. It hasn't rained in weeks.

Tally leads the way out of the compound. We live in four floors of concrete and steel, on stilted metal legs. Like some spacecraft landed years ago to refuel but never managed to lift off again. The legs have been surrounded by seawater so many times during floods that they're starting to corrode.

Even the concrete's cracking now, imploding from the inside. They built it cheap, Mum says. They didn't reckon on the wind and the heat and the salt. They should have

3

built it further back – it's too close to the sea.

"It's not too late to change the plan," Lucas continues, looking back at me. "Your mum won't want extra points."

We're standing under the board where all compound families are listed and where civil disobedience points go up against the names. For shirking shifts or missing quotas or going over the boundary, or a long list of other things Central deem impermissible.

Even when everyone's been compliant, peacekeepers still come from Central every so often to take away the top offender for the prison ship. It's a deterrent and reminder. Never forget the rules.

"Mischa better watch out," Tal says, whistling. "His dad's three off the top."

I hate that list. Our friends and neighbours, their names blur together when I look.

"We won't dare Mischa," I say quickly. "Not this time."

"Or Eli," Lucas cuts in. "His family's not far behind."

Tal shakes her head. "Nah. Sara and Luna, that's who we'll pick. Their families barely have any points at all. Those girls know how not to get caught."

"We could always do fifth field instead. We haven't done that in ages," Lucas says. He's still trying to give me an escape, but there's no way I'm backing out now. Not in front of Tal.

"Where's the fun in that?" Tally's already saying. "Fifth field is just like first field, and second and third." She lets her voice drone on for emphasis.

"No," I say, determined. "It's Billy Crier's windmill. Just like we said."

"Cool," Tally says breezily, and lifts her bike down the last few steps.

The mirrored fields dazzle you when you come out from the compound's shadow. Fields of silicon stretching away either side of Drylands Road, until everything becomes sky. There's shortages of most things round here, but sky we have in abundance.

Most people went inland during the floods. When the seawaters rose, they drowned whole villages and towns, sweeping people right off the edge of the earth, spreading disease and famine. But some people were brought back to the bay after, when the wind pumps were working again, draining seawater out of the land. Edible Uplands and the solar fields were built, and our compound, with its housing, service shops and school. Those are the things our district is known for. Them and the prison ship, brooding out on the horizon, representing everything bad about the sea.

"Race you!" Tally calls, jumping on her bike, and Lucas and I ride after her, our bike tyres cartwheeling over the maintenance tracks.

Even when there's no wind, there's something. Energy, from the ground maybe. It builds in the rotating wheels and passes up into you.

We leave our bikes stashed under one of the panels in third field. We make sure they're hidden, so no one recognizes them as ours.

I used to love these fields. It was a novelty to be out of the compound at all and we'd spend whole days tramping through them. The fields felt alive – electrons bouncing round the silicon panels, taking sunlight, parcelling it up into electricity. It's pretty miraculous. The shine just wears off after a bit.

"Looks like we're clear," Tally says, scanning the field either side. We have to be careful. If you're caught in the fields, it's one civil disobedience point. Points for minors go up against your parents. You only get your own chart when you start your shifts. No one wants to risk their parents being sent to that ship, to spend the rest of their days at sea.

We proceed on foot, single file between the panels. Tally first, then me, then Lucas.

We've flagged most places there are to flag already. All around the harbour, Customs and Immigration and Edible Uplands. Last year a flag was left at the top of the growing tower and all the kids in the compound were grounded for a month. Every single one, because no one would break ranks and say who it was that had climbed the rickety ladder. Flag rivalries aside, growing up in the compound makes you pretty tight.

Billy Crier's windmill isn't like the growing tower. The danger isn't just in the climb.

It's older than the other wind pumps. It predates not only the floods and the Hunger Years, but the Decline, and even the Greedy Years before that. It's from when the land was still healthy enough to farm, before the poisons and the saltwater got in.

"It's just a story. He was probably never even real," Lucas says, as the windmill looms closer, black and broken.

"Yeah?" I say, looking back.

Lucas nods emphatically. "Dad says they only tell about Billy Crier to keep us out of the fields."

"Liar," Tally pronounces, staring back at him defiantly.

Lucas blushes. "Well, the ghost bit at least."

"I guess Nat's going to find out," Tally says, crooking her neck ghoulishly and making an eerie kind of cry.

I laugh, to show I'm not bothered.

Billy was the same age as us. He was a runner for the smuggling gang that operated in the bay in the Hunger Years. People were so desperate for food they were dragging eels out of the marshes. If customs officers were coming, runners got the windmill operators to stop their sails at a diagonal cross, so the smugglers knew to sink their goods. It was a throwback to another time – some ancient signalling system.

The night Billy Crier was running, his dad was in the

marshes, in one of the little wooden boats. There'd been a delivery from the next district and Billy's dad was taking packages of food up to the old town.

Billy got word customs officers were coming, but when he got to the windmill, the operator refused to go up. A summer storm was coming and the brakes for the sails weren't working properly. It was too dangerous. Only Billy thought it wasn't as dangerous as it would be for his dad to be caught out on the marshes, with a full shipment of food, so he climbed up himself to stop those sails.

All the kids in the compound know the story. A freak gust of wind blowing in from the sea. Billy losing his footing. His necktie getting caught on the sail. They say he only wore that necktie to look older, like his dad.

The storm meant it was three whole days before they could get his body down. Or so the story goes.

Lucas glances across to me. "You don't have to do it, you know."

I don't say anything. We're standing at the bottom of the windmill. It's like you slip through to a different time here. No one comes, not even maintenance. Green straggly vegetation has grown up, and though the gulls barely bother with the land, sometimes they come here and sit at the top of the sails, watching.

Lucas's grandmother says the gulls are the souls of all the people that drowned in the floods.

"Nat, mate, did you hear?" Lucas says, determined to give me the chance to back out. It doesn't matter to him that Tally's listening.

The panels have started up with their whistling. It makes my heart skip a beat or two. There's a film of sweat on the back of my neck. "Do you think Billy was scared?" I ask suddenly. "The night he climbed?"

Tally's gone ahead into the doorway. Her face is dim in the shadows. "You know Crier wasn't his real name?" she says in a lower tone than usual. "It was 'cause of all his crying that night."

Lucas giggles nervously. "Well, he can't have cried for long, can he? Not after a fall like that." He does the same neck twist that Tally did earlier.

A gull screams at the top of the windmill and flutters up into the sky. "Something scared it," Tally says, looking at me intently.

I push past her into the windmill. I want it done with. I want that flag up there and it to be someone else's job to get it down.

I peer up through the space in the ceiling where the steps used to be. Someone took them out years ago to deter climbers, but they didn't do a great job 'cause the next set of steps is still there. And the set after that. More like a ladder than actual steps, but still there. You can see them all the way to the top, like snakes and ladders.

The noise of the panels has got up outside. A pinging, like someone repeatedly twanging an elastic band.

"You got the flag?" Lucas checks.

"Course!" I show him a flash of red from my pocket.

"You don't have to climb out properly," Lucas says, scared now. "As long as you can see it from the outside. The flag doesn't have to be right out on the sails, does it, Tal?"

Tally shakes her head. She looks scared too, just a tiny bit, and a shiver runs down my spine. Tally shrugs when she sees me looking. "It's just a flag, isn't it? We could even leave it down here. The others would still be too scared to come in."

We all nod. This place is taboo. There are no names sprayed on the walls like you get round the compound – bored kids, proving their existence. Billy's windmill is totally empty. Just the few odd stinging plants – nettles and thistles. Sometimes the plants grow round Edible Uplands too, before maintenance get paranoid about pests or disease and rip them up. Nothing can jeopardize the growing tower. It's what keeps us all alive.

"Right, I'm going up. Catch me if I fall," I say, stepping through the doorway.

Lucas tuts disapprovingly, but comes forward to give me a leg up to the first floor. I scrabble on to the dusty floorboards above.

TWO
Nat

It's dark inside and there's an odd creaking that sounds throughout the building. The sails don't turn any more – they were permanently braked years ago – but it feels like they're going round anyway.

"You all right, Nat? Are the steps sound?" Lucas's voice trembles slightly. He hates flag days. If it were up to him, we'd leave all our flags in the compound.

I put my hand on the iron rungs to the next floor and give them a shake. They groan, but don't wobble enough that I can back out.

"What's it like?" Tally calls.

"Dark. Dusty," I say.

"And? Is there anything there?" she says impatiently.

"Nothing," I say. "Some old sacks. Names on the wall."

"Names?" Tally shrieks. "Someone's been up?"

I laugh quietly at her indignation. "Not for ages. They look old. Carved in the wood." I run my fingers over the letters. I shiver – it's like fingers walking down my spine. "Billy's here," I whisper.

"What?" Tally shouts.

"Billy," I repeat, louder, uncomfortable now, like I'm trespassing somewhere sacred. "His name's here."

"Billy Crier?" Lucas asks.

"Just Billy. And his mates, I guess." I read them out. Billy's last on the list. *Jones, Yusuf, Mara, Olive, Billy.* The names are written together, but in different writing, like each of them scratched out their name themselves.

BILLY. The letters are jagged and deep. It could be any Billy, but I know it's him. I feel it. Billy Crier, up here one summer's day with his mates, or at night, after the windmill operator had gone home. Billy, carving out his name by torchlight. Never imagining what would happen.

"Nat, you going on up?" Tally says. "We don't want to hang around longer than we need to." She sounds nervous.

I'm almost on the third floor when there's a scrambling noise below. "Nat! Nat!" Lucas shrieks. "Someone's coming. Uplands people. Hide!"

Tally swears loudly. "How did we not see them coming?"

"Lucas? Lucas!" I hiss. But there's silence below. Tally and Lucas have already scarpered.

I'm about to leg it back down when I hear footsteps outside. Voices.

I pull myself up the rest of the way on to the third floor, wincing when the ladder creaks. The voices outside carry on uninterrupted.

I crawl along the wooden floor to where there's a little window at floor level. I lie horizontal and peer out to the ground below.

There are two people. A man and a woman. They're both workers from the Uplands, I recognize them. They're wearing white, wipe-clean, seamless suits, that are anti everything – bacteria, virus, fungus, general grime. The woman's got a box and is looking down into the thistles like she lost something. She picks something up with gloved fingers and holds it out to the man. I can't make out what she's saying.

They seem to be transferring leaves to the box. The man keeps pulling a face and rubbing his hands on his legs, like he's touching something unpleasant. The woman lifts up a leaf to her face and stares at whatever she's seeing on it.

"That's all of them, surely? Don't know why Central are so bothered. Not if the things die anyway," the man says, louder now. He sounds bored.

The woman gazes to the top of the windmill. "I swear I saw something. Some movement."

I retreat back into the darkness, willing myself invisible.

The man's looking now too. "They say this mill's haunted. That boy who was strung up on the sails, back in the Hunger Years." He laughs nervously.

"Billy Crier, poor lad," the woman says sadly, before they both head off down the maintenance track with their boxful of whatever it was they were collecting.

I jump back down the ladders. Both flights to the first floor, then a final leap down and out into the sunshine. My eyes blink after the dark of the windmill.

"Tal? Lucas?" My voice sounds emptily across the fields. There's nothing but the hum of the panels.

I crouch down next to the thistles. I've never noticed the leaves before. They're pointy, with prickly hairs on them, like the nettles that grow round the compound, before maintenance come and rip them all out.

No one would come out here for thistles. What was it they were collecting?

I rifle through the plants. They're just leaves. I'm about to spring up, to get away from this place, when I notice it. A creature – moving, living. A tiny black thing with miniscule hairs. It's inside a sort of webbing. It looks a bit like a maggot, the kind you see when the vacuum packs of meat are left open too long. But from the way the woman was looking at the creatures, boxing them up, they can't be maggots.

There's a prickle on the back of my neck, as if someone's

watching, and I look round again for Tally and Lucas, but they're nowhere in sight. There's no one there, just me, and Billy's ghost.

I go through the thistles again, quicker now. There are more creatures further on, huddled together on a fresh set of plants. The man and woman must have missed them.

I drop one of the creatures from the leaf on to my palm. Its little, segmented body soft against my skin. It tickles.

There are always scary stories about pests or fungus coming to the bay. About the Hunger Years coming back with a vengeance. Mum gets angry when I don't take them seriously. "*You don't know what it's like, Nat. To know hunger like that.*" The adults have the Hunger Years etched deep in their heads and their bellies. That's why they put up with all the rules.

"Are you dangerous?" I whisper to the tiny creature.

I take out the red flag from my pocket and spread it over the ground and then transfer the creatures into it. There must be two dozen or so. I add some leaves, because from the holes in them, I think that's what the creatures eat.

I don't know why I take them. Perhaps it's because the Uplands people want them. Or maybe it's something to show Tally, to make up for not hanging out the flag.

THREE
Pearl

16th July
Weather still and hot. Blue sky. Not a breath of wind.
A good day for a wishing.

We're painting the exterior of our cabin – yellow against the blue sky. It's weather protection, but we might as well make it colourful. Clover picked up the paints from the hardware shop on the mainland. She chose a whole rainbow but her enthusiasm is less bright than yesterday, when she had clattered off the motorboat with a toppling stack of cans.

"It's the hottest it's been in ages, Pearl. I want to go swimming." Clover's looking over the water longingly. There are four sleek, grey bodies breaking the surface – turning like little wheels.

"We have to paint a bit every day, otherwise it will never get done. Like Dad says."

"Does he?" Clover says, furrowing her eyebrows. "Does he really say that any more?"

There are snores from inside the cabin and I blush on Dad's behalf. He's flat out on the sofa.

Clover's voice sings out. "I can't remember the last time Dad helped with anything."

"He took you ashore yesterday, didn't he? He just needs more time, after that winter…"

I shudder, thinking about the winter. Ice formed all the way round our platform. We had to break it up with axes to get to the oysters. Even in April, we were still breaking up the ice.

"It's been warm for ages now," Clover says dismissively.

"I know, but the cold gets to Dad more because he's older, and…" My voice trails away. I inhale a deep breath of sea air. It's thick with salt. Tangy.

If you look towards land, the mudflats are already appearing, like a magical kingdom rising up from under the sea, all green and gold. It'll be glorious out there today. A perfect day for mudlarking, where we find washed-up treasure in the sand that's exposed when the tide goes out. The finds twinkle extra sparkly when it's sunny.

"I'm going to do a wishing," I say. "Later. When the tide's full out."

"You've got to leave off with the wishing, Pearl. You're getting too old," Clover preaches in someone else's voice. Somebody from one of her books maybe. Clover's always imagining a life other than our own. She wasn't so annoying before she could read.

I pull a face. "Mum wished."

"It was a game, Pearl. She was playing a game for us," Clover says, kindly now. My ten-year-old little sister, telling me I should have grown up by now and found some other way of forecasting our future than using the things that turn up in the mud.

"Grey!" I say, looking past her. Clover runs to the edge of the platform and throws herself flat on her front, her fingers trailing down into the water. Grey nudges up to her, wanting fish.

You shouldn't have favourites, but Clover and I love Grey best. The round, smiling bulk of him.

"The wishing brought Grey, didn't it? And the others," I say.

Clover rolls on to her back, her head hanging over the side of the platform, yellow hair streaming into the water like beams of sunshine. She's laughing and Grey's prodding her. "Maybe. Maybe it did," she says playfully.

When Grey first came, Clover had wished for a friend. It was a couple of years ago now. She did it out of spite because we'd argued, but it was still a bona fide wish.

She'd used her best treasures. Things we'd found on the flats, larking – the cracked face of an old porcelain doll, a broken comb, a swirly black marble. She'd laid them in a ring of periwinkles and left them for the tide to take, whispering out her wish to the sea. "A friend who'll understand me," she'd said, looking at me deliberately as she spoke.

And that was the day they came, gliding in from beyond the prison ship, like they'd always been here.

Clover noticed them first. She's never forgotten that the first two mammals in my sea ledger were her spot.

"Mermaids!" she'd yelled certainly across the deck. Dad was inside, sleeping. Even back then he'd sleep a lot. I'd been shucking oysters, so intent on the knife in my hands that I hadn't noticed the squat little bodies surround our sea platform, breaking the surface with their triangle fins.

"Mermaids!" Clover had screamed again, jumping up and down with delight.

Dad had guffawed when he made it out on to the platform. "They're not mermaids! They're a type of cetacean. Porpoises."

I'd repeated the word softly. *Porpoises.* Harbour porpoises, Dad had said. All I really knew about were the bivalves we farm in the lantern nets under our platform, and down in the cages on the floor of the sea. I hadn't set foot in the prison library back then.

We weren't sure what else might exist. I don't think we thought anything else could, so much had been lost in the Decline.

"Harbour porpoises?" Clover had said curiously.

"That's right. Sorry to disappoint you, my little legume." Dad had used her favourite pet name and flung her up into the air. He'd had more energy then. "You and Pearl are the closest this bay will ever get to mermaids."

"Are they sisters, like Clover and me?" I'd asked excitedly, but Dad had shaken his head. It was a mother and a child, he'd told us, and Clover and I had gone all solemn.

"It's a blessing to have them back," Dad had said, as he tucked us into our hammocks that night. It was a happy thing, but Dad's voice had been sad. "You should be recording this, big one." Big one is me, and because Dad doesn't issue many instructions, and because the porpoises seemed so happy, I had started my ledger the next morning, backdating it one day for accuracy.

Grey's the little one, all grown up now. His mum swam on at some point, but Grey's never gone away.

Once I found my way into the prison library during a delivery to the ship, I found out all sorts about our new friends. Olive, a prisoner who sorts the books, found the perfect book. *Cetaceans of the UK – Whales, Dolphins and Porpoises*. The books in the mainland library are all new – any old ones were washed away in the floods – but the good thing about a library on a ship is that it floats. Their books may be yellow and ancient, but they survived.

Sometimes Clover will bring back more up-to-date reading material when she goes ashore with Dad for supplies. Some pro-compound propaganda pamphlets about working your shifts, the greater good, not wasting food, loyalty to Central. Clover studies them like they're engaging even though I can tell she's bored. She's much happier with the old novels I sneak back from the ship.

Cetaceans breathe air, like we do. They're aquatic mammals and give birth to live young. The writer of *Cetaceans of the UK* says harbour porpoises are shy and retiring, but ours aren't. There's nothing shy about porpoises when they want food. They come for the schools of fish that gather under our farm. Dad says our farm's a veritable coral reef.

The book says people used to call porpoises puffing pigs because of the noise they make when they breathe. I never heard a pig, but I can imagine them from hearing the porpoises.

I can hear Grey now. *Choo, choo, choo*, like he's sneezing. Clover strips off into her pink cotton swimsuit.

"You can't!" I cry aghast. "We've got to finish this paint coat. Storms don't stop because it's summer!"

She beams. "They will if you command them to, Pearl.

Can't you wish for that? A summer of no storms?"

"Clover! You know it isn't like that!"

"Can't you wish anything you want if you leave the right offerings?" She puts her hands into a prayer sign.

"Clover!" I repeat, though I'm already loosening the ties on my shorts.

"Come in with me! The painting will wait. Look at that sky!"

Clover raises her arms up above her head. She flicks me a smile as she dives down into the water, where Grey's waiting to greet her, snorting away.

I can't help but smile too, looking up, looking all around us, because when you live at sea the sky's everywhere. It's a fifth element. And today there's not a cloud in sight. Clover's right, the painting can wait.

I press the lid tight on the yellow paint pot, then I'm diving in after her, unable to ignore the sea's call any longer.

FOUR
Pearl

We swim round the platform. We swim in circles and figures of eight. Butterfly, backstroke, front crawl, breaststroke. All the ways Mum taught us to propel ourselves through the water.

Grey doesn't stick around for long, and nor do the others. The fish must have moved on. "Farewell, Grey. Goodbye, Smile! See you later, Salt! So long, Snort!" Clover calls.

Dad laughed at us for not picking more eloquent names, but I think they suit the porpoises.

We lie on our backs like starfish before diving down, pulling ourselves deeper along the rope lines of the scallop nets and mussel socks, to the oyster cages and clams at the bottom. With a big enough breath of air, we can make it right down to the seabed where there's barely any light left.

Some of the cages are full – crammed with big, fat shells,

hardly any space between them. We need to bring them up; they're ready for harvest.

I gesture to Clover at the cages. She was meant to have separated these oysters out last week. She told me she had.

I shake one of the cages pointedly and the water darkens around us. Clover pulls a funny forgive-me face and starts making her way back up to the light.

I wait for a moment, the pressure of the sea drumming against my ears. Clover and I used to have competitions to see which of us could stay down the longest. We'd count out the seconds, holding hands, gazing into each other eyes. I learned every fleck of green in her blue irises.

Clover's lost interest lately. She's always up first, wanting to surface.

I kick my way up, after her.

"Race you!" Clover cries, as I break the surface, and she shoots on by towards the flats. Butterfly stroke, fast, to make me laugh.

"We have to do those cages," I say when I reach her, sprawled languidly out on the mud. "The algae's bad again."

Clover pulls a face. "Later, though? We'll do it together, after larking."

I nod and take her hand to pull her up. We can never resist the flats on a day like today.

Clover and I used to mudlark all the time with Mum.

Even when she was sick, Mum would summon up the energy for larking. She said the finds gave her energy.

I think she was looking for the right thing. She didn't know what it was, or at least she wasn't able to put it into words, but maybe if it had washed up on the sand before her, that would have been the turning point. Then she'd have started to get better.

Only it didn't turn up, whatever it was she was looking for, and the doctor from the compound hospital came and said there was nothing left for him to do. He told us Mum ought to go to the mainland so they could better manage her condition. Only they didn't actually mean that, they meant better manage her dying. Even though it was the land that got her sick in the first place.

"Look, Pearl. A face." Clover's voice is clear as a bell.

I tremble a fraction. We get our fair share of faccs, though now it's almost always just the bones underneath. The floods washed so many people away they'll be washing up forever. Eventually they'll be fossils.

But Clover's not found anything ghoulish. She's sunk on her knees and is digging with her fingers.

It's an old doll. Plastic. The eyes have long washed away, so there are just two hollow sockets and a little snub nose, which is surprisingly intact. The doll's got two arms but only one leg, and even that's missing a foot. She's in need of a mermaid's tail. I'll carve one out of driftwood before I send her on her way again.

"You could paint it," Clover says. "It would be good for your wishings."

She's smiling at me sweetly and I nod, trying not to notice how she always calls them *my* wishings now, when they used to belong to us both.

After years of larking you end up with too many of certain things. Mum started the wishings as a way of giving them back to the sea. We'd lay things out at low tide and wait for the water to take them, sending our wish as they went.

In the beginning, we laid the offerings in circles, but after Mum died we got more adventurous. We found an old book in her office. *Rituals, Magic, Witchcraft*. It's about white magic, or Wicca, which is magic to do good. The book's damaged – whole pages bleached out from seawater or sun – but somehow the gaps make the surviving sections more important.

We wish to get better when one of us is sick. For a winter without the sea freezing over. For the geese to come back in October.

We wish for things we want too. A new dress for Clover. A notebook or pencil for me. Those things don't turn up very often, but sometimes they do. Not washed up by the sea, but once in a while Dad will bring something back from a supply run.

Pretty much all our spells and chants come from the Wicca book. The shapes too. Triangles and stars.

Pentangles, five-pointed stars, are my favourite. Five points for spirit, water, fire, earth and air.

Water is the sea all around us. Earth the poisoned land. Air's the sky where the gulls fly.

Fire is the Decline. Here it was floods and the rising storm water, but elsewhere it was fire. The world got too hot. Fire burned forests and villages, whole cities too.

Spirit is everything that was lost. For us spirit is Mum, because she got lost too.

Clover's digging efforts have paid off. She lifts the doll from the mud triumphantly. "Ta-da! She's a pretty one, isn't she, Pearl?"

"Yeah, she's pretty," I say nonchalantly.

"You can have her." Clover holds the doll out to me, her arm stretched tight. "Take it. She's more your thing than mine."

I take the brittle figure but I don't say anything. I run my finger over the smooth face. All the places the sea has touched. I place the doll down on the sand and start marking out a pentangle with my toes.

Clover turns cartwheels, her shadow turning alongside her so she looks like two people. She's coming deliberately close to my star.

"Careful!" I say, irritated.

"I wish something exciting would wash up," Clover says. "Something we've never seen before. I'm so bored. B. O. R. E. D."

Clover writes the letters in the sand with her finger. One straight line of capitals. She does this a lot lately. She'll write FED UP, or RESCUE ME! Like someone might see. Clover's always wanted to be noticed.

Then she flops down and lies on her back, looking up at the sky.

"Watch your eyes," I say automatically. In winter we worry about the wind, but in summer it's the sun that can be the enemy. It glints off the sand particles and burns your skin. Burns your eyes too, if you aren't careful.

Clover sighs and turns over, so her face is flat on the sand instead. Her voice comes out muffled. "I'm going to ask Dad to send me to school in September."

I stare at her, open-mouthed. Clover stays still, face down, listening for my reaction. I can't think of a single sound to make.

"I need to learn, Pearl," she says, still speaking into the sand. "I'll never achieve my dreams stuck out here. You know how much I want to see other places and meet new people. I'm going to ask Dad."

"Clover, you can't! You're a secret!" I gasp.

"*One* of us is," Clover says purposely. "*One* of us is a secret. There's one school place, if we ask for it."

"Don't you dare!" I cry, outraged. "Look what the land did to Mum!"

Clover's silent for a moment, but she turns reluctantly on to her side to look at me. She spits out a mouthful of mud. "It's just going to school, Pearl. Like every other kid in this entire bay except us."

"But we're not in the bay, are we?" I exclaim. "We're at sea. The compound school wouldn't want a sea girl!"

Clover sits up, her eyes lit with fury. "Don't call me that. We're no different from them. *I'm* no different."

"That's not what they'll think," I say meanly. The first time Dad took Clover back to land, a kid called her a sea witch right to her face. She won't let us talk about it, but she's never forgotten. Only Clover's not like me. The landlubber taunts don't make her want to stay away – they just make her want to prove them wrong.

"I deserve to go to that school. Just because you..." Clover's voice fades out.

A gull flies above. We watch its shadow on the sand, cutting between us.

"Just because you never wanted to go," Clover finishes.

"You won't fit in," I say quietly.

Clover's voice trembles. "I'll make myself fit in."

"Dad's a better teacher than they've got, I bet."

Clover laughs bitterly, her eyes wet. "You're joking, Pearl? Dad barely gets out of bed! When was the last

29

time he got the books out?"

She turns away from me to look out to land and I follow her gaze, to the upright cylinder of the crop farm and the stilted compound where the workers live. That's where the school is that Clover's become so obsessed with.

Clover's right. Our schoolbooks were put away in a trunk before a storm months ago and none of us have bothered to get them out. We've dropped any pretence of schooling. But how can Clover want to go to land? To give up our freedoms and obey all the rules the compounders have to live by?

Rations.

Curfew.

Shifts.

"I want to make friends, Pearl," Clover says, quieter now.

"You've got Grey, and the others," I retort. And you've got me, I want to say. Only I don't, because I know she'll throw it back at me. Clover can be as cruel as the sea in a storm sometimes.

"People, not porpoises," Clover says, enunciating each word deliberately. "I want proper friends."

"Olive would like you. You should come to the ship, for the deliveries," I grasp.

Clover rolls her eyes. "I'm not making friends with prisoners, Pearl. Old cronies."

I let out a sharp breath of air. "Olive's not an old crony.

Don't say that!"

"She's ancient, Pearl. You can't deny it."

"She's no crony."

"Yeah, well," Clover says stubbornly. "You don't know what she even did. She must be there for a reason!"

"Olive wouldn't have done anything bad," I say fiercely.

When the seas rose, the authorities said land was too precious for anyone who didn't deserve it. All kinds of people were put on that ship. Hungry, desperate people. When I try and talk to Olive about it, she goes blank. I don't think she even remembers.

Clover shrugs. "I'm going to go to school, Pearl. You can't stop me. I want it more than anything in the world."

FIVE
Nat

There are five computers in the compound library. You're meant to book ahead to get time on one, but they're not popular enough for that. They're slow and break halfway through doing anything. All you really need to do to get one is smile nicely at Mr Rose, the librarian.

The machines are in a narrow space running along the back of the compound. Tally says Mr Rose put them here to keep them hidden. Out of sight, out of mind. There's mostly just old games on the computers, but there's an old encyclopedia too. Random facts about life before the Decline that maybe Central wouldn't want us knowing.

The encyclopedia's why we're here now. Tally insisted we research the creatures I found.

"It's loading," Lucas says.

"Sounds like we're breaking it!" I say, as the machine

cranks through its old memory.

"It better not break," Tally says from the window.

I go and stand next to her. You don't get this view from anywhere else in the compound. The compound was built to face inland, out of respect to everyone that died in the floods, but the low, wide windows of the computer corridor look out to sea.

You can see the lines of razor wire, then miles of mud and sea with only the weird oyster farm breaking the grey, and the prison ship after that.

"Look at her," Tally says. "The sea witch is out."

I strain my eyes. Sometimes it's hard to tell where the mud stops and the water begins; it blurs into one and plays tricks with your eyes.

But there is a smudge in all the grey. A tiny, moving vertical.

"She's got her ghost with her," Tally says.

I laugh. "Don't let Lucas hear you say that."

I can feel Lucas rolling his eyes behind us and I wait for his voice to pipe up about reflections and shadows. He hates the ghost stories. He says they offend his scientific brain.

"You shouldn't call her a witch," is what he actually says.

Tally doesn't even blink. "It's not an insult, is it? I'd swap places with her in a heartbeat. I'd be a witch if it meant I could live out there. Or a ghost. I'd haunt the peacekeepers.

I'd haunt all of them."

"Tal!" Lucas warns.

"What? You're not going to tell on me, are you?" she teases.

I laugh. Tally's hatred for the peacekeepers is well known. When she was eight her parents had an illegal second child. They knew from the beginning the baby would be taken, and Tally's mum cried her way through the pregnancy. She died soon after the baby was born from some freak infection. Our District Controller, Ezra Heart, said that as Tally and her dad had lost her mum, they might be able to keep the baby. He said it was worth a try. A test case, he said. He appealed to Central for them – for leniency.

The appeal dragged on for almost two years, which turns out is way too long to live with a little kid and not fall in love them. And not just for Tally and her dad. You don't get many babies in the compound and we all loved Barnaby. But when the decision came back from Central, the answer was no. Tally's family couldn't keep a second child. The peacekeepers came to take Barnaby to the Communal Families to be raised for shift work inland.

Losing Barnaby broke Tally and her dad's hearts most of all, but all our hearts broke a little. And after that Ezra Heart stopped even trying to push back against Central's demands. He must have decided it wasn't worth it.

That's when Tally, Lucas and I started hanging out more

in the solar fields, and here in the computer corridor, playing old games the processors can still handle, like *Lemmings* and *Space Invaders*.

"It's up," Lucas says, reading from the screen theatrically. "'Welcome to the World. All-new reference guide. Comprehensive and up to date. All your questions answered!'"

"Budge up then," Tally says, squeezing into the seat next to him. Her fingers flutter over the keyboard and *butterflies* appears in the grey search bar.

"You really think that's what they are?" I whisper, looking over my shoulder to check no one's nearby. "They don't look much like Mum's picture."

We have a painting of butterflies in our kitchen, above our table but low on the wall, so you can look right into it when you eat. Bright-winged creatures flying around trees of pink blossom. It's Mum's prized possession. It used to belong to her grandmother. Mum brought it with her when we were posted here from inland.

"They look just the same as the caterpillar in that book I used to read to Barn. Honestly, Nat. I swear they do." Tally's voice doesn't miss a beat when she talks about her brother, but she goes slightly robotic. Like she's removed herself a little from what she's saying.

"It starts with an egg," Tally says. "There's an egg on a leaf and it hatches into this caterpillar that doesn't stop eating.

35

It eats holes through all kinds of weird things. I don't even know where the book came from, but I swear the caterpillar looked like yours. Except this one was green."

"Here," Lucas says, leaning into the screen. We're sat in a row in front of the cranky computer. "Butterflies," he reads out. "Insects in the order 'lepidoptera'. They undergo complete metamorphosis."

"Meta-what?" I ask.

"Metamorphosis. Change," Lucas says, continuing to read. "The egg hatches into a larva, or caterpillar, which grows bigger and sheds its skin through a series of moults, before hanging upside down and spinning itself into a chrysalis."

"Exactly!" Tally says triumphantly. "Like I told you. It eats and sleeps on repeat. And then it turns into a butterfly in the cocoon thing."

"Shush," I say. "If they are butterflies, we've got to be careful. They're on my windowsill, remember." I can feel my heart racing. Butterflies are property of Central District. All sightings must be reported.

Tally ignores me. She's peering at the screen. There are labels for four separate life stages. Egg. Caterpillar. Chrysalis. Butterfly. But the pictures aren't loading, there's a slowly flashing icon of a grey paintbrush instead. "They stole the pictures," Tally says angrily.

"Why would they do that?" I say. "Pictures aren't going

to hurt anyone."

"They make us think about the past, though," Lucas replies, matter-of-fact. "Stops us looking to the future."

"'Be future thinking'," I mutter, reciting one of our school values.

"Falsifiers," Tally declares murderously. "Do they think we can't handle knowing what we're missing out on?"

"Red Admiral," I say, reading the caption under one of the flashing paintbrushes.

"There were lots of different types," Lucas says, scrolling down the page. "Peacock, Common Blue, Meadow Brown, Holly Blue, Brimstone, Painted Lady, Speckled Wood, Gatekeeper, Swallowtail, Skipper."

I shiver at the old names. You can hear the computer winding through its memory but the paintbrush icons stay grey.

"How can we tell anything without the pictures?" Tally sighs, frustrated. "We need an actual book. I'm going to ask Mr Rose!"

"Tal! You can't!" I call after her, but she's already striding down the corridor and turning back on to the main library floor, where Mr Rose sits behind a stack of pamphlets ready for repair.

"We're looking for books about insects of the order lepidoptera," Tally pronounces.

Lucas groans into his hands. "If anyone finds out you

took those things from the fields, Nat!"

"They won't find out, will they?" I snap nervously. "Unless someone tells…"

I creep to the end of the corridor to listen. Tally's not shut up about the caterpillars since I showed her. It's all she's talked about since she sailed up to my room with no apology for abandoning me halfway up a windmill with a ghost – just questions about what Uplands people wanted in the fields and then total fascination with the creatures. She calls them ours, even though I'm the one the points would go to. Or rather Mum, which makes it a hundred times worse.

I should hurl the creatures down the rubbish chute. I might have done too, except Tally makes us go for fresh leaves every day and they're eating and getting bigger. What kind of person would I be to throw them to their deaths now?

Mr Rose's eyes twinkle with amusement. "Where have you dragged that one up from? Lepidoptera? It's a long time since I heard that word."

"You know what it means then?" Tally says, her eyes dark and shiny.

"Lepidoptera. Insects with scaled wings. Butterflies and moths." The words float out of Mr Rose's mouth, like he's enjoying saying them. Our parents were all kids when the Decline happened. Bees and butterflies were already gone.

Mostly our parents just remember the hunger. But Mr Rose is older. I wonder if he remembers skies humming with insects?

"Butterflies are pollinators, aren't they?" Tally says pointedly.

Mr Rose gazes at her, surprised.

"They are, aren't they?" she presses.

Pollinators are symbols of the Recovery. It's in the small print, in the rules plastered all over our compound. If pollinators return, it's a sign the Recovery has begun and the siege state laws that govern every bit of our lives will finally be relaxed. That was the promise Central gave when they took control of the districts.

"*Were* pollinators," Mr Rose says sadly. "They *were* pollinators."

"I knew it!" Tally smiles back at me and puts her thumbs up. "We want to see pictures. The computer won't show them."

Mr Rose shakes his head. "Images like that won't have survived. You're lucky you found anything. Why are you interested anyway?"

He looks over to me curiously, sensing me watching. I freeze.

Tally shrugs. "There was a butterfly in Barn's favourite book. I sent him off with it, to the Families. I wanted to see a picture of one, to remember…"

Mr Rose's face moulds itself into an expression of sympathy and Tally scowls. She doesn't think Barnaby should be anyone else's sadness but hers and her dad's.

"This library's useless," she says, and Mr Rose flinches a little.

"Tal!" Lucas groans again beside me.

"If you tell me what you want to know, perhaps I can help, Tallulah?" Mr Rose prods gently.

Tally pulls a face and stomps back to us. A couple of kids nearby who've listened to the whole thing snigger into their hands. Tally glares at them furiously.

Back in our corridor, she goes straight to the glass, her face pressed up against it. Tally looks out to sea way more than anyone else. She's not scared of it, not even when the storm clouds form, like a giant hammer, and the siren's sounding for us all to take cover in the bunker halfway up our compound – the safest place from floods and high winds.

Tally would absolutely run away to sea, if she could. Anything to get away from the district and its rules.

"Sorry, Tal," I say awkwardly.

"I swear sometimes there are two of them," Tally murmurs.

"Huh?" I reply, confused.

"The sea witch and her ghost. Look," she says.

I follow her gaze. You can barely see the figure – a thin

shape moving horizontally against the wide expanse of sand. It'll be the girl from the oyster farm. I often see her walking out there. She's hazy in the heat.

"Can you see, Nat?" Tally presses. "Two of them?"

Maybe there are two figures. They never come close enough to land to really know.

I rub at my eyes. "How can you even see that far?"

Tally sighs loudly. "You just got to grow those caterpillars, Nat. Let them do their metamorphosis thingy. That can be our proof that the Recovery's started. Our district's been kept down long enough. Even without a picture, Central can't pretend they don't know what a butterfly looks like, can they?"

I shrug. "But they must know already. What they are, I mean. Or else why take them?"

"That's obvious, isn't it? Central don't want proof that the Recovery's begun, not out in the districts anyway. They want things to stay the same – us stuck here, our parents working in the growing towers, while they get the best of everything. It's working out fine for them, isn't it?" Tally bangs her forehead deliberately into the glass. Her fists too, knuckles pressed white. "They don't want butterflies in the bay, they want to keep them all for themselves. They've probably got glass palaces full of butterflies in Central, collected from pathetic districts like ours, so we can be kept down. I can't stand it. And our

41

useless District Controller's not going to change anything, is he? Old Ezra!"

She turns round and stares at us. "Those caterpillars are our chance to do something! Nat? Lucas?"

I get this shiver of excitement. We've never had chance to do anything before.

"It doesn't mean you'll get Barnaby back," Lucas says quietly, still at the computer, staring down at the keyboard. "Even if those things are butterflies, all it says is siege state laws will be relaxed. It doesn't say revoked or anything. Central will make it mean what they like."

Tally stiffens but doesn't say anything.

"I just don't think you should get your hopes up," Lucas says, his face red. "That's all."

Tally turns her head to me, pointedly. "I'll see you by the bike sheds after school, Nat. To get more thistles."

She doesn't even look at Lucas as she goes by.

SIX
Pearl

20th July
The sea's holding on to the heat. We saw another pod of porpoises, far out – they didn't stop.

Magwitch and Pip are always flying off inland and they're catching more fish than usual. Could they have a nest somewhere? Maybe we'll have cormorant babies this summer?!!

Dad's playing with the oysters on his plate. He's not meeting our eyes. I know he's got something to say, because if not he'd up and leave back to his cabin. I can't remember the last time we sat down and had lunch together.

Clover's not noticed anything is wrong. She's reading a new pamphlet from the compound library. *Rosa's Resolve*. Some insipid tale of working hard in the districts and making the best of what you've got, written by some person in Central who's probably never even seen the sea.

I wonder when Clover's going to bring up school, or whether she will at all. If I can persuade Dad to start with the teaching again, she might let it go. I should at least get the textbooks out of the trunk. Clover's convinced education is her path off our farm.

"I've some news for you, girls," Dad says finally, slamming his hands down either side of his plate.

Clover looks up, surprised.

"We're going to have visitors." Dad's voice is flat.

"Visitors!" I say, my jaw dropping in astonishment. "What do you mean, visitors?"

Clover shuts her book and sits up straighter. "People, Pearl! You know, of the Homo sapiens variety! Who, Dad?"

"Some researcher from Edible Uplands. And her child. They're going to stay with us for the summer."

I stare at Dad open-mouthed. "Stay? You mean, live here?"

"Guests!" Clover's squealing. "New people!"

"What about us?" I cry. "No one can see us together. No one! You're the one always saying it!"

Dad glances across at me with downcast eyes. "It'll be all right, Pearl!"

"What do you mean it'll be all right?" I scream, my heart racing. "We'll be discovered!"

Dad sighs. "Ezra Heart says no confidence will be breached. He cornered me the other day on land.

44

We can trust her, he says. This scientist of his." He slams his fist on the table again, softer this time, defeated.

I breathe new air. Taste salt on the roof of my mouth. "No confidence will be breached… You mean he knows?" My voice rises hysterically. "Ezra knows about us? About me and Clover?"

Dad nods miserably.

"How can he know?" I fire back.

Dad gives a tired shrug. "Your mum worked there, didn't she, at the Uplands? Vita was their researcher once. Their best one." Dad's voice crackles with pain, splits open with it. "Anyway, she's coming. This scientist and her child too. I can't stop it."

"What are their names? How old is the child?" Clover's saying. She puts her book down and sidles closer to Dad. She's drumming her feet on the floor and the platform rocks a little faster than usual.

Dad purposefully doesn't look at me. "It's a boy," he says. "Your age, or maybe closer to Pearl's age. He goes to school at the compound."

"A compound child, to tell tales on us and call us sea witches? And we're letting them come? Just like that? Landlubbers!" I splutter.

Dad winces. "Don't call them that. Like they're a different species."

"Well, they are, aren't they? As good as!" I say. It feels we evolved differently out here, Clover and I. Seal skin, strong lungs, mermaid's hair. Sometimes I look down at my toes and imagine them webbing together.

Before Clover goes to the mainland, she washes her hair out. She washes it with desalinated water and tugs a comb through it, complaining about the seawater that has tangled it up into knots. I love how my hair is black like the mussels when they're wet and thick with salt and wind. I flick it back now over my shoulders.

"I don't know where they'll sleep," Dad mutters.

"The old office," Clover pipes up. "I can clean it out for them. And there are those old mattresses in the store. We can put them on the benches for them to sleep on, and—"

"That's Mum's space," I cut in.

Clover stops mid breath. We both look at Dad for support.

"It is, though, isn't it?" I press. "Dad?"

Dad stays silent.

"Not any more," Clover says quietly. "It hasn't been for five years. Has it, Dad?" She grips his arm, willing him to be on her side.

"Easy, girls," Dad says wearily, looking from one of us to the other. "We just need to bear these visitors for a month or so. Maybe less. Maybe they'll discover our oysters are useless to them and go home sooner!"

"I think it will be good for us," Clover says haughtily. "It'll stop *some of us* living in the past. *Some of us* forget there's a whole world out there. Anyone would think we were on the prison ship, the way we live."

"Clover, Clover!" Dad says, trying to soothe her.

My eyes mist with angry tears and I look out through the oblong windows of our cabin house. The sea rocks slowly from side to side, like a picture edging its way out of a frame.

Clover's eagerness for new people in her life makes me queasy.

"I don't know what Grey will think. And the others," I say. "Strangers will scare them away."

"No, they won't," Clover says quickly. "Not while there's fish to be had."

"Girls." Dad sighs. He looks at me, his eyes still lowered. They're red and his brow is glistening with sweat. I wonder how long he's known about all of this. George the boatman has been bringing letters for weeks now. Yellow ones, stamped *From the District Controller* – is this what they've been leading up to? Dad refused to even open them. Ezra must have had to corner him on land.

"Dad?!" I say again, plaintively.

"I don't want them to come either, Pearl," Dad says. "But we don't have a choice. Ezra Heart has spoken."

"But that's not fair!" I yell. "If other people come out

here, they'll ruin it again. The sea's only just starting to get better. It's *ours*, Dad. It's *ours*." I run my fingers through my hair. How can Dad be saying all this? Dad hates the land and landlubbers more than I do.

He leans forward, shaking his head. "No, Pearl. It isn't. That's where people went wrong before. The sea doesn't belong to anyone."

My fingers clench at the shells I wear threaded round my neck. "The platform's ours, though, isn't it?" I say. "This place. Why are you giving up on it? Why do you give up on everything?" My voice falls into a sob and Dad's face breaks up desolately.

"Pearl," he says softly. "Big one."

"I'm not the big one," I scream. "*You* are!"

I slam my hands down on the table like he did and stride out of the cabin to the edge of the platform. I don't even bother pulling off my clothes. I dive into the water, my tears mixing with the sea. Saltwater and saltwater.

"Watch the tide!" Dad's voice calls after me. "It's already on the turn."

SEVEN
Pearl

Dad's right – the tide is already on the turn, but he doesn't follow. I don't look back, knowing he's not even watching as I swim to the flats, my clothes dragging heavy after me. The argument will have been too much for him. He'll be turning into his cabin to sleep away another day.

I scream into the air. Sometimes I'm as angry with Dad as Clover is.

The gulls answer in a cacophony of screams.

I rip off my sodden T-shirt and shorts and hurl them on to the mud. Underneath, my swimsuit's blue, or it was when I made it last summer out of an old dress of Mum's. Part of our gradual appropriation of Mum's wardrobe, because Dad forgets facts like daughters grow.

The swimsuit is duller now, more grey than blue. Clover will dye it some new colour when she inherits it.

Some violent shade of pink or orange or yellow.

I ache inside, thinking of my sister. The less we see of Dad, the more Clover and I have to argue about. And now she'll get what she wants – new people to be on her side. She'll barely need me, and one day she'll leave the bay for good.

I walk along the mudflat, parallel to the land so I don't have to look at it. When the tide comes in, water floods in from either side, but this sandbank will still be exposed for a while. Not quite solid but not quite liquid either, until some tipping point is reached and the water surges in fast, deeper than you'd ever think possible.

Every so often, I look back to our platform – a clash of colours on top of the sea. Mum used to feed us stories, that our sea farm with its rusting section of oil platform and tied-together old boats was a moated castle. She said Clover and I were halfway girls. Not mermaids or selkies, but not land people either. She said there was a magic to this place. She said it would keep us safe. That Clover and I would be safe here forever.

I head over to the wreckage on the foreshore. Things from the Decline and the Greedy Years before that. Old doors. Shopping trolleys. Metal cars, two of them. The open ribcage of one of the last ever whales.

Sometimes the wreckages will disappear – the sand will shift and suck them further down, or bank up over them, and I'll wonder if they're finally gone. But after a storm, or quite by accident, they'll reappear like they never went away. Or they'll turn up in a new resting place. The flats are always being remade.

The sea's pooling around me, like liquid moon. It's warm and makes the sand softer. My feet sink into it. I listen to the crackling of the mud shrimp. A million lives under my feet. It sounds like water draining away, like the whole sea is evaporating, but really it's the shrimp snapping their claws to stun prey.

I coil a strand of emerald-green seaweed round my hair, to keep it out of my eyes, as I climb into one of the old cars.

Dad calls the cars vehicles of destruction, but I'm strangely drawn to them. Sometimes I think they're as beautiful as the whale. All rusted and barnacled and covered in algae. They've given themselves up to the sea entirely.

There are always finds to be had in the cars. I reach down into the gloopy mud to pick things out, one by one.

A burnt gold button.

A child's yellow building brick.

A shiny metallic packet. *Walkers*, letters spell out faintly on the silver foil.

A small tube of clay pipe.

A rusty old nail.

I line the things up on the sand. I've got to do something.

Landlubbers coming to sea. Land rules encroaching

on our farm.

And Ezra knows about Clover. Ezra Heart, lawkeeper for the whole South-East District, knows about Clover and me. That there are two of us. Maybe he's blackmailing Dad with it. Maybe that's why Dad can't say no to the scientist coming.

Dad should have given me those letters Ezra sent to wish away. Blot out the words with seawater, or let them burn.

I trace a pentangle in the sand and pick one thing for each point.

The packet I put as earth – for the walkers, their feet heavy on solid ground.

The clay pipe represents air.

The nail is fire. The thick ancient nails would have been forged by a blacksmith, Mum told us, when we first started larking. *Fire hot enough to melt wrought iron. Imagine that, girls!*

The toy brick I put as spirit. I wonder what child played with it and what things they built, and where their spirit is now.

Water's easy – I pluck a black periwinkle out of a tiny tidal pool. Little horns retreat back into the spiral when I pick it up. It'll leave the pentangle when it's ready, but it'll play dead for long enough.

The centre has to be something special, for the wishing to be a success. I dig down into the buttoned pouch

I sewed into my swimsuit. Some finds I keep on me always.

Pieces of sea glass.

A section of pottery with a woman's face on.

I take out the wentletrap. The intricate, tightly wound spiral shell, perfectly intact and beautiful. I found it with Clover one hot day last summer, when we'd been swimming with the porpoises for hours. Dad had been in his best mood for ages and we'd barbecued scallops on the flats in the late-night sun. Clover and I had choreographed elaborate dances.

It had felt like Mum was watching us. That she was almost with us.

"Is it really worth the wentletrap?" a voice says behind me. Clover. She's surveying the offerings, her head to one side thoughtfully. "We haven't ever found one as complete as that. You don't really think you can stop those people coming?"

She's not cross any more. Clover's moods go in and out with the tide. "It isn't real magic, Pearl. You do know that, don't you?"

I look away. "Yeah, well," I say non-committedly.

"We were never going to hide out here for the rest of our lives without anyone coming. Look at this place, Pearl!" Clover sticks out her right arm and does one of her 360-degree spins. If Clover was growing up in a normal age, she'd be a ballerina. She was made for people to watch.

"People were always going to come here. It's too beautiful to leave alone, isn't it?" she says, and gives me her biggest grin. Like sunshine.

I smile back instinctively, because no one gets this place like Clover and I do. Not even Dad.

"They ruined it before. They'll do it again," I say helplessly.

Clover shrugs. "It wasn't them. Most of those people weren't around back then." She's bending down and pocketing shells. Empty ones – mussels and periwinkles and the tiny tallins you have to be careful you don't crush as they're so delicate. "You've got to be future-thinking, haven't you?"

I flash her an angry look. "You got that from one of those compound pamphlets, didn't you?"

"No, I didn't!" Clover retorts fast, so I know she's lying. "I'm going to make their cabin up. Guest quarters," she says proudly. "I'm going to decorate it with shells. That wentletrap would be perfect." She eyes it greedily, bending down to caress its spiral.

"Don't you dare!" I yell. "It's too good for them. And what do you mean, guest quarters? We don't want them to be too comfortable."

"I do," Clover preens. "I want them to stay long enough to teach us things. Land things."

"I don't need to know land things!" I exclaim indignantly.

"You might, one day. Dad won't want to stay here forever," Clover says nonchalantly.

"Of course he will!"

Clover arches out her back, her belly up, and tips her hands over her head back down to the sand. She walks sideways on all fours like a crab. "Then why does he spend all day in bed, snoring? He's not happy. And I'm not either."

She collapses cross-legged on the sand, watching me.

I go on with the wishing, walking round my pentangle, chanting.

"*Mother Sea,*
Sister of the Moon.
We are your daughters,
Our tears are proof of it."

"Are you really sure about that shell?" Clover says after a while.

I glare at her. "The sea's taking it," I say. Even though part of me does want to snatch it back. Keep it.

In the prison library, there's a book about old churches. That's what the wentletrap looks like to me. Like an old church spire, before the sea tore them all down. The shell really is a special thing to let go, but then our farm has never come this close to being invaded before. I go on with the chant.

"*Leave the sickness on land,*
Take the infection back to shore,

Leave us clean and pure."

Clover stands and stares at me without saying anything, then turns and walks, light-footed as a wader, across the incoming sea. I turn my back to her, lowering my eyes so I don't have to look at the land. If anything was going to destroy the magic, the concrete ramparts and banked-up rocks of the sea defences would.

"Cleansed and blessed by the salt,
Take our treasures
As proof of our devotion.
As we say it, let it be."

I scatter sand over the offerings. It's meant to be pure salt. *Salt to purify*, it says in the Wicca book. But salt in a swimsuit pocket isn't practical.

Seawater's good anyway. Whenever Dad took me to visit Mum in hospital, we had to immerse ourselves in the sea before we got back on the platform. Fully clothed, to wash off the land, so nothing of its poison could infect us.

Dad and Clover never bother with that any more after their trips. Maybe breaches like that have allowed land people to come here.

I think of an Uplands scientist on our platform. Picking through our cages, pulling ribbons of seaweed out of the water. Maybe it isn't the oysters they want. Maybe it's us, our whole way of life.

"Make her go away," I whisper frantically. "Turn

her round and send her straight back to land." I stand watching for a while, as the sea washes around my ankles. The treasure is already lifting up at the edges.

Sometimes we see the things again. Sometimes they reappear in the exact same place, caught in a crevice of one of the old cars, or behind the ribs of the whale. But most of them get taken somewhere else. That's why it's important to send them off right. Give them a proper goodbye.

"*As we say it, let it be,*" I repeat, watching.

When everything's submerged in the bronze sea, I turn back to our farm. For a moment I think I see Dad, calling me, but it's not him. It's just some strange trick of the opaline light. There's only Clover, head bobbing in the water, almost back at the platform.

EIGHT
Nat

Mum and I are in our kitchen, sitting opposite each other at the little scratched table. Kids' indignant voices float up from the caged court at the centre of the compound. There's a basketball game in progress. It sounds like there's some dispute over rules.

My summer hangs in the air, about to crash. "We can't go to sea!" I yell. "Has Ezra finally lost the plot?"

"On the contrary," Mum says. "He's thinking ahead. It's a good idea."

"The sea's poisoned!" I cry. "What about the rotting dead carcasses of fish and birds, and people too? You can't want us to go out there?"

"Things are better now," Mum says gently. "We have to consider the sea's potential. It's risky, to rely on one food source. What if disease got into the growing tower?

It's happened in other districts, Nat. And Central won't help; we'd be on our own. No one wants to go through the Hunger Years again."

I think of the Uplands people, picking up the caterpillars with their gloved hands. Are they really worried they'll bring disease? Is that why they hand them all over to Central?

"We saw Uplands people heading out into the fields…" I venture.

"Nat, you didn't!" Mum snaps. "I've told you about playing there!"

"We weren't!" I lie. "We were on the bike tracks. But what were the Uplands people doing?"

"They were following up on a sighting," Mum says wearily.

"Sighting?" I ask.

"An insect. There was hope it might be significant."

I gaze at her questioningly.

"For the Recovery. Bringing us out of the ecological Dark Ages. There was hope it might be a pollinator."

"And?" I say, with bated breath.

Mum shakes her head sadly. "They're not viable. We first found them a couple of summers ago. They can't survive here. It's toxins from the ground we think. Poor things."

She smiles at me pitifully as she says the last bit, like I'm a poor thing too.

"Then why were they collecting them?" I ask, frowning.

Mum shrugs. "It's protocol, after we reported them to Central District that first time. Central want all pollinators, even if they're not viable. It looks like we're a long way off having pollinators again, but the sea... The sea, Nat. We've ignored it for so long, but what if that's where we should be looking? What if that's where the Recovery has started?"

There's a strange quality to Mum's voice. I wish I could tell her about the creatures on my windowsill. How can they not be viable, the amount they're eating? Central must see that too, surely, if they make any effort to keep them alive. Maybe they're lying to us, like Tally says. Maybe if Mum wasn't so tired and busy she'd see that.

But I can't say anything. Mum freaks out at any mention of the solar fields. I'd mess everything up for her if I was caught out there. Ezra can't have a science advisor with high points.

I lean over our windowsill to watch the kids down in the court. There are blooms of crusty yellow lichen over the concrete, like bursts of sun. There seems to be more every year.

"I don't have to come with you, though, do I?" I falter, changing tactic with Mum. "I mean, I can see the oyster platform, if I look out the back of the compound. I can stay here and you can come home in the evening so you know I'm all right. I'm thirteen, Mum. I don't need looking after!"

Mum sighs. "The tides don't work like that. You can't always get out to the farm. Half the time there's not enough water in the bay to take a boat, it's totally cut off. I can't be that far away from you. Not in the summer, without school on. What would you do all day on your own?"

"I won't be on my own, will I? I've got my mates!" I think of the summer with Tally and Lucas. Cycling through the fields, with flags to be laid and found and laid again. No work. No classrooms. It's the best time of the year.

"Doing what, Nat?" Mum says brusquely. "Trespassing in the solar fields? Climbing the growing tower?"

"No," I say, my face hot.

"Do you think I don't know? Do you think I don't know what you and your mates get up to?" Mum sounds tired and deflated suddenly.

I flush with guilt. "What will I do all day out there?" And the caterpillars, I think, who hatched in the fields and eat thistles. What will they do at sea? Or should I take them back to the windmill, to be picked up and sent to Central and labelled 'not viable'.

"A girl lives there," Mum says. "On the oyster farm. She must manage it."

I bow my head at the thought of meeting the girl. She and her dad come to the compound for supplies every so often. Everyone laughs at her behind her back and makes fun of the odd clothes she wears and the way the sea has washed all the colour out of her hair.

Sometimes, when a storm comes and keeps us all inside the bunker for hours, or whole days even, kids say the girl and her dad sent it. Some of the adults say it too.

But I remember what Tal said. *I'd swap places with her in a heartbeat.*

"It will be *new*, Nat," Mum's saying. "It's a whole new landscape for us. Isn't that what you're always dreaming of?"

Her hands are squeezed together tight. Mum's right. I might be excited too, if I didn't have the caterpillars to worry about. But they're mine now – I'm responsible for them. I can't go out to sea.

"It's a few rotting boats tied together with rope," I say dully.

"And this is a concrete block with a few fields of silicon panels," Mum bites back. "Which you've already explored within an inch of your life."

I look at Mum oddly. She's never said anything like this before. It's the compounder way to acknowledge how grateful we are. We survived. We're alive and our stomachs are full. Never mind that there's a different kind of hunger. I didn't think any adults got that. They're always reminding us that the rules were brought in for a reason.

"I thought you'd be pleased for me, Nat. It's a vote of

confidence. Ezra picked *me* for this. He's recognized how hard I've been working."

"Will I have to live off seaweed and oysters?" I mutter, softening a little, realizing I'm fighting a losing battle.

Mum grins. "Don't worry, we'll pack food you like!" She rises on to her tiptoes, to kiss me on the head. "You're growing so fast. I won't be able to reach you for much longer."

"Mum!" I groan.

Mum laughs. "Why don't you go and join them in the cage? While you still can?" She gestures down to the games court.

I shake my head. "I can't be bothered. Tally might come round. Can you let her in?"

Mum nods and smiles gratefully. "It's only for a few weeks, Nat. It'll fly by. You'll see."

I go to my room and pick up one of the jars from behind the curtain where I hide them. I've punched holes in the lids for air. The caterpillars have already eaten themselves out of three or four different skins, which lie discarded on the bottom of the jars.

"Not viable," I whisper slowly. Does Mum really believe that too?

If the information we found on the computer is correct, the next step will be for them to hang upside down from the top of the jar and spin themselves a cocoon to wait out the rest of the change. That's the bit I find hardest to imagine. Anything can eat and get bigger – humans do that – but to spin yourself a sack, sprout wings and fly? Maybe there's a reason those pictures didn't show up on the computers. Maybe it's all made up.

NINE
Pearl

I wanted to be right out of the way when they arrived but I can't make myself go. Someone's got to know what they really want. I hide round the side of the cabin, out of sight.

If they've come to seize our home, they're not looking very fierce about it. The woman is small and thin. Her eyes dart round our platform. The boy keeps his head down, intent instead on a small box that he grips with both hands.

George is hauling boxes of equipment up from the boat on to the platform. He looks slightly bemused by his new passengers. Usually it's prisoners he carries, to the ship. Once Clover asked what the prisoners were like and George said how quiet they were on the way over. He said he always tried to make their ride as smooth as possible.

"But they're prisoners! They don't deserve it!" Clover had said, aghast.

George had been disappointed in her. "You don't know what it's like, living there," he'd said quietly, gazing back to land. "Some rules are hard to keep." Clover had burned bright red with embarrassment.

I wonder what the woman and boy's trip was like. They're both looking a bit green.

Dad puts out his hands to take the box from the boy, so he can grip the guide rope as he comes on to the platform, but the boy shakes his head ungratefully. "It's OK, I can manage." I watch him look inside our cabin disparagingly, before he clambers awkwardly across the makeshift gangway.

The woman's more graceful. She puts her arms out for balance. Still, a flash of worry travels across her face as the platform bobs slightly in the water, adjusting to their weights.

"It's good to be here," the woman says, when she's far enough away from the edge to breathe normally again. She stands still, feet slightly apart. "It's good of you to have us. I know it's an imposition, unwanted guests." She laughs gently, like a trickle of water from the desalination tank. Light, with all the salt taken out. "I'm Sora. You must be Atticus."

"That's right," Dad says gruffly. He looks uncomfortable. He's wearing a shirt for the first time in months but it's creased and stained with rust.

Clover steps forward, determined not to be left out. She's brushed through her hair so many times it's flying out, like strands of magic thread, catching the sunlight. She's wearing her one dress. It used to be yellow when it was mine, but it's white now – bleached by so much sunlight. For some reason Clover's never wanted to dye it. She looks like an angel, or a ghost, with golden sun-touched skin.

Clover sidesteps from one foot to another. She's excited. She's been hanging out of the crow's nest all morning, watching out for them. "Sora. That's such a nice name," she gushes. "Like flying. Soaring, like the gulls."

Sora looks up to the birds in the sky and laughs, and I creep forward to get a better look at her. Her dark eyes glisten like periwinkles when they're wet. "Wouldn't that be amazing?" she says. "Actually, my name means sky. It's a Japanese name. Some of my family were from Japan. A long time ago now. Before... Before everything changed..." Sora's voice dies away.

Clover nods soberly and hangs her head, because she thinks that's expected of her when people talk about the past.

"And what's your name?" Sora asks, a new smile brightening her cheekbones.

"Clover. It's a plant, from before. A plant with three leaves."

"Or four for luck!" Sora says.

Clover's face lights up. "You know it?"

Sora nods. "It grows around the edges of the compound. In the solar fields too. You must have seen it, Nat?" She turns to the boy. "It has little white flowers with pink tips."

The boy, Nat, is standing in the exact place he came off the boat, and still clutching his box.

George says when landlubbers think about the sea, they think of drowning. It's a nightmare that went right into them. They can't ever forgive the sea. Even on the brightest, calmest day, they're still thinking of everyone that got washed away.

The boy's mouth curls up at the edges and he sighs pointedly. "I wouldn't know about the solar fields, Mum. You know that!"

Sora laughs. "He's not meant to go there," she explains. "Only sometimes I think he gets led astray, by his friends." She leans in to Clover, as if she's telling her a secret.

"Mum!" Nat protests, though still with that mouth curl. "No one leads me astray!"

Sora grins. "If you say so. Anyway, I think Clover's a very pretty name indeed. How lovely to be named after a plant!"

"I think so too!" Clover sings. "We're so glad you've come! I've been wanting new people for ages."

I retreat back again round the corner of the cabin.

There's a clatter as I knock against a crate of empty bottles, and Clover looks directly at the space where I was.

The others don't seem to have heard. Dad's shifting his feet impatiently. "We'd better show you where to put your things." He nods his head when Clover jumps up and rubs her hands together with excitement. "Lead the way then, my fine legume. This is your moment."

TEN
Nat

"Welcome to your quarters! I got them ready all by myself," the girl, Clover, says, bouncing on ahead. She looks at me expectantly.

It's a boat, or part of one. Except for the main platform, which Atticus says was once part of an oil rig in the North Sea, the whole farm is a collection of boats all strung together. This looks like the smallest, most ramshackle one of the lot. It rocks as we step down into it.

"Is it safe?" I ask through clenched teeth.

"Oh yes, it is, I promise," Clover says seriously. "We wouldn't put you anywhere that wasn't safe!"

There's a wooden bench either side, and if I stood in the middle and stretched out my arms, my fingertips would touch both walls.

"It's a narrowboat," Atticus says gruffly.

"I can see that," I say under my breath.

Clover laughs lightly. "That's a type of boat. It was built this size on purpose, for canals."

"Man-made waterways," Mum says, anticipating my question before it's even out of my mouth. She smiles at Atticus. "Growing up in the compound you're not given much information about life before the Decline. It's not considered…" She pauses. "Necessary."

"Safe," I say at the exact same time.

I see Clover glance between us.

A mattress on each bench is made up with sheets and old woollen blankets covered in shells of dead sea creatures. The air's hot and stale.

I look round for a place to hide the jars of caterpillars. There's no windowsill. Nowhere to hide them where they'll get any light. Surely in all these different boats there would have been somewhere for me to have my own space. Why do I have to share with Mum like I'm a baby again?

Clover crowds in close to me and bumps up against the box. I snatch it back into my chest.

"Look," she says, pointing at the shells laid over each bed. They're arranged in a heart shape.

"Oh yeah," I say, taken aback.

"It's from a book I read," Clover says. "An old one. There was this big manor house and when the girl – the heroine – arrived in her room at the top, in a turret, there were rose petals on her pillow. I didn't know where to get rose petals, but…" Her words tail off and she stands awkwardly, looking at the shells.

I don't know what a turret is but I wish I had a room in one – at the top, out of the way, and I wish the girl would go away. And Mum and Atticus. They're waiting for me to be appropriately grateful.

The box feels heavy in my sweaty hands. The caterpillars don't weigh a thing, but what they mean, that's heavy. I brought chrysalises to sea. What's going to happen to them now? And what if someone discovers them? My heart rattles in my ribcage like the jars sliding around in the box.

"I wanted to make it nice for you," Clover says, quieter now. "It was stupid of me. I should have known you wouldn't like shells."

"Shells are better than rose petals," says a new voice, bright and brittle. There's a chiming sound and a girl steps into the room, pushing past me to stand next to Clover. My jaw drops open.

"Ah, you must be the other daughter," Mum says, just like that, like it's no surprise at all.

I gasp, looking around at everyone. How can there be two girls here?

The new girl glares at me. "You look like you've seen a ghost."

"I… How… Who are you?" I splutter.

Clover squeaks beside me. "Ezra told Dad you knew about us!"

Mum puts her hands on my shoulders and smiles reassuringly at Clover. "Don't worry, your secret's safe. I just hadn't told Nat yet. I thought it best to wait for him to meet you both in person." She smiles at the girls. "The rules are so strict in the compound. A word out of place and…" Mum lets the implication hang in the air.

I stare at her, feeling betrayed and horrified, and then again at the girls, standing side by side. "You're sisters, aren't you?" I say to them, still hardly believing what I'm seeing. And then to Mum, "You didn't trust me? You really thought I might tell on them? That I would do that?"

"Of course I trust you, Nat," Mum says easily. "But because of the situation with Tally, it felt … sensitive. And you were so upset about coming here."

"We didn't want you to come either," the new girl says coldly. She looks a couple of years older than her sister. My age, probably.

"Pearl!" Clover shrieks, red-faced. "Ignore her!" she says to me. "We did want you to come. I did. Pearl's just in a mood. You'll find that out about her. Pearl's stormy. She doesn't like land people."

Atticus pulls a face. "Pearl had a bad time," he says,

blushing a little. "When their mum, Vita, was…" His voice cracks. "It was a bad time for all of us, but Clover doesn't remember it so well."

"I do remember," Clover says indignantly. "You and Pearl always say that, but I do. I remember everything." Clover stretches 'everything' into an accusation.

"Tally said there were two of you," I murmur, still gazing between them, from one to the other. "When we saw you in the distance, out on the mudflats. We thought you were a ghost!"

Atticus tuts loudly. "Haven't I told you girls about getting too close to land?"

Clover ignores him. She's smiling proudly. "Did you really think there was a ghost? Is Tally one of your friends?" she asks, savouring the word. "What a brilliant name!"

"Pearl's a lovely name too," Mum says kindly. "Like the stones you find in oysters, yes?"

Clover waves her hand dismissively. "You don't find many pearls. They're pretty much a myth, like mermaids and selkies. Don't get your hopes up."

Pearl looks like her younger sister, except taller and darker – where Clover's hair is gold, Pearl's is almost black. The expression on her face, that's darker too. "This was our mum's room," she says.

"Pearl," Atticus says warily. "Your mum would be glad to see what a nice job Clover's done."

"Would she? Do you honestly think that?" Pearl steps towards me and I stumble back. "And do *you* like it?" she asks.

She has a necklace made of shells – that's what the clacking is as she moves. She smells of salt and seawater and her feet are bare. "Clover spent days getting it ready for you. Days! And those shells aren't as easy to find as you might think. You should be grateful." She flicks her hair back off her shoulders. There's actual seaweed twined through it. She stoops over Clover like she's protecting her from something. From us. From me.

"I think it's lovely," Mum's saying tactfully, behind me. "I think you've done a very good job indeed, Clover. We're honoured, aren't we, Nat? And very pleased to meet you too, Pearl. It's kind of your family to have us." Mum looks at me pointedly, telling me to make an effort.

Pearl doesn't even look at Mum. She's already decided who she's picking her fight with. I get this flash of Tally, how she was in the days after Barnaby was taken. Angry, coiled up, ready to pounce.

"It's not kindness," the girl says. "It's compulsory. Ezra Heart made us."

"Ezra Heart made us too. We didn't want to come to your weird sea farm," I retort.

"Nat!" Mum admonishes. "*I* wanted to come. I'm excited about finding out what you do here." She turns to Atticus and smiles apologetically.

"Pearl's nervous about it all. About what it means for us," Atticus says in the doorway.

Pearl stares out of the window deliberately. Next to her, Clover's tearful and disappointed. This obviously wasn't what she had in mind when she got our cabin ready.

I pick up a shell from the bed. I press my fingers into it and it doesn't yield. When the sea turned acidic it dissolved shells and killed loads of creatures, but this one's like stone. I run my finger over its ridges. "What's it called?" I ask.

ELEVEN
Pearl

He's slid the box under his bed thinking we're all too stupid to notice. Dad tells Sora he'll show her the rest of our farm before the tide goes back out. Some of the molluscs get harder to reach at low tide.

"Are you ready, Pearl?" Dad asks me. "I'll need you to bring up some of the lines."

"No, thanks," I say coolly. "I'll leave the diving to you today."

Clover suppresses a stream of giggles. It's a good couple of years since Dad went down. He trained us up good and proper so he wouldn't have to.

Dad looks surprised at my refusal. "She's here specifically to see the produce."

"Well, you'd better get on with it then, hadn't you?" I say.

"We could go tomorrow instead, if that's better for

Pearl," Sora ventures.

"No," Dad says, shooting me a look of fury. "I'll show you myself. There's no point stretching this out." He storms out to the main platform where the motorboat is.

Sora looks back unsure then smiles at her son reassuringly, before she heads out after Dad.

Clover plonks herself down on the bed next to Nat. "That one's a plain old scallop," she says about the shell in Nat's hand. "And look, these white spiral ones are whelks."

"Do you eat them?" he says, pulling a face.

"Only the inside bit!" Clover says laughing. "And you fry them up first, in the skillet. They're good, I promise, especially if you use some butter."

I draw in a breath, angrily. Butter! Clover adores it but we only get a small packet once every couple of months if we're lucky. Why's she offering it up to him?

They carry on going through the shells together. Cockles. Periwinkles. The purple-blue mussels. The boy says the oyster shells are 'iridescent' inside and pronounces the pearly top shells to be 'like jewels'. I wonder what jewels he ever saw. It feels strange, watching his landlubber hands on them.

"These are my favourite," Clover says, "and they're too small to eat." She holds up one of the tiny tallins on the tip of her finger. "They come in different colours. Look!

Aren't they the prettiest?"

She gathers up a few – pink, grey, orange, green, like a subdued rainbow. Sometimes you find them open in the sand, like tiny wings, but they almost always separate once you've picked them up.

The boy nods. "They're nice."

Nice?! He picks up a long straight shell that looks a bit like a knife. "What's this one?"

"It's a razor, isn't it, Pearl?" Clover says, trying to include me. "Pearl's learned them all. She goes to the library. There's a whole section of books there about sea life."

The boy's face crinkles, confused. "In the library?"

"Not your compound library," I say dismissively. "Out there, on the ship. They have a proper library with real books." Nat looks through the porthole where I'm pointing. You can see the prison ship on the horizon, the rusting, barnacled bulk of her. She's weighed down with the biggest anchor around.

"The prison ship!" Nat breathes. "You go there? What about Benjamin Price?"

Clover shudders at the name of the ship's governor. Benjamin Price runs that ship with an iron fist.

It started off as a detention centre, for people coming across the sea from flooded lands, who thought the bay might be a safe place to land. Then after siege state laws were brought in, other people started to be sent there too.

"Course!" I say, trying to sound casual, pleased to have the chance to impress him after the way he looked so dismissively at our farm. "Who do you think our shellfish are for?"

I don't say that the governor has land food taken across for his own plate. He won't touch our produce.

"Aren't the shellfish full of poison? Don't they make you sick?" Nat asks.

"Do we look poisoned to you?" I snap.

The edges of the boy's lips curl up again in that funny lopsided smile. "I guess not." He kneels on the bed and puts his face up to the porthole window. "I can't believe there's a library out there. At sea!"

I shrug. "Stands to reason, doesn't it? There are people there. People want to read. Know things."

Clover looks at me strangely. I know what she's thinking. Most of those prisoners never set foot in that library. Olive's only allowed because she's skilled at cataloguing.

"But to have books about sea life?" Nat says. "I was told there wasn't…" He stops and blushes. "The librarian at the compound told me there aren't books about old things."

I look at him scornfully. "Of course *you* don't have them. Your books got washed away. No point making books now about dead things, is there?"

"Not everything died," Nat says, staring at me. "The clover's come back, like Mum says. And other things.

I could show you one day, if you wanted."

"Pearl doesn't go to land," Clover says, matter-of-fact.

Nat looks at me oddly.

I pull at my necklace. I feel the blood rush to my cheeks – little pricks of heat. I frown at Clover, irritated. "I can't, can I? Not since you started going. People can't know there are two of us."

"But you go to the ship?" Nat asks.

"I do the ship, Clover does the land," I say.

"Maybe I could come with you one day, to see the library?"

I stare back at him disdainfully. "Benjamin Price would have a field day if a regular landlubber like you clambered on board. You might never get off."

"Pearl!" Clover says, shocked.

The boy doesn't look bothered. "How come you're allowed into the library anyway?" he asks. "The library doesn't need shellfish, does it?"

I toss my hair back. "I got special permission." Pride edges into my voice.

"She made friends with a crazy prisoner," Clover explains.

"She's not crazy!" I say. "And you shouldn't use that word. None of us know what she's been through."

"No, but everyone thinks she is. You did too, Pearl, don't lie." Clover turns to Nat to explain. "This old prisoner barely talks to anyone. She works in the kitchen where

Pearl delivers our shellfish and seaweed. Pearl made friends with her, which is a miracle as Pearl's the most antisocial person you could get!"

"Her name's Olive," I say, ignoring Clover, because the boy does actually look interested. "She noticed the log—"

"That's Pearl's record of what produce we take to the ship," Clover says, jumping in to explain. "Olive saw she was good at recording things."

I shrug. "She wanted help sorting the books out. They were all over the place. The whole room full. A big room too. She's letting me catalogue them with her."

"Catalogue them?" the boy asks.

"You know, group them. Put the right ones together. We're still going through them."

"You should have seen them, in the beginning," Clover interrupts. "There were mountains of them, thousands, about everything you could ever think of. And there are stories too, old ones. Proper novels. They'd been ignored for a hundred years, but Benjamin Price started to think they might be worth something. At least that's what we think he thought."

"He keeps the books prisoner too," I say bitterly. "Like everyone on the ship."

"Are there books on insects?" Nat asks.

I look at him curiously. "Entomology," I say.

His face crumples into confusion and Clover giggles

at him. "Ento what?" he says.

"Entomology," I repeat. "The study of insects. Why do you want to know?"

Nat looks out of the window again, towards the ship. "No reason. I just saw something. Something I wanted to know more about."

"In the solar fields?" I ask.

He shakes his head quickly. Too quickly. "Just something I remembered from school once."

TWELVE
Nat

"I'll show you round the rest of the farm, Nat," Clover says, gathering the shells and arranging them back on the pillow. She's grinning. "I've been waiting for this moment!"

My face falls. I wanted to check on the creatures. They're hanging from the tops of their jars now, already in their cocoons. It felt cruel to put them on that rocking boat that stank of fish. I wanted to check they survived the journey.

"You don't have to, if you don't want to," Clover says quickly, clocking my face and turning red.

"I do. I do want to," I say, guilty now. I've obviously offended her. "This place is going to be my home for the next few weeks, isn't it? That's what Mum says."

The smile returns to Clover's face. "This way then," she says. "I'll give you the guided tour. I've got it all planned."

"Great!" I say. The caterpillars will just have to wait. At least looking round the farm might give me an idea where to hide them.

I expect Pearl to slink back to wherever she came from but she follows us. She doesn't trust me enough to let me out of her sight.

It's a relief to step out into the fresh air again after the staleness of our 'quarters'. I look back the way we came, to the main platform where we landed, where our bags are waiting for us. It has a living area in a kind of hut. The walls are made of wood and the roof looks like tin, except for a structure built on top of it – there's a ladder up the side of the hut, to a high little hideout on top.

Half of the hut is faded pink, the other half fresh and yellow like the sun.

"We call that the cabin," Clover says, following where my eyes are looking. "That's where we cook and read and draw and hang out. We've been painting the walls bumblebee yellow. And can you see our crow's nest on top? That's our pirate lookout. You'll see it properly later. We've got a special dinner planned. Let me show you the outlying areas first." The words spray out of her.

"Outlying areas?" I say, laughing. "You make it sound like a whole country."

Clover smiles. "Pearl and I pretend that it is, sometimes."

"Do peacekeepers come?" I ask.

"Nah," Clover says easily. "We're off their radar out here."

Each area of the farm is held together with rope and you have to jump from one section to the next or, if it's too big a jump, make your way along the rope.

Clover watches with concern as I try and tightrope to the next boat. My stomach twists and turns. It would be so easy to slip under one of the boats if you fell in. It feels like you could disappear forever down there.

"We're so used to using the ropes, we didn't think about other people," Clover says doubtfully.

"It's OK, I can manage," I bluster.

I feel Pearl's eyes burning into me.

"If you put your hands out, you can balance," Clover says. "Like a bird, wings outstretched. You know what a bird looks like when it flies, right?"

"Course I do. I can manage," I say again loudly, then swear under my breath as I slip and grasp at one of the vertical poles in a cold sweat. The girls look on piteously.

My cheeks burn furiously. If only they could see me on my bike, freewheeling through the solar fields!

Here the ground's not entirely steady and the dark water beneath laps higher when I put my weight on the rope, like it's trying to get at me.

I take a running jump instead and land on the next section – another platform which tilts unnervingly when

I land, and which is mostly empty save for coiled-up piles of rope and netting and a couple of cages. The smell of fish gets stronger.

"Look," I yell suddenly, noticing something in the water. Something big, with a triangular, glossy black fin. I run to the side of the platform. "A dolphin!" I cry.

Clover laughs. "It's not a dolphin. That's Grey. He's a harbour porpoise."

"A porpoise?" I say. I've never even heard that word.

"It's similar to a dolphin. Ish," Clover says kindly.

"There are no dolphins left," Pearl says starkly behind me. "Don't you know what your people did? What they destroyed?"

"Pearl, don't say that." Clover sighs. "It's not Nat's fault, is it, what people did a hundred years ago?" She turns to face me and smiles. "Ignore her! A porpoise is a type of cetacean. An air-breathing sea mammal."

"Why does it live in the sea if it breathes air?" I stare at the glossy creature weaving in and out of the grey water like it's part of it.

Clover shrugs. "The sea's its home. It belongs there and that's where the fish are. Grey loves fish. Oh, look!" she says, pointing out across the water.

I follow her finger to Mum, out in the boat with Atticus. You can hear the motor thrumming across the water. Mum's peering over the edge of the boat, trailing her hand in the water. It makes me feel odd watching her, my air-breathing mother in the middle of the sea.

The boat's stopped by one of the yellow balloons that are dotted around the bay, and a small cloud of gulls circles overhead. Noisy. It sounds like the compound courtyard after school closes.

It's the last day of school today – Mum took me out early. I barely got a chance to say goodbye. Just to Tally and Lucas, who snuck out at break to find me. Tally gave me new leaves in a sealed bag for the caterpillars.

"What are those things?" I ask, watching the yellow balloons bob in the water.

"Seagulls," Clover says easily.

I can't resist laughing. "I know what seagulls are. We do look at the sky sometimes! I mean the yellow floats."

"Oh, them! They're buoys," Clover says.

"Boys?" I repeat uncertainly. The boat's on the move again, making new waves which lap higher up the platform. I take a couple of steps away from the edge.

"Buoys," Clover says, giggling now. "With a U. B-U-O-Y." She writes the letters in the air with her index finger. "The buoys mark the tops of the lines where the shellfish are. That's why the gulls are following – they think Dad's going down for a harvest." She pauses. "They'll be disappointed – that line's seaweed!"

"Seaweed?" I repeat.

Clover nods. "We grow it. The cook on the ship makes it into noodles."

"Mum's talked about seaweed," I say thoughtfully. "But not to eat." I grimace at the prospect of that. "Mum thinks we should be using it on land, for the Uplands. To feed the crops."

I feel Pearl stiffen behind me. I decide to ignore her if she can't be bothered to make any effort to be nice.

"So the seaweed's underwater?" I ask Clover. "I thought it just washed up on the sand."

Clover nods enthusiastically. "There are ribbons and ribbons of it. Like an underwater forest. It's like swimming through trees. We can get the boat out later and show you. You've got to see our farm from the edges to really get it."

"You've got to go down to really see it," Pearl says, coming forward. "You do swim, right?" Pearl says it darkly, like it's a dare.

I shake my head, surprised. "Why would I have needed to swim?"

Pearl stifles a snigger and Clover glares at her. "Well, why would he? Land people don't, do they? It doesn't mean he's stupid." Clover turns back to me and smiles kindly. "I can teach you, if you like. While you're out here."

"To dive as well?" I ask.

Clover grins. "Well, once you've got the hang of

swimming, why not? Dad says you're here the whole summer."

"Yeah," I say uncertainly.

"Lucky us," Pearl retorts sarcastically.

"Ignore her!" Clover chimes. "Like I told you. Antisocial!" She jumps across into the next boat.

"How do you even do that?" I exclaim, impressed.

Clover doesn't care that there's water underneath. She doesn't care about the gaps between the different structures, or that the ropes are all frayed. She doesn't care about the underwater forest and dark creatures swimming in the depths.

"You'll get used to it!" she sings back to me. I decide I much prefer her to her sister. I don't know why Pearl's got it in for me, but she clearly has.

I clamber after Clover, clinging to the side of one boat as I stride across to the next one. It feels like the water's got inside me too. My stomach rolls, like it's trying to find its level.

Pearl's watching smugly and I pull myself taller, determined not to give her the satisfaction of seeing me throw up.

"You like it colourful out here," I say to Clover, pausing for a moment to breathe in a fresh gulp of air. The boat we're on is painted in strips of different colours. Like a rainbow, except one that's shedding colour.

Clover beams. "We wanted it to be cheery. I get the colours from your hardware shop."

"The compound one?" I ask surprised. In the compound everything's grey and metal. Colour is considered too celebratory, or disrespectful, after so many lives were lost in the floods.

"The shop man orders them in specially," Clover says. "He lets me pick them from a catalogue from a supplier in Central. He's lost the colour chart so I never know what I'm getting till they come, but I choose from the names. Like bumble bee. I wanted to see what colour a bumble bee would be."

"I never pictured Central as colourful," I say.

"It must be. I bet it's like a palace," Clover says dreamily. "That's where I'll live when I'm grown up. At least some of the time. I'll go other places too of course. Everywhere you can get to." Her eyes fix determinedly on the horizon.

I get this sudden stab of envy for people in other places, and for the bright, colourful lives of the Central Districters, not having to worry about floods and storms, or working shifts, or meeting targets, or accruing disobedience points. Getting all their food delivered by the outlying districts. There are rumours that Central are even allowed second children now. District rules might have had their place one day – to keep us safe and protect what resources we had left – but things aren't as bad now. The sea has receded, no one actually goes hungry any more. I wonder why we still need all the rules if Central don't?

Clover's floating on obliviously. "That's pink parasol," she says about a boat that's 'mostly storage'. "We call it the plant room. It's where the water tank is too," she says. "If we run out."

"How can you run out of water at sea?" I peer into the pink boat, full of pipes and containers. It all looks like it could do with a good clean.

"You're very welcome to get your water directly out of the sea, while you're here," Pearl says.

"Don't do that!" Clover says to me alarmed. "You know you can't drink saltwater, right?"

I smile. "It was a joke! Calm down. I'm not from the Dark Ages. The district has its own desalination plant. A huge one. Some of the compounders are bussed out there for their shifts. That's where I might be sent, when I finish school…"

Clover looks at me pitifully. Working at the desalination plant suddenly seems the worst job in the world. Even Pearl looks sorry for me, if that's the most exciting future I can hope for.

I go on, edging round another narrowboat, this one the colour of rust.

"That's where Dad sleeps," Clover says dismissively. "Don't look in. It's M. E. S. S. Y."

My eyes dart in immediately – through a half-open door to a dark interior. There must be blinds or curtains pulled across the windows, but even so I can see the floor's covered in stuff. Mum would be livid if I left my room like that.

Pearl slams the door in front of me angrily, the shells on her necklace clacking sharply. "That's private," she says icily. "That's the third rule of life out here. People need their space."

I think of the narrow cabin I'm sharing with Mum. I guess that rule doesn't apply to us. "What's the second rule?" I ask.

"No shirking work," Clover recites. "Everyone does their tasks. Except Dad lately. Oi!" Clover shrieks as her sister prods her with her hand.

"Dad's been tired," Pearl says defensively.

"OK," I say, looking from one to the other. The tension between them is so sparky it feels you should be able to see it, like lightning. And the way they predict each other – it's like there's some connection between them, like an invisible thread. I wonder if all siblings have that? "What's the first rule?" I ask, uneasily now.

"All hands to the deck when a storm's coming," the girls say in unison.

"Got it," I say, gulping, as my stomach turns over again.

Clover pats my arm gently. "You've gone green. Don't worry! You came for the best bit of the year. We don't have to worry about storms."

Pearl opens her mouth to say something but decides better of it. I think of Billy Crier and the freak storm in summer, but that was years ago. The storms and floods aren't like they used to be.

"What's in here?" I ask, peering into another boat, painted green and low down in the water.

"That's just paperwork now, and broken things. Some of the things from your cabin went in there. It all needs sorting," Clover says dismissively, walking on ahead. "Mostly we just live on the main platform and in the open air when we can. It's good for your lungs!" She inhales a deep breath and I copy her, smiling.

"You're lucky," I say. "All this space! No peacekeepers in sight!"

No one to spot the creatures, except for the girls themselves. I'm starting to think I'll need to let them in on my secret. Clover seems so excited to have someone new around, I can't imagine her leaving me alone anytime soon. Pearl obviously doesn't trust me enough to let me out of her sight. Can I trust them both about the butterflies? They've had to keep their own big secret all this time...

Clover's already turning back to the platform, like the tour's over, even though there are still a couple of sections we've not got to.

"What about that one?" I ask, pointing to a see-through

dome on a raft all of its own.

"Oh, that," Clover says, slowing down and changing her course towards the transparent room. "That's our mum's greenhouse."

"A greenhouse?" I ask, confused, because the boat isn't painted – it's like a misted-up plastic bubble.

Clover jumps on to the edge of the bubble boat, before turning back to me. Her expression's changed   wistful now. "We call it the greenhouse. It's an old term for somewhere you grow plants. Our mum was into flowers and herbs and things. This was her dominion."

She opens a cut-out door on the side of the plastic dome. It creaks.

I make the leap over too, awkward and flustered. Pearl comes across right after me, her stride effortless, but her face full of agitation. Her chain of shells seems to snap angrily.

"Your mum grew plants? Like in the growing tower?" I ask, stepping between bits of broken panels and cracked pots. There's a strange smell – dank, earthy – that makes me think of the solar fields after it's rained.

Clover shrugs. "All sorts! She had loads of clover, of course. Clover was her favourite. Some of it had four leaves."

"Did it?" Pearl says. "I don't remember that."

Clover hangs her head and her eyes glisten a bit more than usual.

Pearl trails me, discomfort radiating off her as I walk around. The greenhouse isn't big, but it feels big because the walls are see-through. Or would be if you scrubbed away the mould and algae. The amount of mould, it's a wonder the whole place isn't hopping with fungus gnats. Even the growing tower with all its whirring fans gets fungus gnats.

Green leaves press against the concave edges of the dome, hungry for light. The girls continue to bicker, like being in here pulled that invisible thread between them to breaking point. I let their voices fade into the background. All I'm thinking is, this space would be perfect for the chrysalises.

THIRTEEN
Pearl

We should have kept the greenhouse out of bounds.

Mum planted herbs for cooking here. Thyme, rosemary, lavender, sage. Dad used to use some of the scrappy bits that were left when he was still cooking properly.

Mum ordered the seeds from Central and they took months to arrive. She almost gave up hope of them coming, but then one day they did. George arrived with the supply run and a small box of brown paper envelopes full of seeds.

I still have the image of flowers in my head, all those bright colours, but I don't conjure it up very often, or come in here. I don't go to that section of the library either – land flora. I let Olive catalogue that one. I stick to sea life.

The soil's dried up now, though the rain gets in sometimes. It's mostly rain that's kept anything alive at all, cycling around – condensing in the sun, falling again at night. In winter the water in the greenhouse freezes and new cracks appear in the panes.

"Pearl! Are you listening? What are these called again?" Clover's calling, pointing to one of the yellow flowers like sunshine that appear every spring.

"Dandelions," I say quietly, Mum's voice in my head.

"*Dent de lion. Lion's tooth, see. Look at the toothy leaves, Pearl.*"

Some of them have gone to seed already. Fat globules of seeds that Mum called clocks.

"*Blow it, Pearl! Be like the wind!*" Mum's voice sounds in my ears like she's here beside me and I'm seven years old again, without a care in the world.

Nat picks up one of the seed heads and blows into it. Seeds scatter like dust. I glare at him.

Clover spins on tiptoe in the swirl of seeds. "It's a snowstorm! Do another!" she cries joyously, and I'm suddenly jealous of Clover's capacity for happiness.

Nat plucks another seed head from the ground and his cheeks puff up as he blows. He looks like a fish.

My teeth grind together. "You'll waste them," I say. "They don't belong to you."

Nat pulls a face. "The seeds want to be spread. That's the point of them, isn't it?"

I glare at him silently.

"You've got nettles too," he says, ignoring me and

bending down over a patch of green.

"Careful!" Clover cries. "Those ones sting!"

Nat takes hold of a leaf firmly between his forefinger and thumb and plucks it off. He holds it out to me pointedly, superior, like I knew a landlubber would be. Though I didn't think someone from that concrete monstrosity over the water would be bothered about our old greenhouse and the few straggly green plants left.

"We get nettles around the compound too," he says, shrugging. "And the dandelions. Sometimes Mum picks them. She puts them in a glass on our kitchen table with the thistle flowers. They'd only be taken away otherwise."

"Taken away?" Clover asks, mystified.

Nat nods. "In case of disease. Spores or fungus. Anything that could get into the growing tower. We have to protect it. It's all our district has."

He sounds like he's giving a speech. The nettle leaf drops to the floor.

"So that's why you want our oyster farm? To add it to your empire?" I ask.

Nat shrugs again. "I don't know. I don't decide, do I? None of this was my idea. I'm the one that had to leave my mates behind. And my bike. I had to give up my entire summer." He stamps his foot against the floor.

Clover wrings her hands and looks depressed on his behalf. "I've always wanted to ride a bike. I can imagine how much you'd miss that."

Nat smiles at her, amused, and starts to walk round the edge of the space, feeling the panes, putting his hands through the gaps. Clover follows in his wake, imitating him.

"We shouldn't be here," I say, desperately wanting us out, most of all him. "This is Mum's place." She could almost be here, in the cloud of dandelion seeds still looking for a place to settle.

"Mum might like to see us here," Clover says.

"She wouldn't," I bite back. "Not with a stranger."

I don't mind Mum's ghost on the flats when we're larking. I don't mind her in the water either, but I mind her here. This was the last place she came. She'd walk here when she was too sick to drag herself out to the flats. If I think of Mum here, she's sick.

It's sad we forgot to water her flowers and that we let storms smash up the panels of her greenhouse. It's sad that Dad forgot to flavour our meals with the herbs and green leaves Mum planted especially.

"It wouldn't take much to fix it up," Nat says thoughtfully. "We could mend it."

Clover squeals excitedly. "Do you think? Do you really think we could?"

I glare at her. "Course we could, if that was the right thing to do. We could do it on our own; we don't need him. What's the point, though, when everything died?"

Nat looks at me confused. "It didn't all die, did it? The dandelions, the nettles. They're alive. *That's* the point. If they can grow, other things can too."

"Like what?" I say, annoyed.

Nat glances around surreptitiously. "I brought something with me. Something secret."

Clover crowds in closer. "A secret!" she whispers with glee. "No one ever told me a secret before!"

I glower. I'm sure I have. I'm sure there have been things between Clover and I that we didn't want Dad to know. Sister things.

Nat looks unsure suddenly. "But you can't tell anyone! Not Atticus and definitely not my mum. It's against district rules. Big time. You'd have to promise not to tell."

"Oh, we would, wouldn't we, Pearl?" Clover says, gripping my arm tightly. "We solemnly swear not to tell a soul. Pearl, you say it too." Her fingernails dig in to me.

"You found out our secret," I say to Nat aloofly. "It can't be bigger than that."

"What if it is?" Nat says, his voice low and slow. "What if it's bigger than anything? What if it could change everything?"

I hold his eyes for a couple of seconds. They don't blink.

"I promise," I say tersely. Clover's fingernails dig in further and Nat raises his eyebrows.

"I mean it. I promise," I say, louder now, pulling my

arm away from Clover. If she presses any tighter she'll draw blood. "Tell us," I say, sitting down on the bench, trying to sound like I don't care, even though I'm desperate to know. Why is Nat keeping secrets from his precious district?

Nat glances again around us. "Caterpillars," he whispers.

I stare at him open-mouthed.

"And not even caterpillars any more. Chrysalises now," he says grandly, watching our faces.

"As in butterflies?" I ask.

Nat nods slowly, surprised at my knowledge. I keep my expression fixed.

"Butterflies!" Clover repeats beside me. "But you can't have! They died out with the bees. Even before the floods!" She looks disappointed, like he's revealed something about himself she didn't want to be there – that he's a liar, that he makes things up.

Nat nods impatiently. "Yes. Only I think they came back. To the bay. I think I found some in the solar fields."

"In the solar fields? With your mates?" Clover squeaks.

"You said you don't go to the solar fields," I say coldly.

Nat meets my eyes, a half-smile flickering across his face, like the candles we light in winter when the generator's down. "All the compound kids go to the solar fields. There isn't anywhere else to go. You just can't let the adults know. It's a penalty against our parents if the district find out."

"A penalty?" Clover asks, her nose crinkled.

"A civil disobedience point. You know, for not pulling your weight, or squandering rations, or breaking border rules, or something."

Clover stares at him blankly.

"We have our rules too," he says, slightly bitterly now. "So the district can function smoothly. Everyone has to cooperate. The rules are meant to protect us."

"So why do you trespass in the fields?" I say. "If you're so into your district rules."

Nat shrugs. "Some rules are made for breaking. The solar fields aren't actually dangerous. Not if you leave the panels alone. There's no actual harm in it. But the district police would get you anyway."

"So that's why your supposed chrysalises are a secret?" I ask Nat, surprised he doesn't think his district is so perfect after all. "Because you were trespassing?"

Nat nods. "And because butterflies are property of Central District. All pollinators are. It's written into the laws. You're meant to report them, so Central can gather them up and keep them safe or something."

"So why did you bring them here if it's against the law to have them?" I ask, accusing.

Nat shrugs. "I didn't know what they were, did I? Not at first. I didn't know they were going to start changing. Almost straight away, they were changing…"

"Changing?" Clover interrupts.

Nat nods. "They were tiny in the beginning. They could have been maggots, though I knew they were something different, more important than that. My mate Tally and I fed them thistle leaves, and they ate and ate and ate. We had to keep going back to the fields for more leaves."

"And then what?" I prompt, my pulse quickening.

I can hear voices out on the main platform. Dad's back with Sora. There's the sound of pans. They must be starting dinner.

Nat looks anxiously towards the metallic clatter.

"Where are they?" Clover says, her voice high and excited. "Can we see the caterpillars?"

"You need to be quiet," I say to Clover, glowering at her. But I turn straight back to Nat. "And then what?" I repeat urgently.

Nat carries on in a whisper. "They started hanging upside down from the lids of the jars I'd put them in. They wove themselves a kind of casing, because suddenly they weren't caterpillars. They're chrysalises now. Or cocoons. I found that out on the computers at school." He looks proud of himself.

"You have computers?" Clover says, impressed.

"They're in that box, aren't they? Your jars of cocoons?" I say, talking over her. "The box under your bed?"

Nat looks nervous, and glances again towards the

104

platform. "How did you know?"

I shrug. "You made it pretty obvious. The way you were holding it, I knew it was important. And now you want to put your stolen creatures in our mum's greenhouse?"

Nat nods. "If we can fix the panels. Ready for the next change."

"Butterflies!" Clover says, her eyes widening beguilingly.

"Won't your mum notice butterflies?" I ask.

Nat shrugs. "She's not noticed anything so far. Grown-ups don't always, do they? And now she's so intent on your oysters and seaweed, and figuring all that out." He stops and frowns. "Though actually she has always been interested in plants. When she finds out about this place—"

"And when your butterflies start flying around," I say, cutting in mid sentence.

"Pearl's right," Clover chips in. "Even our dad would notice butterflies."

"Maybe. Maybe you're right," Nat says, his forehead rippling. "If they start flying around, like they're meant to, I guess they'd notice that. But by then it'd be too late. They'd already have changed, and anyway, Mum likes butterflies. She has a picture of them in our living room at home." He pauses. "So if they really are butterflies, Mum will understand."

"What, because she has a butterfly picture in your apartment? Even if your mum is that stupid, Clover and

I don't want to be involved in stolen pollinators. We don't want them on our farm," I pronounce.

"Pearl!" Clover gasps, mortified.

"We don't, Clover. We're breaking enough rules here. You break the rules by even existing!"

Clover winces like I struck her.

"Don't worry," Nat says to her, looking at me strangely. "We'll be careful. The chrysalises are tiny, I promise. I'll show you. If you see them, you'll understand why I couldn't just leave them to shrivel up and die on my windowsill."

"Let him, Pearl. Please! I never saw a chrysalis before, or a caterpillar. You could put them in your ledger. Please!" Clover's sea-blue eyes are wide as they go. If they were the sea, the water would all spill out.

"If we get caught—" I start.

"We won't, will we?" Clover says. "Not out here! We might as well be at the end of the world!"

"So much is at stake," I say. "This place…" *You're at stake*, I think, but Clover's expression melts me – her big eyes, her downturned lips.

"Haven't I been wanting something new for ages now, Pearl? This could be what we've been wishing for," she says.

"A wishing wouldn't come from the land," I grunt, glaring at Nat again.

"All the finds came from the land sometime! All your

dolls. Your clay pipes. Your precious sea glass. It's all from the land once!" Clover says indignantly

Clover's voice tugs at my heart. She hasn't been this passionate about anything lately, except school.

"OK," I say grudgingly, softening. "Get them then," I say to Nat. "Go and get your precious chrysalises."

FOURTEEN
Pearl

There are dead, shrivelled leaves at the bottom of the jars Nat brings out of the box. The creatures look dead too. Like folded-up bits of paper with slight spines in strange webs. Some hang down from the jar lids. Some lie curled up among the leaves.

"Oh!" Clover says, not hiding her disappointment. "Are they … alive?"

"Yes," Nat says defensively. "They probably didn't like the boat journey. But I had to bring them, didn't I?" His eyes search out mine.

"Couldn't one of your 'mates' have taken them?" I say abrasively.

"No," he says flatly.

"Why not?" I fire back, feeling strange and uncomfortable. The creatures – if they are creatures – aren't like anything

I ever saw before. They're as dry as dust. If they came from the land, maybe they brought the land's poison with them. Maybe that's why they're not moving.

Nat shakes his head. "They just couldn't. Reasons." He takes a dandelion leaf to scoop up one of the peculiar forms, and places it gently on a green nettle plant on the floor of the greenhouse. "You don't know what it's like in the compound," he says, his eyes still on the creature. "The rules. Even if they are for our own good. Everything you do, you have to think about the rules."

There's a dull anger to his words.

I imagine life in the compound – in the grey grid of interior spaces, with a library that only has pamphlets. I think of a kitchen table with yellow dandelion flowers and purple thistles, but nothing else there alive. Despite everything, I feel sorry for him. We have the seagulls around us all the time, and the cormorants, and the fish and porpoises every time we jump into the sea.

"You did the right thing, bringing them here," Clover says, peering into the box.

Nat nods gratefully. "This is the stage after the caterpillar, the last one before they turn into a butterfly."

"How do you know?" I ask.

Nat shifts a little. A smile flickers high up on his cheekbones. "My mate, Tally. There was this book she used to read to her baby brother—"

"Brother?" Clover gasps, sucking in a stream of air. "You're not allowed!"

Nat's face falls. "No. You're not. The baby, Barn, was going to be taken inland when he was born, except Tally's mum died..." He pauses. He doesn't think he can talk about dead mothers. "Anyway, her dad thought they might be able to keep the baby. Because they were a three-person family again, like you are. You'd think that was fair, wouldn't you?"

"And could they?" I ask, scrutinizing his face, desperate to know the answer. "Could they keep him?"

"No," Nat says, his eyes firmly on the chrysalises. "The decision took ages. But no, they couldn't keep him.

Clover looks horrified. "So Barn was sent away? Just a baby?"

Nat swallows. "Barnaby. He was two by then. They promised he'd be looked after. You know, by the Communal Families, inland." He makes his face hard, like there aren't tears misting up his eyes. "They raise surplus kids. Make sure they acquire the skills to do their shifts, when they're older."

"The Communal Families! Do you think that's where I'll be sent?" Clover wails.

"If you insist on a school place they will!" I say. Trust Clover to make someone else's story about herself.

I turn back to Nat. "So that's why you think these

creatures are butterflies? Because of a baby book?"

Nat shakes his head indignantly. "Not just from that. We found out what we could at school, on the computers. Only they weren't that much use," Nat says. "Not really. There were no pictures. I asked my mum too."

"You said your mum doesn't know about them!" I exclaim.

Nat shrugs. "She doesn't. But it was easy to ask her, because of the picture. The Sakura painting."

Clover and I both look lost.

"It's Japanese. My grandmother grew up in Japan. The cherry trees blossomed every spring and they called it the Sakura. She used to tell Mum about it, when Mum was little. Butterflies flocked to the blossom like it was candyfloss."

Clover hangs her head dramatically. "Spun sugar. Pearl and I haven't ever tasted it."

Nat laughs. "Well, I only did once. I was about seven. A travelling circus came from one of the northern districts. Years ago now. Nothing like that ever happens any more. It was soon after the circus that Ezra stopped bothering. He gave up on us all." Nat sighs angrily and looks through the transparent panels to the sky. "The cherry blossom in Mum's picture looks a bit like the clouds," he says. "Except it's pink. And there are blue and yellow butterflies all over it."

"I wonder what colour your butterflies will be." Clover peers over Nat's jars longingly and picks out one of the chrysalises from the bottom of one. The creature shakes alarmingly. Clover gasps and drops it.

"Look at that!" Nat says, rescuing the strange little package of life, relief swelling in his face, and pride too. "They don't like being touched!" He puts it down on our nettle plants.

Clover beams. "They really are alive! They're alive, Pearl! Actual butterfly babies!"

"You better be careful," I say, fixing Nat with a hard stare. "You and your mum might think this is your science lab, but it's our home."

Nat smiles. "I know. That's why you two have got to help me fix up this glasshouse. So we've got a place to hide them."

FIFTEEN
Pearl

Dad's at the stove, bent over a steaming pot of mussel soup. We don't normally bother with proper mealtimes, but yesterday he said we had to make an effort on their first night, even if we didn't want visitors. "We don't want them thinking you're not being looked after," he muttered, not meeting our eyes.

Clover made ship's biscuits, only she cheated and used some of our precious store of butter to make them soft.

I picked samphire earlier at the shoreline. Mostly because it's my favourite, and because it takes all of two minutes to cook. It doesn't need anything extra. And because it's one of the best things I could show them.

Sora's perched on the edge of our frayed shabby sofa. She's already told us they're not used to seafood, but she's trying to be nice about it anyway. "It's smelling

113

good. I'm excited. It'll be something different," she says for the tenth time.

Nat's at the kitchen table playing with the dominoes Dad made, when he still used to do things like that. It was Dad who got me started on the mermaids, showing me how to carve a fish tails out of the pieces of driftwood we collect on the flats. To remake the old dolls as something new. Something better suited to the sea.

If Nat and Sora weren't here I'd be starting on the new doll Clover found. She's sitting on the shelf above my hammock. Empty eyes, waiting. I've named her Miranda after a book of paintings in the prison library. The caption said Miranda was banished to an island when she was three to live with her father. She had wild red hair. I wonder if the doll had any hair once.

Nat tiles the dominoes on top of our table methodically. It annoys me, seeing the wooden blocks in his hands.

"I've told you, Nat, haven't I? Your grandmother grew up eating seafood," Sora is saying, in that excited voice I'd hoped the boat trip with Dad might dampen. "She was always sad she couldn't give it to me when I was a little girl. The seas were in such a state. She'd be pleased to see us here now, about to tuck into a seafood feast."

Nat doesn't look interested in the grandmother he never met. His eyes are on the dominoes. Instead of dots, Dad carved fish. One fish, two fish, three fish. Cod, bass, sole, mackerel, whiting. Nat's putting them together into a shoal and Clover's beside him, watching, as if he's performing alchemy.

Dad swears loudly in the kitchen, and there's a hissing sound as boiling water sloshes over the edge of the pan into the flame.

"Dad!" Clover chastises, embarrassed.

"It's this damn foot," he says, lifting up his right foot and standing on one leg like a gull.

"What happened?" I ask, rushing into the kitchen.

"Argh, it's nothing. I got it caught in the winch head, pulling up one of the lines." His face contorts with pain.

"When?" I ask, my blood racing ever so slightly faster. "How did your foot get near the winch head?"

"It wasn't working," Dad says. "I was kicking it into action."

Sora looks over, concerned. "I didn't realize it was serious or I would have made you rest it. Sit down, Atticus. Let me take over dinner."

"That winch works fine. You've just got to ease the line in right," I say, talking over Sora.

"It's easy you saying that. You refused to come, didn't you?" Dad says. "It wouldn't have happened if you'd been there to help."

Sora looks surprised at Dad's sudden flare of anger. My face reddens. Dad's right: I should have gone with them. I only stayed to make sure Nat didn't tease Clover. And because I didn't see why we should be helping Sora anyway. Why should we make things easy for her? She could be a spy, not a scientist, for all we know.

"Don't blame Pearl," Clover blurts out to Dad from the kitchen table. "That line's easy. If you ever did it any more, you'd know."

Sora looks between us, perturbed at the fizzing tension. I watch her make eye contact with Nat, who's still at the table, turning over the dominoes silently.

"It's nothing," Dad says gruffly, then gives another stream of curses as he tries to put his foot down and stumbles. Shame washes over me. He's already on his third bottle of beer. I take the wooden soup ladle from his hand.

"I'll do it," I say frostily. "Go and put your foot up, like she said."

"Perhaps I can help?" Sora asks awkwardly, edging into the small galley kitchen. "Pearl?"

"You'd overcook it," I say, not looking at her. I take the lid off the saucepan and a cloud of steam blows up near Sora's face.

"Pearl!" Clover admonishes.

"She said they don't know about seafood! We don't want the mussels tough, do we?"

Sora smiles diplomatically. "I'll get out of your way then, Pearl. If you're sure."

"Set the table, Clover!" I yell. "Those dominoes are in the way."

Dad made mussel soup because it's simple. Mussels don't need much else to taste good. Still, Nat's face falls when I slam a bowl down in front of him and cloudy liquid spills over the side.

"They're in shells," Nat says, peering into the bowl. Sora's looking just as unsure despite her supposed seafood heritage.

"Yeah, well, obviously you don't eat the shells," I say scornfully.

"Watch me," Clover says. Nat's jaw hangs open, as Clover noisily sucks out the flesh from a mussel and throws the shell into a bowl at the centre of the table.

She giggles at his reaction. "It's food of the gods, I promise. The sea gods anyway."

Sora gingerly starts to eat and takes care to make appropriate 'ooohs' and 'yums', even though it's obvious she's forcing herself. Nat nibbles at one of Clover's biscuits, like even flour and water out here are too weird for him to stomach.

"I saw your porpoises, girls," Sora says. "I had no idea we had them in the bay. What an amazing discovery! Sea mammals back in Blackwater Bay!"

"They're not ours," I say brusquely.

"They're our friends, though," Clover says immediately. "So they are sort of ours." Then she blushes and looks at Nat. "Well, not real friends obviously. Not like your Tally."

Sora beams. "I'm so happy you've all been getting to know each other. Nat was very miserable about leaving his friends behind. It's wonderful he has the two of you. Do you think Nat and I will get to know the porpoises too? I'd love to find out more about them."

I shake my head fiercely. "They won't like strangers."

Clover ignores me and starts rattling off the names of the porpoises, describing every little thing about them, and everything she does for them, like she's the only one they ever come for.

"Nat wants to repair Mum's greenhouse," I interrupt.

Nat stiffens opposite me.

"Pearl!" Clover says warily, jabbing me with her foot under the table.

"That's what you both said," I say. "*Mum's* greenhouse." I turn to Dad for backup. Out of the corner of my eye I see Nat staring at me strangely.

Dad barely looks up. "Sure," he says. Mussel soup dribbles into his beard. I sink back into my chair, deflated. Clover breathes a noticeable sigh of relief.

"A greenhouse?" Sora asks keenly. "For plants? Oh, I'd love to take a look. What did your mum use it for?"

I glower. First marine mammals in the bay, now a greenhouse. If I'm not careful, Sora will never go back to land.

"Mum," Nat groans. "Can't you leave this one thing to me? I need some independence! This could be my project while I'm here."

Sora smiles easily. "If you insist! I'm sure I can trust these girls to keep you in line. I'll leave you to your repairs and I'll look forward to seeing it when it's all fixed. I'd love to discover what can grow out here." She turns to me. "Your dad mentioned your sea ledger, Pearl. I was wondering if you would mind showing it to me?"

I gasp. It's like a kick to the stomach. How can Dad have told Sora about the ledger? *My* ledger? All the secrets the bay keeps. "The ledger's not for looking at. It's just sightings, that's all."

"Precisely!" Sora says. "A record. That's why I think it could be useful. Scientists need records. You need to be able to measure things, so you can spot patterns and see changes."

"It's not even accurate," I lie. "Some of the sightings weren't even definite."

"I'd still love to see it," Sora says.

"Why's our farm so interesting to you?" Clover asks, her head to one side.

Sora smiles at Clover, and I go back to my soup, glad to

119

have her eyes off me. "Truth is, we need more food sources to rely on, especially in the bay," Sora says. "I'm excited about what your shellfish and seaweed could offer us. If we could scale things up, increase yields, we could feed more people."

She looks round the table, as though wondering whether to go on. Dad's slumped further into his chair.

"With more food security, we'd have to worry less about Central." Sora gives another cautious glance to Dad. "We'd be less reliant on it. I know your mum had some very exciting aims, when she was involved at the Uplands."

I tense up. Sora's got no business talking about Mum like she knew her.

"We feed *Aurora* already," Clover chimes.

"*Aurora*?" Sora asks.

"The ship," Clover says. "That's her name. When she was a cruiser. When she was still grand. George says people were served lavish meals under crystal chandeliers and had loud parties and danced in ballrooms 'til past midnight."

"He didn't put it quite like that!" I say.

"Did George always live in Blackwater Bay then? Before?" Sora tilts her head to one side. "His apartment's right at the edge of the compound. He keeps himself to himself."

"George has been in the bay his whole life," Clover says, her eyes still burning with longing, dreaming about that ship. "I wish I had lived then!"

120

"What? In the Greedy Years?" I say scathingly.

Clover sighs sadly. "It would have been nice at the time. To dance past midnight."

Sora looks at Clover indulgently, a twinkle in her eyes. She's caught Clover's charm. "I'm sure you will dance after midnight one day, Clover. I feel certain of it."

Clover smiles back adoringly, like Sora might be just the person to make her wishes come true.

"Things will get better again, I'm sure," Sora goes on, though it's me she's looking at now. "I know you girls have been through a lot. Your mum is missed at the Uplands too. I wasn't lucky enough to meet her, but from what I've been told by colleagues, she was quite a woman. A pioneer. People were really sad about her passing."

Dad, Clover and I stay silent. Passing makes it sound like Mum got on one of the big ships to somewhere else. Not that the land poisoned her.

Sora smiles. "But I'd love to know more about your lives now, and what kind of creatures you have round here. Your ledger could give me a head start with all this, Pearl."

I stare down at the table, feeling everyone's gaze back on me. Even Dad's watching now.

"I know we must feel like intruders. But we haven't come to interfere. I've come to learn from you, that's all," Sora presses.

There's a hot, uncomfortable quiet.

"The ledger's a mess. You couldn't use it for science," I mutter.

Clover stares at me but doesn't say anything.

"You're not eating," I say to Dad, to deflect the attention away from me.

"It's this foot," he says annoyed. "I'm going to sleep it off."

Dad clambers up awkwardly. Clover carries on parroting about life before the Decline. Things from the books she's read. And things she's just made up because they sound good. Sora listens politely but her eyes follow Dad as he limps away noisily. When did he start looking so old and worn out?

"I think he should take antibiotics," Sora says after Dad's gone. I look down at my bowl, because I know Sora's directing it mostly to me. I'm the oldest, the *big one*.

"Do you know what antibiotics are?" Sora asks.

I scowl at her. "Of course we do."

"The winch your Dad's foot got trapped in. It was awfully rusty," Sora goes on. "The foot could get infected. It's not worth the risk… I offered him some tablets, from the first-aid kit I brought with us, but…"

"Dad doesn't take medicine," Clover says quietly. She stirs her remaining soup intently.

"But if it helps," Sora presses.

"Doesn't matter if it helps, Dad doesn't take medicine."

Clover's shoulder blades hunch together as she speaks

"He does sometimes," I start to say.

"Not real medicine," Clover says dismissively. "Not from land. He thinks anything from land is bad. He won't even eat the butter. Even Pearl eats the butter!"

Sora's face creases uncomfortably.

"I'll help Dad with his foot," I say. "I'll wash it with seawater. The salt will stop the infection."

There's an awkward silence. Sora opens her mouth to speak again but then stops. She smiles brightly. I listen to Clover's spoon circling her empty bowl.

I push the plate of samphire in front of Nat pointedly. "You haven't tried it. I picked it specially."

"What is it?" Nat asks, looking queasy.

"It's a sea vegetable. Marsh samphire. It grows on the flats," I say.

"It's delicious," Clover says, smiling now. "It's the saltiest thing ever. I promise you'll like it."

Nat's face goes slightly green.

"Go on," Sora says, laughing. "I think you will actually like it."

We all watch as Nat picks up one of the green nodules and drops it into his mouth. He pulls a face but doesn't actually spit it out. "Hmmm, yeah, it's salty all right," he says through gritted teeth.

Clover laughs. "That's why Pearl and I love it so much.

It tastes just like the sea, doesn't it, Pearl?!"

"And that's a good thing?" Nat says, grimacing but laughing back at her.

I get up from the table, scraping my chair hard against the floor.

"Pearl!" Clover voices. "Don't go! I wanted to play dominoes, all of us together!"

I shake my head. "I'm tired."

"I'll play," Nat says.

"I knew you would!" Clover answers happily, already sweeping the bowls aside to make room.

The sun's a low orange blaze in the sky. A reflected trail of light shimmers back in the water and I'm tempted to leap right into it, to wash off today. The visitors. The crinkled illegal creatures the boy brought from land. Dad's accident. All of it.

But I have to check Dad's OK. I can hear him as I get closer to his cabin, groaning with pain through the night air. His door's ajar and I stand in the doorway, in the dim light.

"You should wash your foot. I could do it for you," I offer.

Dad grunts from his bed. "Ah, it's nothing."

"She thinks it could get infected, Sora does. She said so."

His voice is angry. "Of course she does. She's from land. Diseases and poisons are everywhere there."

I step further inside the room and Dad's voice softens a bit, and slurs. "I washed my foot in the sea, Pearl. We know that's the best medicine there is, don't we? Vitamin sea!"

I smile weakly. "So you don't need anything?"

"Sleep. Peace! I've been with that woman all afternoon, answering her questions. She wanted to see your mum's old papers. What right does she think she has?" He gives another yelp of pain as he stretches his leg out. "Maybe get me another bottle or two from the larder. Would you do that for me, big one?"

I bite my lip. "You should sleep. Those bottles won't help."

"They always help," Dad says.

I walk out but not to the kitchen. I'm not going back there, to Sora and Nat's pity and Clover's desperate attempts to win them over.

I jump into the sea. The water folds around me, smooth and cool.

I won't take Dad another bottle, to drown his pain and his sadness, and make him sleep even later tomorrow, leaving the new visitors to me and Clover to deal with. It isn't fair. No wonder Clover's got so fed up with him.

I swim the perimeters of the platform. Counterclockwise like the moon around the earth.

It's getting darker and we're not meant to swim on our own in the dark. That was the first rule once – safety in the water – but Dad never checks any more.

Clover's dominoes game didn't last long – I can see her in the greenhouse now, with Nat. She's lit a couple of storm lamps for them. They're sat on the bench, laughing. Sora's in the cabin, washing up.

I swim round and round in the dark until the lights go off on the mainland, then I pull myself up out of the water, grabbing a towel from the line we've strung up outside the cabin.

The platform's quiet. Everyone must be sleeping. Two extra heartbeats where there should only be ours.

Inside the cabin, the empty mussel shells remain on the table. Clearly Sora didn't know how to deal with them, and Clover didn't stick around to help. I take them to the edge of the platform, where I drop them down to the bottom of the sea.

SIXTEEN
Nat

Clover and I are on the wide expanse of sand that has revealed itself, fresh and wet, after the water has been pulled back out to sea. The mudflats.

There are tiny fish, darting in shallow pools of water. "Do you eat them?" I ask, bending down to get a better look.

Clover laughs. "What, the tiddlers? They're not even a mouthful!"

I feel myself turn beetroot-red.

"Besides," Clover says, more seriously now, "we don't go after the fish, not really. Dad says that's why the porpoises come here, because no one's after the fish."

She catches a brown fish in her palm and we watch it go still. Warm mud oozes up between my toes. Clover made me leave my trainers in the little wooden boat she brought us in. "The mud will ruin them," she insisted.

I was scared about how it would feel to walk on the sand, but it's better than the boat at least. Clover laughed at how green I went, even that short distance.

"Playing dead," Clover says, indicating the fish. "Because of our shadows, see?"

She moves her hand out of the darkness our bodies create, and the fish starts swimming again in her palm, wanting to be free. Clover pours it back gently into the shallow pool. The water's hot. It's only mid-morning but the sun's already boiled it right up.

"It's clever," I say. "The fish. It's doing the opposite thing to the chrysalises. They moved when we touched them. The fish goes still."

"Does your mum want to restart the fishing?" Clover asks, looking at me, her brow all furrowed. "And Ezra? Is that why he sent you?"

I shrug. "I can't speak for Ezra Heart, I barely even see him, but not my mum. That's not why she's here."

Clover smiles with relief. "That's why Pearl didn't want to show your mum the ledger. Pearl draws everything. Fish, crabs, birds, shellfish, tiny things, not just the porpoises. Pearl's worried if your mum sees the ledger she'll just see things for catching."

I shake my head. "It's the seaweed Mum's interested in most, because it captures carbon. And the oysters.

Mum says they clean the sea. And because you can eat them both, I guess. Everyone needs to eat, don't they?"

I watch the little fish, the tiddler, darting in its ring of water. Funny how it got left here by the tide. If all that water got evaporated by the sun, what would happen to the fish then?

Clover holds up a piece of glimmering blue stone. The girls have jars of it in a cabinet above their kitchen table, separated out into different colours – blue, green, white, brown, violet. "Sea glass," Clover says. "Rolled and washed and smoothed by the sea over hundreds of years." She hands the piece to me. "It's yours," she says. "Your first ocean treasure."

"Are you sure?" I ask, turning it over in my fingers. It feels like an actual piece of sea.

"Yours," Clover repeats, and lies on her back to absorb the heat. "Our mum had plans for all of that stuff," she says almost shyly, like she doesn't think she should talk about it. "The seaweed especially. She was the one that made us grow it. Properly grow it, in lines and everything. I found papers with Mum's diagrams and notes when I was cleaning out her office for you."

"My mum would love to see all that, I bet. They still talk about your mum, at the Uplands..." I hesitate, sensing I'm on precarious ground.

Clover looks at me almost hungrily. "Do they really?"

I nod. "Mum gets frustrated with Ezra because he doesn't try hard enough. To change things. She says he was different when we first came to the bay."

"Did you come from Central?" Clover asks excitedly.

I shake my head. "Nah, just some other district inland. We were moved on because they needed more workers here. Central's demands were already growing. Maybe that's what wore Ezra out. Mum thinks he should fight back more. It's like he's given up."

"Why did he send you here then?" Clover says, turning to me, her head on one side. "If he's given up?"

I shrug. "The yields in the farm have been falling. The plants aren't as strong as they used to be. Ezra still has to feed the entire compound. He has to think of other ways." I smile. "Though I'm not sure landlubbers would take to eating seaweed and slurping oysters."

Clover feigns outrage. "I don't slurp!"

I laugh.

Clover frowns suddenly. "Pearl shouldn't call you that," she says.

"Landlubber?" I say. "She doesn't like us, does she, your sister?"

Clover shrugs. "Pearl's not used to other people. She'll come round. She's good, you know. Kind. She doesn't mean to be … well, like she is." She's making patterns in the mud with her index finger.

"It doesn't bother me," I say nonchalantly. "Providing she doesn't spill about the butterflies."

"I hope she's not mean to your mum today," Clover says, looking out to sea.

"Mum can stick up for herself," I say. "Look how she persuaded Pearl to take her out." I look for Mum and Pearl too, but their boat must be hidden behind the oyster platform.

Clover shakes her head dismissively. "Pearl just didn't want Dad doing it. Not after yesterday. She blames herself for him hurting his foot."

I nod silently. Atticus was still in bed when we left the platform. It didn't seem unusual from the girls' reaction.

I think about Mum, when her Uplands shifts start early, even in winter when it's pitch-black when she wakes and pitch-black when she comes home too, and she always leaves me food out for every meal. I've always just taken it for granted – that Mum will make sure I don't go hungry. She wants my childhood to be happy, before my shifts start. But she must get tired. She's always working so hard.

"Shall I show you the whale?" Clover asks, leaping back on to her feet and turning a sudden cartwheel on the sand.

"A whale?" I ask with astonishment.

"We call him Moby Dick. After some book Dad used to read, about a boy and a whale."

"A whale?" I ask, stunned. "I thought they were all dead.

Pearl said—"

Clover's face falls. "Oh, it is dead!"

The word hangs heavy in the air.

"I didn't mean to get your hopes up," Clover ventures. "I thought you knew... The porpoises are an exception. A miraculous one, but..."

She looks at me dolefully. Pearl's words yesterday ring in my ears. *"Don't you know what your people did? What they destroyed?"* Even though it was a hundred years ago. I don't see why I'm any more to blame than she is. We're both human.

"So it's a dead whale then?" I say to Clover, trying to recover the situation since she looks so stricken. "That sounds a bit gruesome!"

"It's a skeleton. You'll like it, I promise. The sea's washed it clean." Clover's eyes light up again. "This way! Follow me!" She runs across the sand like her feet have wings.

"Is it safe?" I call after her, looking back at the wooden boat. The water's changed around it. The boat's stranded in the middle of the mud – we'll have to drag it to the waterline when it's time to go back.

"You're fine on this bit," Clover calls back. "You'll be all right if you follow me."

"You're sure?" I ask, remembering the stories from the Hunger Years, which some of the compounders tell, when people used to climb over the sea defences to gather cockles.

132

People were stranded. Drowned.

"Run!" Clover calls at the top of her voice. "I dare you!"

I tear after her, the sand crackling beneath my feet, and a cry comes from deep inside me, loud and wild and alive.

Clover leaps into the air and cries back to me. "We're as fast as the gulls!" she yells.

"Faster," I cry. "We're flying!" I imagine pairs of bright butterfly wings flying next to me. Surely even Pearl will be impressed with them then.

I slow as we get closer to land. Thick stubs of grass prick at the soles of my feet, and broken shells, sharp and jagged.

"Ow!" I cry. "How can you walk on them?" I ask. "It's like walking over knives!"

Clover laughs. "You get used to it. Be lighter on your feet." She leaps up and down to demonstrate, like there's barely any weight to her at all.

We pass wreckages of cars and other washed-out bits of land rubbish that look vaguely familiar, but I've no idea what a whale skeleton will look like. I've never seen the skeleton of anything before.

It's half buried in the sand. Elegant white arches like someone crafted them out of stone. Clover crawls inside.

"This was the ribcage," she says, from the whale's inner chamber. "And that's the tail." She points down a line of pillars, sticking up out of the sand. "And the head," she says, of the beaklike structure in front of the ribcage.

I run my hand over the smooth arches. This giant creature that used to swim the sea. "So they were real then, whales?" I say. "They seemed impossible, when the older compounders talked about them. None of them had actually seen one. Sometimes I wondered if they were—"

"Make-believe," Clover cuts in.

I nod.

"Pearl thinks this was a fin whale," she says. "Because of its size. Or it could have been a blue whale. They were even bigger. They were the biggest mammals that ever lived."

"How do you know all this?" I ask.

"Because of the ship's library," Clover says assuredly. "There are books on everything there. Anything you could imagine."

I picture shelves of books on everything that ever existed. Preserved, like the skeleton, only not in the mud but on the ship that's always been the thing we feared most. I think of the people I know who've been taken there over the years – friends' parents, a couple of teachers from school. Do they get to read the books?

I bend down near the mouth of the whale. Imagine it moving through the water like the porpoises do.

"I like the stories in your library too," Clover adds, kindly. "They're exciting as well. Did you read that series on the star voyagers?"

"Some of them." I smile. It seems strange to think of

Clover with those pamphlets. "The librarian, Mr Rose, he says that when they built the compound – he was just a child then – the kids all thought they were building a spaceship to take them to the stars. They thought the scientists had found somewhere for them to go. A new planet to start again on."

I expect Clover to laugh but she listens intently. "And was there one? A new planet?" she asks.

I shake my head. "No. There wasn't," I say. "There wasn't anywhere else to go, was there? Planet Earth's all we've got."

Clover nods thoughtfully. "I still like those books. I like dreaming about all those other places. Rao and Vega and Capella and Solaris."

"And Gallifrey and Ego and Dune," I continue.

I stopped reading the star series a couple of years back. Tally says the books are lies. She says they're to stop us from thinking about our own situation. "*I don't know why they don't have stories about real life. About parents being too tired to get up at the weekend, or babies being torn away from their families, or what life is really like in the Communal Families. No one ever writes about that, do they?*"

"This could be a new land," I say to Clover, gazing across the sands. "This could be a new planet."

"Sometimes Pearl and I pretend we're on the moon," Clover says, animatedly. Then her voice dulls a bit. "Or used to. When we were small."

I smile and make big moon leaps across the sand, wanting to lift the sadness of the dead whale and our compound, still stuck tight to the land, cracking and rusting. Here is what matters, right now – the wide-open space, far from any rules or peacekeepers. Clover laughs and joins in with the moon leaps. She goes higher than me, surer of where her feet will land. "So you don't mind being here?" she shouts, mid-air. "Even without your friends?"

"I mean I miss them, but out here, I don't know. It's not what I expected. I feel…" I stand still for a moment, unsure how to sum up the feeling in my head. Like all the light and the space got into my brain. "I feel free," I say. "It's a bit like being in the solar fields, except in the fields it's all quiet and still and the same, and out here it's … it's just. I don't know. It's alive, isn't it?"

Rays of sun catch in my eyes and make me blink. Maybe here is the perfect place to spend the summer after all, especially if we can keep Mum away from the caterpillars.

Clover smiles back happily. "I knew you would understand. As soon as I heard you were coming, I knew you and your mum would be the right people!"

She vaults up on to the skeleton – tiptoes across the backbone of the whale. She's like the acrobat that came with the travelling circus – graceful and powerful all at once. I wish Ezra had got it to come back. I only saw that one show, but I've dreamed about that circus ever since, and all the places they must have visited.

"Did you know there was once a whale with a horn, like a unicorn?" Clover says.

"A unicorn?" I ask uncertainly. The word flickers somewhere deep in my brain.

"Yeah. A unicorn was a magic horse with a pointed horn spiralling out of its head. And the horned whale, that was called a narwhal," Clover says.

"A narwhal?" I repeat, unsure if she's playing a trick on me. Trying to see what crazy things she can get me to believe.

"Only it wasn't even a horn, it was a giant tooth!!" Clover laughs as my face cracks open with disbelief. "It's all true, I promise. One day I'll get Pearl to bring the book from the ship and show you!"

SEVENTEEN
Pearl

We're back on the farm now. The motorboat is moored in its tiny harbour – a little space cut from the platform, with floats to stop our two boats banging against the side. The rowing boat's not there – Clover must have taken Nat out. Dad's still sleeping.

Sora wanted me to sit with her in the kitchen to measure and weigh the shellfish, and help her test them for contaminants. She's testing for fertilisers and flame retardants and dioxides and metals and plastic and arsenic. She has a whole list of ways our molluscs could poison her. I'm surprised she ate dinner at all last night.

"You could be my research partner," she had said brightly, as I helped her carry one of her equipment boxes to our table. "Photograph them with me. Keep reminding me what everything is!" She'd smiled at me, ingratiatingly.

I'd shaken my head.

The boat trip had been OK, out in the water, sea and sky all around us. The porpoises had joined us. Salt and Snort tailed the boat, thinking we might have fish to throw them.

Sora had dipped her fingers in the water. She touched Salt's grey back and I watched her smile at the porpoise's smooth slipperiness. She can't get over the fact we have mammals here. That the sea's healthy enough for that.

"You're lucky," she'd said, as I got ready to dive. "To be able to swim with such beautiful creatures. To enter their world like that." She'd sounded almost envious.

I hadn't answered. I'd disappeared into the depths to collect the shellfish. But Sora's right, it is a different world. I can forget the things I don't want to think about. Mum not being with us. Dad staying in bed all day. Clover's growing dissatisfaction with our lives here. All those things disappear and there's just saltwater and seaweed and fish. And our shellfish, like sunken treasure.

But Sora's equipment, taking over our kitchen table, frightened me, and I didn't want any part in that. I'd climbed to the top of the cabin, to the crow's nest.

This is where I do my best carving. I've brought up the doll Clover found the other day, Miranda. Her name doesn't suit her yet but it will when I'm finished.

I take the little knife from my pocket. Small, but sharp as anything. I use it for cutting seaweed and samphire and splitting open the shellfish. I slice off Miranda's one remaining leg. "I'm going to make you new," I say to her empty face.

I pick a piece of driftwood out of the box I keep stashed under the bench in the lookout and I start to carve. Getting the size first, and the basic shape. Once that's done, you can work on the detail. The forked tail. The intricate scales. The ripple of muscle underneath. I always make my mermaids strong.

The final step before she's ready for painting is to attach the tail on with wire. Thin, pliable wire, which I wind round and round, tight as I can, so the doll and tail don't ever separate. Long after the paint's worn off, the mermaid will still be swimming.

"Hello! Nat! Clover!" I hear Sora shouting beneath me on the platform, and chattering bright voices – Clover and Nat, back from the flats. I can hear it in them. The freshness of the finds.

She's taken him to our kingdom already.

I peer down through the worn slats of the crow's nest.

"How was it?" Sora's asking, walking out from the cabin to meet them. Her cheeks are flushed.

"*I can't tell you how good it feels to be out here in the fresh air,*" Sora had said on the boat. She hadn't been seasick at all. She's stronger than she looks.

"Amazing!" Nat replies. He does look a bit green from

the boat, and is taking exaggerated gulps of air. "We saw a whale skeleton. It's so cool, Mum. There's so much space out there. We could run for miles. There were crabs and a massive bird that looked like a flying dinosaur."

"Magwitch. She's one of our cormorants," Clover says, giggling. Her cheeks are flushed too. The flats aren't new to her, but having someone else to explore them with is. I bet she didn't miss me at all.

"Have you seen your sister?" Sora asks her.

Clover shrugs. "I thought she was helping you."

"She was. She did a great job. But I think she wanted time on her own. I checked your cabin, but she didn't seem to be there... I didn't want to go right in." Sora sounds unsure.

"Pearl will be off swimming," Clover says casually.

"On her own?" Sora asks, alarm spreading across her face.

"Sure!" Clover answers, surprised. "You don't need to worry. Pearl's an expert swimmer. We both are. Dad says it's like we were born in the water. Water babies."

Sora nods slowly, though the fear lingers there. "Your dad's still sleeping. I hope he's OK."

Clover nods unconcerned. "He will be!"

"I thought I should look at his foot this morning," Sora says tentatively. "Make sure there's no rust left and see how the wound's looking, in case he needs stitches or anything."

Clover's face clouds over. "I'd leave him if I were you," she says. "He gets cross when you wake him."

"He sleeps a lot then?" Sora's eyes are quick and furtive as she glances towards his cabin.

Clover opens her mouth to speak, but I spring down in front of her from the crow's nest. "I'll check on our dad," I say stiffly. "He won't want strangers."

"Pearl!" Sora smiles with relief. "There you are! I was getting worried. That sounds like a good plan about your dad." She pauses. "Only you must feel you can come to me. If you're worried, or you think someone else should look too. It was a nasty injury…"

"I can handle it," I say abrasively, feeling Nat's eyes boring holes into me. I turn to Clover. "Did you find anything, on the flats?"

Clover digs in her pocket to show me – a dull red bead, a cracked piece of green porcelain, the golden clip from a brooch. I nod.

"Oh, and Nat got a couple of pieces of sea glass," she adds. "Show her, Nat."

The boy opens his palm to reveal the smooth pieces. "Do you like them?" he asks eagerly. Proud.

"Blue's common. It's nothing special," I say shrugging.

"Why do you keep jarfuls of it then?" Clover says. And to Nat, "Pearl loves sea glass more than anyone. The pieces in the cabinet are all hers."

I glare at her.

"It's lunchtime, I think," Sora says neutrally, clearing her throat. "Did you girls have plans?"

"Lunch?" Clover says vacantly. "No."

I shake my head.

Sora smiles. "Maybe Nat and I can prepare lunch for you then? After that delicious seafood feast you made last night, it's our turn."

Nat's face drops. He'll be wanting to check his precious chrysalises. He was in there first thing as well. "We were going to start on the greenhouse repairs, Mum. Remember you said we could? Can't you do lunch without me?"

"It's for our hosts, Nat," Sora says, disappointed. "It's the least we can do."

"You don't need to make anything for us," Clover says blithely. "Pearl and I don't bother with mealtimes. Last night was just because you were here."

"But I'd like to cook for you. You have to eat. Regular meals are important," Sora says, her face open with concern.

"I'm not hungry. And I'm going to see Dad," I say, striding off in front of her. I don't want her kindness and her looks of pity. I want my wish to come true. I want them back on land where they came from.

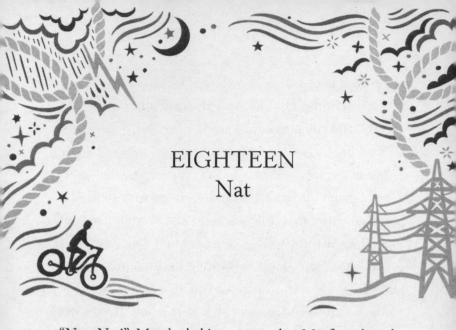

EIGHTEEN
Nat

"Nat, Nat!" Mum's shaking me awake. My first thought is the greenhouse and the chrysalises. She's found them. "I need you. Now!" she barks, already turning back to the platform.

I pull on some clothes and stumble out of our narrowboat blearily. My stomach turns at the dark water but I leap across the space to the main platform and venture inside the cabin.

Mum's at the table with Clover. She's got her arm round her. Clover doesn't look at all like the bouncy, smiley girl from the last couple of days. She's crying.

"Morning," I say awkwardly, hovering in the doorway.

Mum gives a faint smile and motions for me to sit down. "Atticus isn't well," she says by way of explanation. "He got worse in the night. His foot – I think the infection's spreading. I've sent a radio message to the boatman to come. I need to get Atticus to hospital. We're waiting for the tide to come in a bit."

"No!" cries a hollow voice behind me. Pearl. She flares into the cabin and slams her hand on the table in front of Mum. It see-saws precariously. "Our dad's not going to the mainland. I told you already. He won't! And he doesn't need to!" Her voice is high and brittle.

Clover's sobs get louder. "I told you! I told you Pearl won't let Dad go." She puts her face in her hands and cries like it's the end of the world.

"Pearl," Mum says, using her gentlest voice, just like she did with Tally after the peacekeepers came for Barnaby. Mum could comfort Tally when no one else could. "We have to do what's best for your dad. We shouldn't take chances. I managed to get a quick look at his foot last night. He'd gone to the kitchen for a drink."

I watch Pearl's cheeks burn bright red. Mum doesn't pause. "I got him to show me, Pearl. The wound's infected. Badly. You don't want that spreading through his body, believe me."

"No!" Pearl says again, her eyes big and wild. "You can't and you won't. It's not the right place for him. You can't take Dad to hospital. It's not safe."

She's stamping her feet and the platform's rocking in response to it. Last night's dinner shifts uneasily in my stomach.

Mum takes a deep breath. I know that steely look in her eyes. "Listen, Pearl, I know you're distrustful of the hospital, but your dad needs proper medical help."

"I'm helping him!" Pearl screams. "Me! I'm helping, and the seawater will make him better. You just got here. You don't even know him. You can't take our dad away from us."

Clover sniffs, between sobs. "Sora thinks he might be really ill, Pearl! You've got to listen to her. Please, Pearl! We need their help."

Pearl's face breaks up a bit at her sister's voice. She stares between us all desperately. "I'll do another wishing. I'll get one ready." She's pulling at her hair. At the fronds of seaweed that are twined through it and I look away, awkward and embarrassed.

"A wishing?" Mum asks puzzled.

"You wouldn't understand," Pearl mutters.

"Try me," Mum says kindly, getting up and trying to pat her shoulder. Pearl moves away.

"It's a healing ceremony," Pearl falters, glancing sideways at me suspiciously.

"Like a prayer?" Mum asks.

"No!" Pearl says crossly. "Not like a prayer. It's..." She stops speaking and turns to look through the window. She's trembling.

"Magic." Clover stops crying and heaves a sigh. "Pearl

thinks it's magic. She did one last night. A wishing. She puts things out on the sand for the sea."

Mum looks from one girl to the other, her face perplexed.

"It's not just the wishings. If we keep washing the wound too, with seawater," Pearl says desperately.

"Water won't help!" Clover exclaims miserably.

"It's not just water and you know it," Pearl shouts at Clover, her eyes glistening furiously. "And the wishings are magic. They are if you do them right! Maybe they would work if you joined in! Maybe it's your fault Dad's not getting better!"

Clover looks crushed and bursts into another round of crying. Pearl turns away from the table and storms off out to the platform. Mum, with her arm back round Clover, gestures for me to follow.

I stare at the retreating figure helplessly. It doesn't feel like Pearl wants anyone else right now, and definitely not me or Mum. Landlubbers!

"Now, Nat!" Mum orders. "Pearl shouldn't be alone when she's so upset."

"Mum!" I protest.

"Now!" Mum hisses. "I need to get Atticus ready for the crossing. Clover's going to help me pack a change of clothes for him."

"But Mum," I try again. She gives me a look of fury, and I turn reluctantly to follow after Pearl.

I keep well behind as she slips from one boat to another, and I don't say anything – this way I can obey Mum and give Pearl the space she wants. I don't think Pearl even knows I'm there, but as she gets close to her dad's cabin, she turns back to me. If I could see her eyes, I think I'd see she was crying, but she's swiped her hair over her face. Fronds of oily black strands and seaweed. Her right hand clutches the shells strung round her neck.

"You don't need to follow," she says in a clear voice.

"I know that!" I say. "But you don't know what Mum's like. She's worried about you."

"My dad wouldn't be injured if she hadn't come here. I knew landlubbers would ruin everything." She spits out the words.

"That's out of order!" I say crossly. "We didn't ask to come out here. It's not our fault your dad got injured. Maybe if you'd helped him, like he asked you to…"

Pearl glares at me and stalks off.

"Suit yourself!" I call after her, bristling with new anger. "I don't want to be around you anyway!"

I crouch down on the ledge of one of the boats and look out over the water, watching the porpoises, arcing in the water. I grow hot, thinking of that first day when I cried out dolphin.

"*Don't you know what your people did? What they*

destroyed?" Like I was responsible. Like I was part of the destruction.

One of the porpoises comes closer. She's sleek and beautiful. Dark on the top, paler underneath. The mouth looks like she's smiling. I imagine Clover's whale skeleton reassembling itself and growing skin and taking back to the sea when the tide comes in. I wonder if there's a part of the world where whales still swim?

From inside Atticus's cabin, I can hear murmuring voices and shouts. Someone crying, or two people. I edge further away. *Privacy is a rule here*, Pearl said.

A door slams hard and the whole farm seems to shake. I grip on to the rope.

Pearl comes and stands beside me. Her hair's come away from her face and there are tears streaming down her cheeks. It feels awful, seeing her like this. Like the hard shell around her has come away, and she's soft inside, hurting. "You better tell your mum then," she says.

I stare back uncertainly.

"To take him," she says. "Dad. He says he should go. He says he wants to."

"I'm sorry," I say inadequately.

"Yeah, well," Pearl says bitterly.

"The hospital's the right place for him. If he's really sick," I mumble, not wanting to meet her eyes directly because they're sore and red.

"It wasn't for my mum," Pearl retorts, though quieter now. Younger. Suddenly she sounds just like Clover.

"I had my appendix out there once. In that same hospital. I got better," I say. Stupidly. Appendicitis hardly compares with whatever their mum had.

Though sometimes appendicitis is fatal, Mum told me afterwards when I was back home, safe in bed in the compound. The medicines for infection, the antibiotics, not many of them work any more. Infections can kill. Mum's concerned about Atticus's foot for good reason.

Pearl stares blankly, then steps off into the water and disappears. I scramble to my feet to look into the dark water. She's completely gone, swallowed up by the sea. There's just a circular trail in the brown water where she must have gone under.

I yell her name. The rings on the surface are disappearing already, closing up. I can't see any shapes or shadows. There's hardly any trace left. Panic ripples through me. "Pearl! Pearl!" I scream over the water.

I'm about to run for Mum or Clover, when the top of a head surfaces a good twenty metres away. Blithely coming up for air.

"Pearl!" I cry. "Are you OK?"

She doesn't even turn back.

"Don't you want to say goodbye? Your dad will be going soon," I shout after her. I can hear the motor from George's

150

boat approaching on the other side of the oyster farm.

Pearl doesn't hear, or maybe she does, because after a few seconds, she dives back down.

NINETEEN
Pearl

They've already gone. The farm feels different. Lighter. Emptier. Sora's gone, but Dad's gone too, and I wished it.

"Take the infection back to shore
Leave us clean and pure."

I wished it on the wentletrap. I thought Sora was the infection – her and her landlubber son – but the sea always decides and the sea claimed Dad too.

The strange thing is, now he's gone, I feel almost glad. Because now he's not my responsibility to get well.

There are voices coming from Mum's greenhouse and I walk over to see what's happening. Nat and Clover haven't wasted any time. They're already fixing the panels. The door to the tool shed is open. Things are strewn over the floor and the air reeks of creosote. It scratches at my lungs.

In the greenhouse, Nat's telling some kind of story,

theatrically, like he's trying to make her laugh.

They stop when they notice me. Clover's face darkens a little and Nat fixes a sympathetic look on his face.

"You spilled creosote in the shed," I say.

Clover's face stays the same. "It was impossible not to. That store cupboard's a mess."

I stare at the tools on the greenhouse floor. The hammer, file, pliers, screwdriver, wrench. Dad was always doing something with these tools, and then oiling them carefully before he put them away. Rust is your enemy at sea but Dad was always ahead of it. I haven't seen the tools for months.

Clover doesn't even stop for breath. "There was a radio call from Sora. Dad'll be gone for ages. Days, maybe. We don't have to worry about them seeing the butterflies any more." She's almost triumphant. "You didn't want to say goodbye?" she adds, accusing.

I don't say anything. Nat glances sideways at Clover. They're allies against me.

"Mum says she'll stay with your dad a day or two, while he settles, to make sure he's getting the best treatment, and..." He sounds embarrassed. "So he's not lonely, I guess."

"How will that help? He doesn't know her," I retort.

Nat shrugs. "Mum's nice. She's kind. She'll look after him. And she'll send us updates."

"You won't want to stay here without her, will you? We can take you ashore. I'll do it now," I say.

Nat shifts his weight from one foot to the other slowly. He looks taken aback by what I've said – the possibility of leaving.

"You can go back to your friends," I push. "And we won't need to babysit you any longer."

"I can take care of myself," he says defensively. "I don't need looking after."

"You don't like being here," I press. "We can see that. You told us yourself you didn't want to come."

Nat flushes.

"Pearl!" Clover protests furiously. "He does like it! When you're not around he likes it!" She swings round to Nat. "You won't go, will you, Nat? You're the best thing that's happened round here for ages."

A new wave of red blooms on Nat's face. Clover might as well fling her arms round him and beg him to stay. "If I'm not in the way, I'd like to … stay," he says tentatively, looking at me, as though asking for my permission. "I could help maybe, now your dad's gone."

"Besides, Sora wants us to carry on with her work," Clover says importantly. "She's entrusted some of the tasks to us. The recordings. Sea temperature, water levels and tide times."

"To you too," Nat interrupts hastily. "Mum wanted to

speak to you before she left, there just wasn't time to wait. She's going to try and get George to stop off tomorrow, to check in on us."

I sigh impatiently. "George knows Clover and I can take care of ourselves."

"I know. Mum's just like that. And I would like to stay, honestly," Nat says.

I pause. If I insisted Nat should go, would he? Would he go back to land, and it could just be me and Clover for a while. Clover would be hopping mad with me for driving her new friend away.

"Suit yourself," I say tersely. "Just be careful with those insects. Don't go getting us in trouble."

I turn away, not sure where to go, but not wanting to be in the greenhouse, seeing how they're changing it already. Even if Mum would be happy someone's bringing her greenhouse back to life, she wouldn't want it to be him. A stranger.

I go into Dad's cabin. It smells stale and empty. I open the tiny porthole windows.

There are bottles on the floor, rolling hollowly from side to side. I collect them up for the crates we have waiting on the main platform, ready for the next trip ashore. Dad can't have tidied them up for ages. Maybe I shouldn't take all the bottles at once, or Nat will get the wrong idea.

I strip the sheets from Dad's bed. They're damp and reek

of sweat and something else. Sickness, I think. Just like this room used to when Mum was last here.

I'll get them washed while he's on land. Washed and wrung and bleached clean by the sun for when he comes back. I wonder if Dad can see the sea from his hospital window.

Nat said he got sick once and the hospital got him better. Their medicine. Their antibiotics. Maybe Dad will come back better than ever – strong and healthy, like he used to be.

I hope Dad knows I would have said goodbye, if my head hadn't been pounding. If my tears could have held. If there hadn't been new people around to watch me cry.

TWENTY
Nat

It's my fourth day on the oyster farm and I'm sitting on the edge of the platform, the water wrapping around the sides of my legs. "Ouch! It's cold!

Clover grins. "If you think this is cold you should try it in winter!"

"Urgh! How can you go swimming in winter?" I say.

Clover smiles. "It's just what you're used to. Pearl says we have saltwater in our veins, not blood."

As if summoned by her name, her sister appears looming over me. "You're going to swim?" Pearl asks slowly, like it's a supremely bad plan.

"Try to," I reply, squinting up at her.

"You're burning," she says, handing me a glass pot of waxy cream. "You should put this on." She turns her head to Clover. "You should find him Dad's sunglasses too."

"Ah, you'll be all right for a while, Nat," Clover says, as I start to unscrew the little pot, unsure what to do with it. "It's still early. I'll remind you after your lesson."

"You better had," Pearl answers. "He'll blister."

I open my mouth to say thank you, but Pearl's already gone. A moment later I hear a motor stuttering into life in the little harbour.

"It's delivery day," Clover says casually, when she sees me looking over. "On the ship."

"Oh. See ya! Thanks for the cream!" I call over to Pearl loudly, to be heard over the jumping engine. It makes me nervous, seeing another person sailing away from us, just as I'm about to enter the water for the first time.

Clover doesn't seem at all perturbed at our undertaking. She's turning in the water, buoyant, like the yellow floats she's set out to help with my lesson. She's made a circuit, though I think she's vastly overestimating what I'll be able to do.

"Put these under your arms!" she says, bringing a couple of extra floats to the platform edge. "They'll support you in the water."

I look at them doubtfully.

"Come on!" she says. "Lower yourself in. I won't let you go under, I promise."

"But I'm heavier than you. How could you support me if I started to go down?"

Clover smiles reassuringly. "It's different in water. The water will support you if you let it. Watch me!" Clover lies on her back, legs and arms out in a cross, floating.

"How's that even possible?" I say with admiration.

Clover turns upright and swims back to me. "Put the floats under each arm," she directs. "And lower yourself off the edge. I'll be right next to you."

There are cylinders of light in the water and I blink as I lower my body right in — feet first, then shins, knees. When I get to my waist I shiver at the new level of cold but I make myself keep going. Just my shoulders remain above the surface, with the yellow packages of air held precariously under each arm.

"You're in, Nat. You're doing it," Clover's saying, her face open with delight.

I grin. "It's gentle, the water," I say. I had imagined being in the sea might be like being out in the rain, but it's not. It's softer than that, silky. It's not like getting wet, it's like I become part of the water itself. "I thought it would sting, with the salt and the acidity. They told us it burns your skin. In the compound…" I stop and pull a face, realizing how gullible I'm sounding.

Clover smiles at me kindly. She doesn't laugh like Pearl would.

I look down and I can see the kelp underneath, with fish darting through it. I move my legs about, like I'm cycling.

"It really is like an underwater forest down there!" I say.

"Told you!" Clover beams.

"Mum and I came through a forest on our way to the compound," I say. "It's the main thing I remember about our journey to Blackwater Bay."

"You're so lucky." Clover sighs. "To have come from elsewhere!"

"Hardly!" I laugh. "It was just another district, and Mum had to leave behind everyone she ever knew because Central thought they needed new workers out here. I was too young to remember. It's just the journey I get flashes of sometimes."

"Still, you made a journey," Clover insists. "That's more than I ever did."

I laugh. The trees in the forest were green and magical, though when I try and picture them in any detail, I can't.

"Are you ready to try floating on your back?" Clover says.

"I'm not sure I can put my head in," I say. My arms ripple and distort as I move them through the water.

"I'll be right next to you," Clover says. "Lean back slowly. You have to trust the water, see, to take your weight."

I pull a face. Part of me wants to go back to the edge of the platform. Surely I've been brave enough for one day? But I picture Pearl returning from the ship, asking how the lesson went. I don't want to have given up on it without really trying.

"I'm right beside you," Clover coaxes. "It's worth it. You'll feel the sun over all of your body. It'll warm you up."

I grit my teeth nervously. I'm covered in goosebumps and I'm trembling with a mixture of fear and cold. But Clover's right – the sun is hot and inviting, and I lean back into its rays, on top of the sea, gripping my yellow packages of air. I'm floating. Undeniably floating!

Clover whoops. "I knew you could do it!" She turns a somersault in the water, and then lies out beside me. Two stars, side by side, warm and weightless.

After floating for a while, I make my way back to the platform edge and Clover shows me how to hold on to the side and practise my kicking. She dives and spins beside me.

"How can you go under like that?" I ask, after a particularly deep descent.

Clover smiles. "You haven't seen anything yet!" Before I can stop her, she gulps a long breath of air and then she's down, deep, till I can't see her any more.

I think about Pearl yesterday and how panicked I was, and then how casually she emerged back again a minute or so later. Still, I shriek when Clover surfaces. "You scared me! How do you breathe underwater?"

"I don't! I hold my breath, of course! You can't breathe in the sea. Then you would drown!"

The word drown makes my heart jump. I pull myself out

of the water and sit on the edge of the platform. It feels I've achieved enough for one day.

"Pearl stays down for ages," Clover says brashly. "Whole minutes! I can too, when I feel like it."

I shudder, thinking of Pearl and Clover swimming at the bottom of the sea in the ribbons of seaweed.

"There was an island in Korea where women dived for seafood," Clover says knowledgeably, coming to sit beside me. "For abalone and conch and urchins and octopus."

I tilt my head. The words coming out of Clover's mouth mean nothing to me. Ghost names, like the list of butterflies Lucas read out from the computer encyclopedia.

"They dived without oxygen tanks and wore white cotton suits," Clover's saying. "They whistled as they came back to the surface." She gives a long low whistle now, which bounces off the water.

"Was it always women?" I ask. "Who dived?"

Clover shrugs. "I don't know. It was just a footnote in some book. The island was called Jeju." She furrows her brow and looks out to the horizon.

"Jeju," I repeat. "Jeju. I wonder if it's still there now, the island?"

"I wonder if the women are still diving. That's a place I could go, when I leave here," Clover says, a new energy in her voice. "Pearl and I would fit right in. Dad says we're like mermaids. Our mum used to say that too."

She kicks out with her feet. "Anyway," she says, as though suppressing some sad memory, "you best put some of that cream on. Pearl's right, your shoulders are going red. She'll be mad at me if you blister."

TWENTY-ONE
Pearl

I sneak into the greenhouse while Clover's starting Nat's swimming lesson. After making such a fuss about the creatures, it feels too awkward to look at them when he's around. A couple of them are still soft and tremoring, but most have hardened and are further along with their transformation.

Nat's removed them from their jars. Some he's placed on leaves, some still hang from the lids, which he's fastened to one of the panels. Sora wouldn't be able to miss them now if she came here. I wonder how she'll react, to her darling son having stolen pollinators?

I can hear Nat and Clover's voices from across the farm. I hope Clover's being sensible – a landlubber wasn't made for the water. I start to make my way over.

Clover's taken the buoys off some of the lines, to use

as floats. Nat's shrieking loudly. "You should try it in winter," Clover's saying happily, delighting in the chance to teach someone the thing she's best at.

Nat's wearing Dad's shorts. His chest is thin and pale, though I can see a redness on it already. His skin's not used to the sun. I grab the sun cream from the storm trunk in the kitchen.

"You'll blister," I say, handing it to him. Clover pulls a face at me. She doesn't want me interfering.

I haven't got the time anyway. I've got a shellfish delivery to do. Sem'll be wondering where I am.

It's funny the way their laughter carries across the water. I can hear it even as the little boat moves into the shadow of the old cruise liner. I wonder if the prisoners hear it too and are jealous of other people and them having reasons to be happy.

The ship's name is still there on the side, if you know where to look for it in the rust. *Aurora*. It sounds like she belongs in the sky, not the water. Sem showed me the top deck once, where there's a sunken chamber that used to be a swimming pool. There's a faded photo in the library of smiling people in fancy clothes, holding shiny glasses and waving flags. The ship set up for one of the parties Clover's always dreaming about. Now the swimming pool collects water when it rains, to siphon off for inmate drinking water. The luxury cabins are cells.

Dad says the prison ship should be closed now. I guess he's right, but I'd miss her if she went entirely. There's something about her presence I find reassuring, floating out there, reminding everyone else to stay away from the sea.

I pull at the chain on the side of the hull. It runs up to a big brass bell outside the kitchen delivery hatch. After a couple of minutes, Sem's face appears above and he throws the rope ladder down.

I was horrified when Dad gave the ship delivery job to me a couple of years ago. But Sem's nice. He doesn't mind that I don't talk much. He appreciates that I'm quick, that I help unload everything and handle it carefully.

"You know the weight of what you bring," he said after my first couple of deliveries. He didn't just mean the number on the weighing scales. He meant the life that I was handing over to him. Sem gets that kind of thing. He's like Dad, who calls it 'Neptune's bounty', and only ever lets us take what we need.

"I hear you've got visitors, Pearl," Sem says once we're in the kitchen, and I'm piling cockles into one side of the weighing scales, under lengths of seaweed hung up to dry. Sem cuts them into noodles to serve in the prison canteen.

"Huh," I say disparagingly.

Sem smiles with amusement.

He packs circular metal weights on the other side of the

scales until we get the perfect balance. I add up the weights in my head, writing the number in the kitchen logbook. Sem never checks my sums because they're always perfect.

"How are you finding it?" Sem says. "Must be strange having new people around after all this time."

"Dad's on the mainland," I say, going straight to what matters most. "He's sick."

"Sick? Atticus?" Sem's expression changes to concern.

"It's his foot," I say. "It got caught doing the oyster cages. In the winch…"

"In the winch?" Sem asks confused.

I nod. "He couldn't get it to work. Normally Clover or me would do it, but…" I stop speaking. I add a new load of cockles to the scales. They clunk together satisfyingly.

"Ouch!" Sem says. "So your dad's in hospital?"

"The visitor, the scientist lady, made him go. He's got an infection."

A shadow falls across Sem's face but he doesn't say anything.

"She said she'll stay with him. She probably feels she needs to. You know what Dad's like." I keep my eyes on the cockles.

Sem nods. "And your radio's working, is it? In case there's news, or you girls need anything?"

"It's working. I've checked."

I pour the cockles into the ceramic sink Sem has filled

ready with water. You have to wash out the sand before you cook them. It's a lot of work for the tiny portion of flesh inside, but they're delicious with vinegar. Especially if they're as fresh as these. Straight out of the sea.

"You must send Atticus my best wishes then," Sem says. "When you next speak to him. I bet he's not enjoying being laid up. I pity those nurses!"

I nod silently.

"The boy's still on the platform with us," I say after a while.

"You're looking after him, are you?"

"He doesn't need looking after," I reply. "He's my age."

Sem smiles. "Not used to the sea, though, is he? That must be quite a change for him!"

"Clover's teaching him to swim," I offer. "Or trying to. He's scared of water!"

Sem's eyes twinkle. "Is he now? He's out of his element!" He winks at me.

"You'd think he'd come to the moon!" I say.

Sem laughs. "You girls better take care of the boy then, if he thinks he's on the moon."

I keep on shaking the colander. Watching particles of sand drain into the sink, before I refill it with fresh water.

"And you, Pearl? You're OK without your old man?" Sem asks.

"I have Clover," I say automatically.

168

Sem smiles. "Sisters, huh?"

I smile back woodenly, wondering if I could tell Sem about the chrysalises. How tiny they are, and the strange casing, like gold plating, which is growing and thickening. And what Nat says is forming inside them. And how all butterflies are pollinators and pollinators belong to Central District and I'm worried Nat has brought trouble to our farm.

I open my mouth to speak but Olive slides into the kitchen and grabs my arm. "Pearl!"

Olive never says much, but she says my name. And she's good at taking my arm, leading me gently to whatever she wants me to see.

"Can I?" I ask Sem.

"Go on then," Sem says fondly. "But don't be seen. And remember you don't have long. Half an hour and the governor will be starting his walk around."

Olive leads me down the maze of corridors. Dark, damp tunnels that Sem calls the ship's intestines. Her legs are stiff and I can tell it's painful for her to walk. Sometimes I think about Olive in water. How she might swim as elegantly as one of the mermaids, if she had chance.

She glances round, to check I'm following. Her body's old but her smile back when she meets my eyes is like a small child's. Sem says the books have given her a new lease of life.

They've been stored away for years unread, getting damper, absorbing sea air. I don't know why the prison governor decided a year or two ago to get them out from their boxes, maybe he was just bored, but it's good to let them breathe again.

Sometimes Olive and I will spend ages on one book, looking through it, working out where it should go on the shelves. What part of the book seems most important.

"I want a book about butterflies," I say now, as we walk into the library. It's a big room, at one end of the ship. It's plush, or at least it would have been. Wood-panelled walls line a vaguely circular space, with a few small reading desks in the centre, and then shelves spiralling out and upwards.

Benjamin Price's illicit store of old knowledge. It must give him a kind of power, a different one, to have the books under his control.

"Entomology?" I say. "Butterflies would be entomology, wouldn't they?"

Olive nods. It's not that she can't speak – she knows all the words – I think she just decided against speaking. Sem thinks it's the trauma: whatever she was brought here for, and whatever came before that, and all the long years here too. Sem says it eats away at you. He should know because he's been here as long as anyone. He was here when the ship was a detention centre for refugees.

Olive's fingers – dry hands, nails bitten down to the quick – search through the spines of our tiny entomology section. She pulls out a small, fat book titled *Butterflies and Moths of the UK. Spotter's Guide.* The cover's worn and faded, like it's been carried around in someone's pocket or left out in the sun.

I climb to my favourite reading spot at the top of the stairwell, where I can sit by the window, facing the grey sea.

I flick through pages of butterflies and moths. The colours aren't as bright as they were once, I bet, but they're still some of the brightest colours I've seen. They rival Clover's paint pots.

There's a map on each page. 'Distribution around the UK'. Shaded areas show where each butterfly used to be found. By the coast. In wooded areas inland. High up north, in the mountains. Some butterflies you used to be able to find almost everywhere, some were only ever in a tiny part of the country. The Lulworth Skipper flew 'in grassy hillsides and cliffs in South Dorset'. The Yellow Swallowtail in 'the fenland of Norfolk'.

I don't know how I'll identify Nat's chrysalises – the little golden parcels that I wouldn't have believed were even alive if they hadn't shaken so frantically when Clover touched them. Like they contained some old magic.

I frown. Nat said his caterpillars had been black. Lots of these ones are green.

I keep turning the pages when a word leaps out at me. 'Migrants'. Migrants are why the razor wire is strung up on the foreshore. *NO LANDING IN BLACKWATER BAY. MIGRANTS WILL BE INTERNED. ACCESS FORBIDDEN. NO ENTRY.*

The signs say it in different ways but they all mean the same. No outsiders are welcome in Blackwater Bay. That's why Sem's still here. Why despite coming for dry land, he's spent all these years locked away at sea.

If Nat's not known butterflies in the bay before, then they're migrants. They've come from elsewhere to lay eggs, they must have. The book lists three migrant species: the Painted Lady, the Clouded Yellow, the Hummingbird Hawk Moth.

I gasp. I don't need to look further than the first entry. The Painted Lady is drawn out in four life stages. A mint-green egg, a black-and-yellow furry caterpillar, then a mottled, brown-gold chrysalis, with the familiar spines. Finally the butterfly itself: a kaleidoscope pattern of orange and brown, with black tips on the top of its wings.

I scan the text, muttering sections out loud. "Regular visitor to the UK... Found in warm, open places." I read that the caterpillars eat thistles and stinging nettles, and adult butterflies drink nectar from flowers.

"Nectar," I say, the word sweet and thick on my tongue.

Olive has come up the steps. She knows when I've looked

172

things up before, it's been for my ledger. Because I've seen things in the bay and want a reference picture to draw from, or to find out about them.

"Pearl!" Olive says, agitated. She looks back at the door and then points to the book. Her brown eyes are small and scared. They flit to the wall where siege state laws are framed and written out in full. Indisputable.

Pollinators are property of Central District.

Just like it says.

No Migrants.

And the worst part.

Households are permitted one child. *Surplus minors are* illegal *and will be taken to live in the Communal Families programme to assist in food production work.*

"Pearl!" It's Sem. He's at the door, hissing at me, annoyed. "The governor! He'll be passing by here. You know he can never resist his precious library."

Olive indicates the book, for me to take it, but I put it back on the shelf next to volumes about wildflower meadows and beetles.

It's evidence. Nat stole those caterpillars and I don't want any part in it.

TWENTY-TWO
Nat

I wander into the kitchen for food. The girls were serious when they said they don't bother with mealtimes. They just grab whatever they fancy, whenever they want it, and it's not like there's many options.

The samphire and the biscuits Clover makes are OK, but mostly I'm eating up the food Mum brought with us. The shellfish make me retch – it feels like chewing part of a body.

Pearl comes in and goes straight to the radio. She frowns at it and turns a few dials. "Why's your mum not called again?" she asks reproachfully.

"Oh, she did, earlier," I say. "When you were at the ship."

"You missed it," Clover says, coming into the cabin.

"And?" Pearl asks.

"Dad's still got to stay a few more days. They're worried

about some blood condition. Sep something," Clover says.

"Sepsis," I say. And then quickly, as Pearl's face blanks out, terrified. "But Mum said not to worry. She won't leave until he's better."

"To make sure he doesn't walk right out, I bet," Clover says, slightly savagely.

Pearl nods emptily. "I'm going to separate the next batch of oysters. Clover?"

She looks at her sister for help, but Clover frowns and smiles sweetly. "Ah, can you take care of it this time, Pearl? Nat and I need to check on our chrysalises. We'll see you later, though?"

Pearl saunters off silently, giving me a dead eye as she goes.

In the greenhouse, Clover and I are carrying on with our repairs. Fixing the broken plastic panes with duct tape, and then arranging them with nailed-down battens to hold them in place. Some of the panels are too cracked to replace so we have to make do with tarpaulin, stretched taut to span the open space. It doesn't let in light like greenhouse walls should, but it'll stop the butterflies escaping.

"What's Edible Uplands like? Clover asks thoughtfully. "Have you been inside the tower?"

I raise my eyebrows. "No way! No one's allowed in who doesn't work there because of the contamination risk."

"Contamination?" Clover asks puzzled.

"Disease, fungus. Anything that could compromise the food yield. We need it," I say.

She stares at me strangely. I look through the panelled roof to the sky of floating white clouds. The sea's like a mirror today, reflecting them back. The girls obviously don't worry about contamination out here. What was it Pearl said? Saltwater cleans everything?

"Why don't they grow the butterflies at Edible Uplands?" Clover asks.

I shrug. "They can't, can they? They're all meant to belong to Central. Anyway, everyone back there thinks they're not viable – that they're already poisoned from the land. I bet if they'd left them where they were they would have grown. A butterfly must have come to the bay to lay the eggs. More than one. I wonder where the parent butterflies went, and why no one has ever seen one?"

Clover pulls a face. "Maybe they weren't looking properly."

I stare at her thoughtfully, thinking about how the solar fields are forbidden and how everyone's so tired all the time from their shifts. Could we just have missed them?

"I should have left them too. These ones," I fret.

"Though they might have come back another day for more, those Uplands people," Clover says, to make me feel better, I think.

176

"At least if Central had them, we wouldn't be worried about someone finding them here. Pearl's right – I've put you at risk by bringing them. No wonder she's angry with me."

"Don't worry," Clover says kindly. "She's just worried about Dad."

I get this urge to poke at one of the chrysalises, to check again that it's alive. It quivers the moment I touch it.

Clover hugs her knees to her chest. "I'm so excited! We've made butterfly paradise. In the middle of the sea! What would your friend Tally think if she could see them now?"

"She'd be beside herself," I say fervently. "I can't believe every single one of our caterpillars has cocooned itself and there's only one transformation left. The final metamorphosis!"

Clover beams. "We're experts, you and me!"

Barnaby flashes into my head. The way Tally cried when he was taken. I'd never seen anyone cry like that. No wonder Pearl's angry with me. She doesn't want anything to risk Clover.

"You miss her, don't you?" Clover asks intently, watching my face. "Tally."

I nod.

"What's she like?" Clover says, her head to one side.

"Tally?" I say, playing for time, wondering how to

sum Tally up. I've never had to before. Everyone knows everyone in the compound. "Tal's like no one else." I smile. "She's brave and funny and smart. You'd like her."

Clover says warmly. "I can't wait to meet her." Then her mouth puckers a little. "She might think I'm strange, though."

I pull a face. "What do you mean?"

"'Cause I grew up here. I don't know land ways, and I stink of fish."

I laugh. "You don't stink of fish."

"Pearl does."

"No, she doesn't!" I say.

Clover shrugs. "So you'll introduce me to your friends then? You won't be embarrassed?"

"Course I won't be embarrassed. You'll fit right in."

"Pearl wouldn't fit in, would she?" Clover says, pleased, swinging her legs back and forth under the bench.

I laugh. "If she wanted to, she could."

Clover nods thoughtfully. "Then she won't. Pearl doesn't want to fit in. She won't ever go to land. Not ever."

"What, never ever? Even if she knew she wouldn't be seen?"

"Never ever ever," Clover repeats solemnly. "Not since Mum died."

"But that's just to keep you safe? So no one sees there are two of you?" I say.

"It's not just that," Clover says. "She thinks the land made Mum sick. She thinks it'll make her sick too. All of us. She doesn't even like me going for supplies."

"Why does she think that?" I ask.

"Dad," Clover says, and kicks her legs back fiercely so they smash against the panels. "Ooops!" She laughs, though her eyes are narrowed into angry slits. "Dad feeds us a load of lies sometimes."

I shrug. "I suppose that's just like us, only the opposite."

Clover looks at me curiously.

"Most people on land won't go to the sea. I mean, you're not meant to anyway, because of border rules. But it's not just that. Most people in the compound won't even look at the sea. That's why the compound faces away from it. We've been taught to be scared of the sea."

"That's crazy!" Clover pronounces.

"Is it?" I ask. "The sea did kill all those people in the floods. People are scared it could happen again. They don't want a reminder that the sea's even there."

"You and Tally look, I bet," Clover says.

I laugh. "Sometimes. Sometimes we do."

"I knew it!" Clover says, jumping up and cartwheeling through the centre of the greenhouse, clattering plant pots aside. "You'll be my favourites when I come to school."

I lie back on the bench, shutting my eyes, letting the sun burn into my face. School seems a world away.

Even Tally and Lucas do. I don't even care who's found the most flags right now. I don't care about any of it.

Clover lies out on the floor of the greenhouse, her legs in the air, pedalling circles. She's getting in practice, she says, so she doesn't make a fool of herself when she tries a real bike. "I can't wait for September," she says confidently. "Now I'll know people, there's no way Dad and Pearl can say no."

"I can't believe you actually want to go to school!" I tease. "All those days shut inside, watching the clock, waiting for the bell. The endless lessons."

Clover pedals faster. "I want to learn things. All the things you already got taught, and more. I don't want to spend my entire life in Blackwater Bay. If I'm clever, they'll give me permission to leave, and I won't have to spend the rest of my life shucking oysters or working in your growing towers."

"Mum's clever," I say loyally, irritated suddenly. Our compound's a stepping stone for Clover that she thinks she can leap right off as soon as she gets chance. She doesn't know how land rules work. How Central won't let anyone leave the bay, unless it's to the polytunnels or desalination plant or factories. Least there's fresh air here, even if it is briny.

"Mum wanted out of the growing tower too," I say. "But she's still stuck in the bay, isn't she?"

"She got a pass out here, though," Clover insists smugly. "She was chosen to research our farm. See, hard work and being clever pay off. That's why I need to go to your school." She springs to her feet and smiles. "And lucky for me too that your mum was sent here, because I got my first proper friend!"

TWENTY-THREE
Pearl

We watch the lights go out across the water. It's curfew. The farm first, then the compound, floor by floor. Only a couple of faint lights stay on marking Customs and Immigration.

NO LANDING IN BLACKWATER BAY.

Would they say that about a migrant butterfly too?

"It's funny," Nat says, standing on the edge of the platform. "Seeing it all from here. It's like the blocks the little kids play with in the compound. Toy houses."

I watch his face in the glow of light. Is he missing all of it – the compound, solid ground, his friends? Or is he just missing his mum?

I reach up to pull the switch.

"Pearl!" Clover groans. "Don't switch it off now!"

"Lights out," I say. "Like they're doing." I indicate over

the water to the line of land that's just like a darker strip of sea or sky.

"You're the one that says we shouldn't obey land rules!" Clover says sulkily.

"They're not land rules. They're Dad's rules."

We have to conserve power. And it's for the insects too. The little clusters of flies that swirl around our lantern lights after the sun goes down. Without switch-off, they'd fly themselves dizzy spinning round all night.

Clover's face is set in a pout. "You're so boring sometimes."

I stare back at her unblinking, refusing to let the tears come that are pricking at my eyes.

Clover shrugs. "Anyway, it doesn't matter. Nat and I are going to sleep in the greenhouse. We'll get a free light show from the stars."

"You're sleeping in the greenhouse?" I ask, unable to disguise my surprise.

"So we can keep an eye on the chrysalises. We can see wings inside. They're about to turn. We don't want to miss it."

Clover stares at me as she says it. Her eyes don't say anything, but I know she remembers. She must do. When the four of us – Mum, Dad, Clover and me – used to sleep under the stars out on the platform in the height of summer, when the air was warm and dry. Or inside the greenhouse on a cooler night – in the misty damp greenness of Mum's plant house.

It was an adventure. Make-believe. Mum would come up with some elaborate story. We'd be explorers on a trek across a rainforest, or stowaways crossing a faraway sea to Paradise Island. We'd keep wild goats and drink coconut milk when we got there.

I'd already learned to be wary of land but Paradise Island didn't count. We'd be happy there forever.

I remember the pile of cushions and blankets and how it felt, against the warmth of Mum's body on one side and Clover on the other.

"That sounds fun," I say.

I wait for Clover to ask me to sleep there too. I know the stars best. I could point them all out to Nat, give the constellations their correct names.

Clover doesn't say anything. She wanders off into the kitchen and calls back to Nat. "I'm going to get us some snacks! We'll have a midnight feast."

Nat lingers, staring at the light. It's quiet now. The flies have gone wherever flies go at night. "I swear I saw a moth," he says. "Just before you turned it off."

"A moth?" I ask, surprised.

"Like a butterfly."

"I know what a moth is," I reply angrily. Even though until I'd read that book earlier I didn't. Not really. There were more moths than butterflies, the book said. People knew butterflies best because they had cheerful colours and flew in the day. Moths preferred the night. They were less glamorous, more secretive than their relations, but they were pollinators too. Just as important.

"Have you seen them?" Nat asks. "Moths?" He's staring at my face.

I shake my head honestly. "No. Just flies."

He nods. "You could come too. To the greenhouse, I mean." He stammers a little. He's embarrassed. "We thought it would be nice, to watch the chrysalises transform. They're really swollen, and you can see colours underneath. I don't want to miss them emerging. I wonder when was the last time someone watched something like that?" His voice trembles slightly as he says it. He's totally besotted with those creatures.

I shrug. "Probably just today," I say, trying not to let Nat see how hurt I am to be an afterthought. "If there are butterflies in Blackwater Bay, there must be butterflies in other places too. Otherwise where did they come from? Someone probably watched one transform just today."

Nat nods. I don't mention the butterfly book to him. I don't say that that's how I know about moths, and that his chrysalises are Painted Ladies and their wings when they emerge will be orange and brown and they'll need flowers to drink nectar from to stay alive.

"When they hatch, you have to let them go," I say. "You have to let them go straight away. We don't want butterflies here, bringing trouble. I have to think about Clover."

"I know that," he says quietly.

"You shouldn't keep living things imprisoned anyway. It's cruel," I say.

"What about your shellfish?"

"People have got to eat. Your farm can't produce enough for everyone. Do you think we should let the prisoners starve?"

"Of course not!" Nat says, shocked. "I know people on that ship. Good people."

I don't like the way his eyes burn into me. He doesn't know if he should like me. If I'm the kind of person you can like. He wanders after Clover and doesn't ask me again about sleeping in the greenhouse with them.

At night I'm jolted awake by the sound of screaming. I sit up, in case Clover needs me. She gets bad dreams sometimes. But it's not Clover's voice. It's coming from the ship, because there are bars rattling too. Someone having an 'episode', as Sem calls it. Shouting out their fury into the night.

The windows for the high-level prisoners are blacked out. They won't ever see the water or the sky. They probably forget they're even at sea. They'll know they're rocking, but maybe without any kind of view into the world, the rocking might just seem like a madness. I'd scream too if I was kept like that.

I stretch out my fingers to Clover's. It's a habit, when the screaming's bad. We hold hands to go to sleep and sometimes when we wake in the morning our fingers are still intertwined.

Tonight I just touch the loose fabric of her hammock.

TWENTY-FOUR
Nat

Pearl's at the table with a bound book and a small stub of pencil. Clover is with the chrysalises, still waiting impatiently for them to change. She barely slept at all last night.

I lean over the table and catch a glimpse of looping, elegant handwriting. Today's date and the chrysalises, blown-up and detailed.

Pearl slams the book shut and glares up at me.

"I didn't mean to be nosy," I say apologetically. "Is it a diary?"

Pearl pulls a face. "I don't keep a diary. This isn't about me. It's more important than that."

"What is it then?" I ask, curious.

"It's the ledger."

"Oh, yeah," I say. "I wasn't sure what a ledger was."

Pearl raises her eyebrows. "It's a kind of logbook, like old ships and lighthouses used to keep."

I nod. Pearl and Clover talk about all kinds of things I don't understand.

"I thought your mum would have called again by now. To update us." Pearl indicates the radio. She's moved it to the table, next to her.

"Me too," I say. "Is it working?"

Pearl nods. "I keep checking it. It's working this end."

I grunt. "Technology's rubbish over there. There are always blackouts, power cuts."

Pearl nods, frowning, but sort of relieved too, that there might be an explanation for the lack of news.

"What's in it?" I ask, looking back at her book. "Your ledger?"

Pearl shrugs. "Things."

"Things?" I press. "*Ledger of Blackwater Bay,*" I read out loud from the front of the book, written in the same elegant handwriting as inside.

"Weather and things," Pearl says reluctantly. "Things we see. Animals, birds. Like the porpoises. Or the seals that come sometimes. And the birds."

"The gulls," I say affirmatively.

"Not just the gulls," she snaps, frustrated. "Don't you ever pay attention? There are other birds too. Look." She flicks through her book to a double page of birds.

It's all grey pencil sketches, but she's right. They're different. Different sizes and shapes, with different-length beaks and legs. I see the big black bird Clover said was a cormorant, Magwitch she called her, but lots of them I haven't seen at all.

"You get all these in Blackwater Bay?" I ask incredulously.

"Some of them are only here in winter," she adds. "They migrate."

"Migrate?"

Pearl stares at me strangely, but her voice when she speaks is patient. "Migrate. It means move from one place to another. Somewhere warmer to breed, maybe. And some of the geese we get in winter come from northern Russia, from proper snow and ice. They wouldn't survive the winter if they stayed there."

I gaze at the pictures. Every mark she's made on the page matters and she's not allowed herself to add in anything extra. There are none of the flourishes her handwriting has.

"I record everything," she says. "Someone should. So we know what's coming back."

"Coming back? From where?"

"Somewhere out there. Who knows? It doesn't matter, does it?" she says.

I stare at her. Does she really think that? That it doesn't matter about elsewhere?

"Do you think some places have recovered?" I press.

"In the compound it's like other places don't even exist any more. There's never news from outside." I look past Pearl, past the prison ship too, into the endless blue and grey. All you see is sea becoming sky. Flat, horizontal. But there's land out there if you could get far enough. Somewhere, between the sea and the sky, there are other places. "Don't you ever think beyond the mudflats?" I ask.

"No," Pearl says curtly.

I laugh. Even if she does, she wouldn't admit to it, I reckon.

"I think about it all the time," I say. "All those other places there are, and when travel bans will be lifted, and when boats will start coming into the bay again. When I get out of Blackwater Bay I won't be coming back anytime soon."

Pearl blinks slowly. "You sound just like Clover."

She turns her head back to her book and flicks forward to where she was working, where she's drawn the chrysalises in every bit of detail. I hadn't even realized she'd looked at them long enough for that. "You're good. At drawing, I mean."

Pearl puts her arm out to shield the page from my gaze. Her face goes blank, like a cloud blew across the sun. I know our conversation is over.

"See you later then," I say. "I guess I should leave you to it."

TWENTY-FIVE
Pearl

28th July
Possible sighting: Moth (caution, witness unreliable).
Butterfly update: Chrysalises have been cocooned for more
than a week now. Metamorphosis imminent?

I slam the ledger shut. It's dangerous to include the butterflies. To write out evidence of them being here.

And now Nat knows I've been looking at them. Creeping into the greenhouse during their swimming lessons, to get a better look. I tear out the page.

I make my way into our cabin and pick out treasures from the box under my hammock. There's a pressing against the back of my eyes. One of my headaches starting. That's all I need, especially with Dad still away.

I reckon I've given the hospital and its medicine enough

time to get him well. I'm going to the flats for another wishing.

I almost bump into Clover as I edge round the side of Dad's cabin. "Have you seen Nat?" she asks.

I shake my head vacantly.

"Where are you going with those?" Clover looks suspiciously at my clasped hand.

I don't say anything. I'm not in the mood for her taunts.

"I didn't think he'd be gone so long," she says quietly. "Dad." There's a fleck of worry in her blue eyes. Like waves coming in.

"He'll be OK," I say. "He'll be back any day now."

"Really?" she says.

I nod.

"It's just…" Clover's face crumples a bit. "I miss him more than I thought I would."

I stare at her, surprised. "Don't worry," I say. "I know it'll be all right. I'm taking care of it, I promise!"

Clover glances again at my hand. She opens her mouth to speak but then must decide better of it.

"See you later then," I press, impatient to get on with the wishing. "I bet Nat's back in the greenhouse."

I lay the treasures out in the shadow of the whale.

One of my favourite pieces of porcelain. A blue bird

with fancy wings and tail feathers that Dad said was a type of pheasant. I lay it down for air.

I put sea glass for water. Blue. Just one piece. Even though it's common, it's powerful. Smoothed for years by the waves and rocks.

For fire, I use the bowl of a clay pipe. An ornate one, in the shape of a woman's head. There would have been fire in it once.

For spirit, a silver ring, engraved on the inside. FREE SPIRIT.

For earth, I lay down a piece of terracotta.

I stand over the things silently. I know what I've got to say – I've been planning it in my head – but it's harder than I thought to say the words out loud. The butterflies haven't even emerged yet and I'm already sacrificing them to the sea.

Back at the farm, Nat's next swimming lesson is in progress. He's flailing about in the water, like the more energy he puts into it, the more buoyant he'll be. Kicking like his life depended on it.

"That's good," Clover's saying. "You just need to relax a bit. Let the water take your weight."

The splashing increases.

"Almost," Clover says. "You're almost there."

Clover catches my eye as I look over. I can tell she wants to giggle, but she holds it in and turns back to her pupil. She's not going to mess this up by laughing at him.

"Oi, Grey!" she shouts. "Leave Nat alone!" Grey's appeared at the edge of the platform, oblivious to the tuition in progress.

Nat grabs on to one of the yellow floats, his face panicked.

I shrink round the back of the cabin so he doesn't see me and sit just out of sight, my toes in the water.

"What if he drags me under?" Nat's panting nervously, backing away from the porpoise.

Clover giggles. "He's not a sea monster!"

"Do you think I'm too old to learn?" he asks, once she's persuaded him Grey's not about to drag him to a watery grave. "Maybe I spent too much time on land already?"

Clover gasps. "No giving up in my class!" she shrieks, clapping her hands frantically. "Get those legs kicking! Now!"

I peer round the side of the cabin for a better look. Nat reluctantly tries another frantic paddle to the floats that Clover's put out at three-metre intervals. He's getting better.

Grey swims by my feet.

"My grey goblin," I whisper, hanging out over the edge so I can look him in the eye. "I missed you. I've not had time for swimming lately. Dad's not here, you see."

I reach my fingers for his smooth skin. I get such a thrill when I touch him. Like he's the spirit of the sea, come to say hello.

Grey blows out his *choo choo* breaths and disappears under the platform.

I gaze out at the water. It's shiny, like glass. The sky's lit with a strange yellow tinge and the air's still and quiet, only broken up with Nat's splashing and Clover's giggles. She sounds happy. Really truly happy, even if she is missing Dad.

Clover got old too quickly lately. She's only ten. I forget she's younger than me sometimes. It's nice to hear her being young and sunny again, even if it has taken someone else to make her act like that.

I go back to our cabin and curl up in my hammock. The blackness is still forming at the back of my eyes. I've been out in the sun too long, and I can't stop thinking about Dad. Why hasn't Sora been in touch again? Or come back?

I imagine Dad, pacing the corridors of the hospital, shouting for bottles of beer. I imagine him held down with chains, locked on a metal bed.

The row of mermaids above my hammock stare back at me. I gave them all sea names. Names I thought were fitting for a mermaid. Ariel, Emily, Cordelia, Daryah and new blank-faced Miranda. They look sad. I've kept them all too long. I'm like Benjamin Price with the prisoners and the books. And Nat and Clover too, taking such pains to seal up the greenhouse. You can't keep things locked up that want to be free.

I lie back in my hammock and fall asleep, clouds of butterflies dancing through my head.

🦋

I wake with a start and run out of our cabin to the edges of the platform. I scan the horizon for something beyond the blueness that I see. I'm hot and sweating. I dreamed a storm had come.

Clover is beside me immediately, her cheeks pink. "Pearl!"

I reach out to her. "Are you OK? Has something happened?"

She looks at me strangely. "No. Why? You were shouting my name."

"Did I? I don't know. I was…" I pause, "dreaming." I put my fingers on my temples where I can feel my blood pulsing underneath, fast and hot.

"Everything's fine, Pearl. Look. It's calm," Clover says, softer now, closer. I feel her breath on my face. She takes hold of my hand, her fingers gentle and warm. I feel her heartbeat in her fingertips.

I squint back to the horizon, determined to find

something. Something to explain the darkness that has seeped around the back of my eyes. The clouds are mostly white, still, waiting.

"But I can feel a storm," I say, insistent.

Clover rolls her eyes, but kindly. "You're missing Dad. You were like this after Mum too."

After Mum died I felt like my head would never be clear again. I thought the blackness would always be there, like the ink the cuttlefish pump out when they're scared.

"Are you OK?" Nat says, coming to stand beside us, a fist of samphire in his hand. They must have been on the flats together after their lesson. He's got the taste for it now.

"Pearl thinks there's going to be a storm," Clover says. Then, when she sees his face tighten, she adds, "But don't worry, there won't be."

I shake my head, exasperated. "You don't know that. Storms aren't predictable." I point into the distance. "You can see the swell." I gulp. "I'm sure of it."

Clover shakes her head dismissively. "It's just shadows. Clouds. There's not going to be a storm, Pearl. Trust the sea, just like I've been telling Nat in his lessons."

"You should never trust the sea," I say, angry with her now. "You respect it. You don't trust it. Even landlubbers know that."

Nat flinches when I say that word. Like he's finally realized it's an insult.

"Grey's not here," I say. "Or any of the others."

Clover scans the horizon. The water's flat as a pancake. "They were here before. They'll just be in some other bit of the bay. You know what they're like. Fickle. They'll have followed a shoal of fish."

"We should start storm preparations," I say.

Clover groans. "Pearl! This is one of the best summers in years. Why can't you relax and enjoy it? We deserve it, after that winter."

"I can feel it, Clover. I saw it in my dream. You know what that means," I say, pleading now, trying to get her to see. She used to get storm headaches too. Never the same intensity, but part of what I felt Clover felt too. Except perhaps it wasn't the storm that Clover felt, but an echo of whatever I was experiencing. Like how if Clover has a nightmare, I always know.

"If Dad was here, he'd be tightening the ropes," I say, trying to get through to her.

Clover's face is tight as a clam. "If Dad was here, he'd be snoring!"

"Clover!" I say.

She blushes angrily. "It's true. Anyway, Nat and I have got the last bit of the greenhouse to do. We think the first butterflies will hatch today. We want to make sure the holes are all fixed before they're born."

"Born? Listen to yourself! And why are you bothered

about holes? If they do become butterflies, they can fly away, and we won't have to worry about them any longer."

Clover narrows her eyes at me. Slits of cold cobalt. She sniffs. "How can you be so cruel? After all our hard work on the greenhouse." She marches off.

Nat lingers a moment beside me. "You really think there's going to be a storm?" he asks. "Wouldn't the siren be sounding, from the mainland? Would we hear it from here?"

"Course we'd hear it," I snap. "We're not on the moon."

Nat shies away, embarrassed.

"But sometimes they get it wrong," I say, quieter now, tired. "Weather's unpredictable. The signs aren't always the same. Sometimes they sound the siren too late."

"The water does look flat, though." Nat puts his right hand up into the air, holding the red flag that Clover's so enthralled with. Red for the hardest dares, he told us, like we should be impressed.

He's feeling for wind. The flag stays completely still. The sky's quiet and empty. Nat shrugs. "Well, I best go. I've got another swimming lesson. Clover's pretty intense as a teacher." He laughs but I turn away from him, angry, and start to pull at the ropes nearest me.

They're slacker than they have been in ages. Knots have slipped and come loose. The ropes tie our farm together like a spiderweb. You have to have the right degree of tension between them, and weights in the middle, to stop sections of the farm banging up against each other when waves and storm surges come.

I need to check everything inside too. It can take days to be ready for a storm. But even then you're never really ready, because you never really know what's coming.

TWENTY-SIX
Nat

"Wait for them to open their wings, Pearl!" Clover says. She's insisted Pearl stop with her storm preparations to come and look at the butterflies.

Wings closed, the butterflies are brown. Kaleidoscopic and full of brown spots like eyes, but brown nonetheless. I couldn't help but be disappointed when the first one pushed its way out of its sack. I thought colourful was a given.

But then it had opened its wings and we'd both gasped, and Clover had called Pearl in at the top of her voice. "Pearl! You have to see this! You must!"

Pearl comes reluctantly. She's been hammering away all morning. Nailing blankets at windows, securing the two boats in their tiny harbour.

Clover insists her sister's gone crazy and to ignore her.

Except for the butterflies – Clover was certain Pearl should see the butterflies.

Pearl crouches next to us. "They actually transformed," she says quietly. Her eyes glisten. I don't know if it's wonder or sadness.

"Wait for one to open its wings," Clover whispers.

The three of us kneel in a row, barely breathing, and one of the butterflies spreads out orange-brown wings.

"It's like a miracle, isn't it?" I say, pleased that Pearl's come too to see them. My whole body is trembling. It's not the rocking of their sea platform, I'm used to that now, it's like the butterflies awakened something inside me. The butterflies give me the same tingling at the back of my head I get when I think about that forest.

Pearl picks at the empty chrysalis with her finger. "It bled," she says, matter-of-factly. There's a brown-red stain around the papery cocoon.

"Do you think it's hurt?" Clover asks in alarm.

Pearl shakes her head. "Mum bled, when you came. Dad washed her sheets and hung them out on the platform. It took days in the sun bleaching to go."

Clover pulls a face. "Eeeww."

Pearl shrugs. "It's nature. Life isn't always pretty."

"I bet you wish Tally could see them, don't you, Nat?" Clover says, a touch of jealousy in her voice, or maybe just pride.

Tally's name makes my mind jump on. Back to land and the rules, and what it means that we grew butterflies. "Why did it happen for us and not for Central?" I think out loud. "Why do they still bother taking the caterpillars if they're not turning?"

"Maybe they are turning," Pearl says quietly.

I stare at her, remembering what Tally said, about glass palaces full of butterflies. "You think Central just don't want Blackwater Bay to have them?" I ask.

"Even though Blackwater Bay was the place they came to," Pearl says.

"Why's it not flying?" Clover says, her right eye up close to the butterfly. "It's flapping its wings but it's not flying. Do you think it's injured?"

Pearl shakes her head. "It's waiting for its wings to dry."

I look at her oddly. Her big eyes, next to her sister's. Pearl's eyes are green. Witch-green. "How do you know all this?" I ask Pearl.

Pearl shrugs. "It's obvious, isn't it? It needs the sunlight to dry out. Get energy." She's not looking at me, just at the butterfly – the lifting wings, beating up and down. Her face is sad. She must be thinking about her dad. Or maybe it's Clover she's thinking about, worrying about, if the butterflies are discovered. If Central are deliberately preventing butterflies from growing in the bay, they'll be more than just angry if we've thwarted their plans.

Clover squeals as the butterfly flutters shakily up to the ceiling of the greenhouse, just as a gruff voice shouts out behind us, "What on earth have you got there?"

TWENTY-SEVEN
Nat

"George!" Clover and Pearl shout out together, before they've even turned round and seen the old boatman in the doorway of the greenhouse.

"What have you girls been doing? What have you done?" He's crossing his right hand over his chest.

The girls and I scramble to our feet. My stomach drops, worse than seasickness.

"Ghosts. You summoned them back?" George is mumbling, still crossing himself frantically with his shaky hand. "From the past?"

"No. No!" Clover says furiously. "Not ghosts. We didn't do anything. It isn't magic, George. We promise!" She's patting at his arm gently, taking charge, directing him to the bench. "Sit down. Sit down. We can explain!" Clover's scared, breathless.

"Not magic? They're not ghosts?" George asks, looking to Pearl for an answer, like he'll only take it from her.

"No," Pearl says quietly. "Not ghosts."

I watch Pearl's eyes flit to Clover. My mouth is dry. What have I done?

"Butterflies. Back in the bay?" George says weakly.

I look again at Pearl, because I don't know what to say. Where our secrecy should end.

She's wearing a pale green cardigan that she pulls tight across her chest. Her green eyes shine like metal and she sinks down to her knees. "George, you have to listen to us. It's important… Nothing was ever this important. Please, George!" She gulps for air.

"I brought them here," I say, interrupting, because seeing Pearl so frightened and serious, I realize that it's up to me to sort this out. It's all my doing. "I found them as caterpillars. I found them in the solar fields, at one of the old windmills. Billy Crier's."

George looks startled. "Billy's windmill? You found them out in Billy's windmill and you brought them here? On my boat? You were dragging me into it?!"

"No, I wasn't. I didn't mean to!" I splutter.

"You should have said!" George reproaches. "You should have told me what you were carrying. What if Customs had searched us that day?"

"I'm sorry," I say, my voice fast. "I wasn't meant to be

there, out in the fields. I didn't want to get into trouble or land my mates in it. I didn't even know what the caterpillars were. Not properly."

"And Ezra Heart already knew about them anyway," Clover says, prodding me. "He knew about the caterpillars already. Tell him, Nat."

"We think he did," I say hopelessly. "Because people from Edible Uplands were taking them to give to Central. I wouldn't even have seen the caterpillars if the Uplands people hadn't been taking them!"

"And you thought you had the right to take them too? When you know what the penalty would be?" George says.

"But why should Central get them anyway? When it was our bay they came to? Why do Central deserve butterflies if we're not allowed to keep them?" I cry.

George has stopped listening. He's stood up, standing on tiptoe, to get a closer look.

"Careful," Clover says. "You could fall." She hovers next to him.

I never noticed George much on our trip over. He's well and truly from before, from before the Decline got to its worst. He's probably old enough to have known Billy Crier even. Surely the boatman can't still be loyal to Central District? Not deep down inside? He can't really think the butterflies should be stolen away from the place they came back to?

Pearl's standing to one side now. "Do you have news, about our dad?" she asks.

George's eyes drop out across the pewter water, back to land. "He's still in hospital. Your mother –" he doesn't look at me, but must mean me – "she sent food supplies for you. She was worried about you not eating. I left them out there on the platform. I called but no one answered."

"Why couldn't Mum come herself?" I ask miserably. If Mum could see the butterflies, she'd know what to do about them. She could bring Ezra to see them, to shock him into actually doing something for once. There are butterflies in Blackwater Bay! Living, flying butterflies, in fields we thought would only ever be fit for silicon panels.

"But Dad's getting better? Isn't he, George?" Pearl says fiercely, dismissing my question, desperate for her own to be answered. "Dad's getting better? George?" Her tall frame swings slightly from side to side like it's blowing in the wind.

George slumps his shoulders. "I haven't heard anything."

Pearl swallows. "What about storms? Have you had news of incoming storms?"

George shakes his head, surprised. "Nothing. It's clear, isn't it?" His eyes look to the dark line of the horizon. There's a yellow hue above it, like a distant sunset.

"Grey and the others, they've swum off, and the birds have gone too, and..." Pearl's voice tails off but she puts her palms on her temples and her green eyes fog up. Like she's seeing things from far off.

"I'll check at the met office, when I get ashore," George says, watching her uneasily. "What's your barometer showing?"

"Fair," Clover's voice sings out.

"I need to be going," George says gruffly.

"And you won't tell?" Pearl pleads, pulling his arm firmly. "For Clover's sake, George? You won't say anything about the butterflies?"

"You think I'd be believed? Butterflies, in Blackwater Bay? You girls are a law unto yourselves!" George gives an odd little laugh, before turning back to his boat.

TWENTY-EIGHT
Nat

Pearl's standing in the door of my cabin, her arms full of blankets. She's resumed her storm preparations and is doing each boat in turn.

There are clothes on the floor, and my bag is open on Mum's mattress. I've never got round to unpacking properly. I was hoping we wouldn't be here long enough, in the beginning at least.

"You need to sort this out," Pearl says. "We're almost out of time. You can't have all these things strewn around."

I lean down to pick up old clothes, as Pearl starts nailing one of the blankets over the window with a hammer.

"So you're sure, about the storm?" I ask. I've barely seen her to talk to since George left yesterday. I think she's deliberately stayed out of my way.

Pearl nods, distracted.

"I'm sorry," I say. "About George seeing the butterflies. You don't think he'll say anything? He's kept the two of you a secret all this time, hasn't he?"

"George wouldn't want to betray us," Pearl says, not quite answering my question.

Just as she's about to leave, she reaches to the shelf above my mattress, where I've put the couple of things I bothered to unpack. She picks up my trail-biking trophy and turns it round curiously.

"I won it," I say, unable to stop a flush of pride showing on my face.

"You won it?" she asks.

"At school. Biking trials, on the maintenance tracks around the compound. It was a competition."

She's staring at me coolly. "And you won?"

I blush. "Well, Tally won. I was second."

"Second." Pearl drops the trophy on to the mattress with a soft thud. "That could be your head, in a storm. Or Clover's head. You're not shut up safe in your compound now, you're at sea. You need to put it out of the way in the storm trunk."

She points to the wooden box at the foot of my bed. I gulp. "You really think a storm's coming then?"

"I know it," she says.

I nod. "I'll help, once I've done my room."

"Get Clover to listen to me," Pearl says. "She's lost her

senses, since you came. Maybe we all have. It's like those butterflies hypnotized us."

There's an awkward silence. "You ought to feed them," she says suddenly. "The butterflies. Your mum sent fruit, didn't she? In that package George brought? You should cut it up for them. The butterflies would like something sweet."

"How do you know?" I start, but she's already breezed out, back on with her preparations, leaving a lingering smell of salt.

I start transferring my things to the trunk. There are straps around it so the lid can't fly off if it's knocked about. I pause as I pick up the trophy. The bike trial was a couple of years ago now. Mr Rose helped set it up. School had marked a cycle route round the compound, and all the way up Drylands Road. Lucas hadn't wanted to do it, he's never been competitive, but Tally entered and it was the first thing she'd been excited about for ages.

Lucas knew I was Tally's only real competition. He suggested quietly, in that way of his, that I should let her win. Tally had been through so much with her mum and Barnaby.

But we literally never get to do things like that in the compound, and cycling is the one thing I'm really good at. It was my chance to show everyone. To show Mum too. I was the best at this. I was the best by miles.

Our parents were watching from the little terrace that stretches round the top of the compound, so maintenance can get to the air ducts to clean them.

It wasn't fair of Lucas to ask me to hold back. Ever since school had announced it, I'd been out every day before and after lessons, training. This was my chance to shine.

So I didn't hold back. I gave it everything I had, and I was there, out in the front, killing it.

But Tally won. She came out of nowhere, fast and furious. She wasn't even out of breath, just determined. Like all her rage over Barnaby had finally found a way to come out. Like sunlight making electricity. Her anger turned kinetic.

I slam down the lid on the trunk and secure the buckled straps over the top. How can Central get away with taking a child from the people who love them?

Out on the platform, Clover's lounging in a hammock, reading.

"*I Capture the Castle.*" I read the title from the front of the book. "Is it any good?"

Clover nods. She's got a plate of oysters and is eating them lazily. Dropping them into her mouth. The oily juice turns my stomach. I still haven't got the taste for shellfish, even when I'm really hungry.

"Are you OK?" I ask. "You look sad."

"I miss Grey," she says, sighing listlessly. "And the others. Pearl said I've been ignoring them since you came. Do you

214

think they got jealous?" She looks at me vaguely accusatory.

"I wouldn't know," I say.

I'm about to try and persuade Clover to help with Pearl's storm preparations, when I see something on the water.

"A boat," I say jumpily. "What if it's coming here? For the butterflies?"

Clover stands and puts her hand above her eyes, to shield them from the sun. "It's George's boat," she says. "A prisoner."

"Is it coming here?" I ask nervously.

Clover shakes her head. "Doesn't look like it. It's heading to the ship. Binoculars, Pearl!" she says, shouting now. "We want to see the prisoner!"

"They're not here," Pearl says from directly above us. It makes me start. I hadn't known she was up there, in the crow's nest.

"The binoculars are always there," Clover says, annoyed.

"Well, they're not now. Whoever had them last didn't put them back," Pearl ripostes deliberately.

I wait for Clover to remember. We were looking for ships a couple of days ago. The rare ships you occasionally see on the horizon, big ones that never turn into the bay. We were pretending one did come, just once, to collect us, and imagining all the places it might take us to. We had the binoculars. We didn't think to put them back. They could have fallen into the sea for all I know.

"Why's George keeping so far from our farm?" Clover asks.

"What do you mean?" I ask.

"Usually he'd come closer. He'd wave at us."

Pearl's silent above us, watching.

"I wonder who's with him," I say. "I wonder if it's a compounder."

I think about the point board back home. Mischa's surname, two off the top.

I stare over the water. It's dark grey today, and as still as metal. The figure at the back of the boat turns their head, as though looking straight at us. I shiver.

The boat cuts a white line through the water until it's swallowed up by the ship's shadow.

"Poor soul," Clover says sadly.

TWENTY-NINE
Pearl

I jump down from the crow's nest and go straight into the cabin to check the radio. That boat's made me nervous. On the table, the radio is flashing a green light for a recorded message and I stab at the buttons to get the message to play.

"Why didn't you hear it?" I yell at Clover. "How long has it been there?"

Clover shrugs. "I don't know. I didn't notice."

"If you didn't spend so long with those blasted butterflies!" I say.

"You could have been checking the radio," Clover says defensively.

"I've been doing the storm preparations, haven't I? On my own!"

Clover shrugs again but comes up to listen with me. The recorded message is crackly, stilted, but there's no

217

disguising the worry in Sora's voice.

"Mum," Nat says, entering the cabin, putting his fingers on the speaker like he's reaching through it to get to her.

But the message isn't for him. It's for Clover and me. Dad's condition has declined overnight, Sora says. He's getting worse, not better.

The crackles pass into my head. I rewind the message to play it again.

"There isn't a date," I say, panic rising up my throat, like a mouthful of seawater. "She doesn't say when it was."

Clover clutches at my arm.

We listen again. *I'm staying with Atticus in hospital until he's out of danger. I'll call soon with more news.*

"What danger? Why would she say that?" Clover screeches.

"There isn't a date," I say again helplessly. My eyes fix on Clover. "When did the machine start flashing?"

"I don't know," Clover says gulping.

"Today? Yesterday? When?" I shout.

"I don't know!" Clover says again. "Why's it up to me?"

I can't think clearly. There are butterflies cluttering up my brain and I forgot what's important. Dad in hospital. Sick. *He's got worse.* Why did I ignore the radio when it's our only link with land, and with our dad?

"Pearl! Your hand!" It's Nat's voice, sharp.

I look down and Clover's hand is in mine, white, because

I've squeezed the blood right out of it.

"We should go and see Dad, Pearl!" she sobs.

"Go and see him?" I repeat slowly, releasing my grip on her fingers. "Sora says to stay here."

"But what if the message wasn't today? I haven't been looking at the radio. None of us have," Clover says miserably.

"Then she'd have called again," I say flatly. "Sora would have called again."

"But what if he's even worse? What if he's dying?" Clover collapses to the floor in a sobbing heap.

Nat stoops down to comfort her.

"You've done enough!" I bite.

"Pearl!" Nat says warily. "Clover's frightened!"

Clover. I crouch next to her and place my palms on her wet cheeks. "It's OK, Clover. It'll be OK."

"I didn't say goodbye," she whispers, the whites of her eyes wide. "To Dad!"

I stare back, confused. "Of course you did. I was the one that didn't say goodbye! You were with him when he went."

Clover shakes her head furiously. "No. I pretended I was, to get back at you for being unfriendly to Nat and Sora. I was worried you'd scare them away. But I wasn't with Dad either when he left. I was too angry with him. For letting himself get sick when he's the only parent we've got left." Clover's voice rises hysterically. "I didn't say goodbye, Pearl!"

Tears spill down her cheeks like rain. "We have to go and see him. We have to go to land and see him!" she sobs.

I hold her and stroke her hair, but I don't say anything.

"Please, Pearl," Clover says, quieter now but looking up at me with new resolve. Her eyes the colour of the sea at its absolute bluest. The most perfect summer's day. "We have to go to Dad."

I shake my head. "The storm's coming, Clover. I can feel it now. I'm certain. We'll go once it's passed." I peer out of the window anxiously. The sky's fallen and the line where it meets the sea is thick and dark.

Clover breaks out of my arms and runs on to the platform. The wind's picked up. It grabs at her hair and swirls it round. She puts her head to one side, listening. "There's no siren yet. We can go before it gets worse. There's still time." She wipes tears away with her sleeve and looks at me expectantly. "We need to go. Now!"

I gulp. "We have to wait for the storm to pass."

"We need to see Dad!" Clover yells.

"Dad'll be all right," I tell her. "I know it. I wished for him."

Clover bristles furiously. "I'm going to him!"

"Dad wouldn't want us leaving the farm, Clover! Not when a storm's coming"

I close my eyes. I can see the storm, or feel it – coming in from the sea, in white-tipped waves. It's big.

"The wishings don't work," Clover's saying, crying out the words. "When will you see that? The wishings don't work, Pearl. I want to see Dad!"

"I want to see him too," I say. "But he's OK. I know he is."

Dad's like an extra beat of my heart, across the foreshore, on land, where I swore I'd never set foot again. It's slow, like the butterfly wings, but I know Dad wouldn't want me taking Clover across the bay in a storm.

For days I've known the storm was coming, days, but it was crafty, secretive, clever. Now it's out in the open and it feels it could rip our farm apart.

Clover's saying something but I can't make out the words, and then she's running, off round the edge of the cabin, to get to where the motorboat is moored.

I grab at her but Clover's always been good at slipping away. She puts her arm out to topple over a stack of oyster cages as she runs, blocking my way. I clamber over them but she's jumped in the boat before I can stop her. She's taken the rope off the mooring pole and is starting the engine. The throbbing joins in with the rising wind. She kicks off with her feet to get away from the edge of the little harbour, and kicks out at me too as I try to fall into the boat after her.

Her gold fairy-tale hair whips round her face. She takes her hand away from the tiller to claw at me. She scratches my arm.

"Clover, Clover!" another voice is calling. Nat. He's next to me, reaching out as she slips further away.

The water's surging now. White where it was grey, and split apart, like someone took a mirror and cracked it all the way through.

Clover's face is smaller, whiter, frightened.

"Don't go! Clover! Please!" I yell. The land looks further away than ever and sometimes the waves surge up so you can't even see it any more. And there's more. I can feel it coming – riding in from the north, galloping to get us. A herd of white horses. It's going to be the biggest storm in ages. "Clover, the boat's not big enough for those waves. Come back. Please!"

She's still struggling with the engine – it's unreliable, this is what will save her, I think – but suddenly it bursts into life and Clover's about to burst away from me too, when Nat does a running leap on to the boat beside her and pulls out the connection. The engine cuts out and Clover screams with frustration. Then a wave crashes over them and for a moment they're both in a wall of water and I'm the other side, waiting to see if the wave takes them.

But when the water clears they're still there. Nat's holding on to Clover's arm, and I meet his eyes gratefully.

He hoists her back on to the platform towards me.

The deep alarm of the storm siren starts from across the water. "Storm drill," I say. Clover nods, barely looking at me, and runs past to get on with it.

THIRTY
Nat

The greenhouse is coming away. The ropes have slipped and it's loose.

The sea's tilting. A giant has got his hands round the whole world and is shaking it from side to side, water frothing up like it's on the boil. Sometimes the greenhouse lurches away from the rest of the farm. Sometimes it crashes back into it.

"The greenhouse!" I scream at the top of my voice. "The butterflies!" The words are ripped away from me the instant I say them. I can't even hear my own voice.

I can see the butterflies – silhouettes on the sides of the panels that Clover and I cleaned and mended so diligently. They're flying around, panicked. The panels are cracking and smashing.

"Pearl! Clover!" I yell again. A colossal wave crashes

over me, drenching me and carrying the greenhouse further away. We're going to lose it. We're going to lose the greenhouse and we're going to lose the butterflies too. Their frantic beating wings appear close up in my vision, even though my eyes can barely see them behind the lashing sea and groaning panels.

"Pearl! Clover!" I summon up all the air in my lungs to call them.

The girls are round the other side of the farm, battling to tether their cabin down tighter. It's their home. That's what's important for them.

My face stings and I'm not sure if it's tears, the sea spraying up at me, or the biting wind. More than ever, I wish I was back in the compound behind its thick concrete wall. In storms we'd go to our bunker. You can barely hear storms inside there, not with all the compounders packed in tight and films playing to calm us. Safe as houses, the older compounders say. Tally always laughed at them. Isn't it crazy, she said, that even after all their houses had been washed away, that's the expression they go back to? Safe as houses.

I wait for the next wave, to bring the greenhouse back in against the farm. If I reach far enough, I can grab at one of the ropes trailing off it. I can loop it back round the poles, knot them off like I've watched Clover do when she's tethering the rowing boat. But the waves have changed and are working against me. Working to rip the sea farm apart and send the greenhouse off into the ocean.

I know what I've got to do and I don't think it through, because if I think about it, I won't do it. If I run round to get the girls, by the time we're back, the greenhouse will have gone too far.

It's only a few strokes, and what was the point in learning to swim if I can't do it when I need to? I think of Billy Crier, climbing up the windmill in the storm. He must have been scared, but he did it anyway, to save his dad.

I plunge into the water.

All points of reference go – farm, greenhouse, land, ship. Even the sky disappears. Everything is replaced with water – dark walls of water, lunging from side to side, taking me with it, and into them. I desperately try and tread water, like Clover taught me. More than ever, I need to stay afloat. The waves are too strong to fight.

Every few seconds I get a glimpse of the greenhouse and try to reach out for it, not to save it now, but to save myself. Then the water comes between us, and over me. I snatch at air, a desperate gulp of oxygen, before the water comes again. My legs frantically keep on moving.

If I stop, I'll drown.

Someone's screaming my name and I can see arms waving over the towering water as I push down against it. My mouth clamps shut to stop me from drowning, and my nose and eyes do the same, closed up against the water. It's out to claim me. What's one more landlubber to the sea?

"Nat! Nat!" Pearl's beside me in the water, arms reaching out to me. Another wave hurls itself at us. Pearl fixes her eyes on me and shakes her head. All I can hear is water.

Pearl turns back to the wave and pulls me down to swim under the worst of it with her. Showing me with her body what she wants me to do. We swim into the wave together, Pearl propelling me alongside her.

On the other side, there's the greenhouse. I grab at it with both hands. I've lost the energy to pull myself out of the water, but I cling on to the edge.

Pearl's already trying to heave herself out of the water. Normally she's in and out effortlessly, but today the sea doesn't want to let her go.

Then a rope is hurled over our heads, and Pearl does a final hoist and is standing on the edge of the greenhouse. She gets the rope in one catch and starts pulling it tight round one of the poles, to lever the greenhouse back towards the rest of the farm. Her face is grimly determined.

She's shouting and jumping up and down, waving her arms. Another rope comes. Clover doesn't need to hear to understand. She's already throwing another rope, and dragging extra buoys to the side of the farm where the greenhouse is tethered.

"Get up, Nat!" Pearl roars at me, and bends down to help drag me out. "I need you to pull with me!"

Pearl puts a rope in my hand and we tug it together, hauling ourselves and the greenhouse back in place.

"Stand back, stand back," Pearl's yelling at her sister. "We'll crash into you. We need another rope. Throw one to Nat!"

And in the lashing, howling storm, we work, the three of us, to pull the farm back together.

THIRTY-ONE
Nat

Exhausted, we pile inside the main cabin. The sea turned on us. It came for a fight. I don't think we won, but the greenhouse is tethered to the rest of the platform again.

Miraculously the cabin floor is still pretty dry, though it rocks from side to side, lurching precariously on the top of the ocean.

The drowning sensation comes back at me. The lack of air. My wet fingers cling at one of the vertical poles holding up the ceiling.

"We're safe here," Pearl says quietly, flicking her eyes across me. She turns on one of the lamps. Just a soft glow.

"Towel, Nat," Clover says, opening up a trunk and throwing me a large brown towel. It's threadbare but dry.

"Thank you," I splutter, still fighting for a proper breath of air.

Clover pats my arm and smiles at me kindly. "Sit down. Catch your breath. We'll be fine. We've survived much worse, we promise."

"Worse than that? Out there?" I ask, still shaking. "Now I know why the compounders face away from the sea. I thought that was it. I thought I was going to…"

"Drown," Clover finishes my sentence dramatically.

Pearl glowers at her. "You saved the greenhouse," she says, looking at me in a way she hasn't before.

"You were so brave, Nat," Clover says proudly. "Jumping into the sea to save our butterflies."

I blush. "It was stupid. Pearl saved them. It was her that was brave."

Pearl shrugs. "I couldn't have saved the greenhouse on my own. I wouldn't have had the strength. Not with the waves like they are tonight. I needed you on the ropes too. That storm…" She lets her voice fade away, and she sinks down on to the sofa.

Clover rushes over with a blanket and covers her tenderly. "I'm sorry, Pearl. For not listening to you." She's got tears in her eyes.

Pearl nods, exhausted. "It doesn't matter now, does it? The usual signs weren't there. And you were brilliant with those rope throws. Brilliant, Clover."

"Do you think Dad is all right? Do you think he knows there's a storm?" Clover asks.

"Of course he does," Pearl says assuredly. "Couldn't miss a storm like this, could you? Even on land. We'll go as soon as the storm's over. I promise." She smiles at Clover. "Dad will be OK," she says. "I know it."

Then Pearl closes her eyes and turns into the sofa, burrowing under her blanket.

"Will she be OK?" I whisper to Clover.

"Yeah," Clover whispers back, her face lit up in the lamplight. "Pearl's always hated storms. She can't understand why the sea boils up like that. Not against us. She thinks the sea should be on our side."

Clover looks up at the skylight where water's battering down, rain and sea spray combined. There is a leak, but just slow drops. She pulls a bucket out from the corner and kicks it into place, though it rolls over immediately.

"It's not normally so bad. Dad used to say we were hurricane proof. He's just not kept up with it lately. He's been ill for ages I think, it's not just his foot." She looks sad and deflated. "We've had to do everything, Pearl and me."

All Clover's brightness and enthusiasm is gone, and she's just sad and worried. She yawns.

"You should sleep too," I say. "Shall I get you a hot drink?"

Clover smiles at me. "Nah, I'll be fine. There are extra blankets you can use, in that storm trunk," she says.

"Do you mind?"

I shake my head as Clover climbs across to Pearl's sofa, and even though I thought Pearl was already asleep, she opens up the blanket for her little sister to curl up next to her.

I should sleep too but my mind's racing. I open up the trunk. There's a whole storm kit here – candles, matches, blankets. I start to lift out the blankets, and notice a stack of papers at the bottom.

I glance over at the girls. Their breathing has changed – they're both sleeping already.

Some of the papers are photos – loose, for anyone to see, and I can't help looking. Clover and Pearl as young children, Atticus looking fit and lean, and a woman who must be their mum – tall and graceful, with long golden hair just like Clover.

Clover's just a toddler – fat, pink arms, moon smile. In some of the photos she's gaping with happiness, in others she's crying. I think of Barnaby. It could be the end of the world if Tally left the room, but show him something shiny and he'd soon start to laugh.

Pearl's more serious in the photos, harder to read. She's not looking at the camera, she's just looking at her mum, studiously, like she's trying to learn everything about her. Like she already knew that storm was coming and she had to make the most of her.

Mum would have had the photos framed and arranged around our apartment for everyone to see. I guess it's different at sea. Harder to keep things safe.

The jars of sea glass are in the trunk too. Pearl must have put them there for safety, even though the sea glass has probably survived a thousand storms already.

Under the jars there's a pile of distinctive yellow envelopes wrapped around with string. *From the District Controller*, says a stamp on the front of each. They look quite new and not a single one's opened. Maintenance isn't the only thing Atticus hasn't been keeping up with. No one on land would dare ignore official correspondence.

I wonder if Ezra's hounding them for rent, or wants them to up their targets for the ship? Or maybe Ezra does want to take over their farm entirely, like Pearl worries he does. It's not my business to look. I take out a couple of blankets and shut the trunk back up, then lay on the opposite sofa to Pearl and Clover and bury down to sleep.

THIRTY-TWO
Pearl

Light from the edges of the skylight presses at my eyelids, but for a moment I don't open them. I just listen. Clover's snuffled, rhythmic breathing – as familiar to me as the waves, with her occasional porpoise snorts.

Nat's almost silent, yet his breathing seems louder than any noise Clover could make because he's still new. Though I am getting used to him. We couldn't have saved Mum's greenhouse without him last night.

The wind and the waves have quietened. The storm's moving on. I leave Nat and Clover sleeping and lever myself out through the door, on to the platform.

I blink. Outside the sea has strewn the platform with seaweed, and it's brown and green and slippery. But underneath its leathery skin our home is intact. The wood stayed together. The knots held.

Later I'll throw back the seaweed and sweep away pools of gathered water, but right now I know where I'm heading. Past the repurposed narrowboats: Dad's, where he should be sleeping; mine and Clover's, which barely looks touched; Nat's, with a shutter hanging off and a smashed plate he forgot to tidy away.

Oyster cages have toppled over. Some of them will have been lost out to sea or fallen down to the bottom. There's always damage after a storm. That's the way of life out here. You're always repairing after the last storm, getting ready for the next.

The greenhouse floats serenely at the edge of everything, like it's forgotten its bolt for freedom last night.

Be alive, be alive, I whisper under my breath.

I was so angry with Nat for bringing the chrysalises. The winged, scaled creatures I offered up to the sea in exchange for our father. The book in the library says they might have come from as far away as northern Africa. Thousands of miles of sky, over mountains and sea and deserts. Of course the sea would want something that's travelled so far.

Be alive, be alive, I repeat.

There are three butterflies on the floor as I go in. Wings torn. Dulled colours. I don't need to get any closer to see that they're dead. Did they come together at the end?

"No!" yells a voice behind me. Nat's. His hair is wet and

tousled from last night. He pushes past me to kneel down beside his precious butterflies. "No!" he says again, a stifled sob behind his words. He looks up at me. "It's my fault, isn't it? I did it."

"It was the storm," I say quietly.

"But I shouldn't have brought them here."

I shake my head uneasily. "They can't all be dead. They can't be."

Be alive. Not for me, but for him.

I walk around the tiny, circular path of the greenhouse. There are other butterfly bodies lying on the cracked tiles – broken, battered. But the sun's rising in the sky, blinking its light through the clouds, and live butterflies spin out of their hiding places.

Nat croaks with relief.

Clover's in the doorway. "How many?" she asks, surveying the broken butterflies sadly.

"Seven, so far," Nat says sombrely.

Clover looks at me with a blank stare.

"We need to clear up," I say, exhausted. "When the tide comes in, we need to be ready. Dad—"

"We should give them a funeral," Clover says, interrupting me. "The butterflies. So we can say a proper goodbye, like we did with Mum."

She crouches down next to Nat.

"That was different," I say. "That was marking Mum's life,

236

because we loved her. We should think about Dad now."

"I loved those butterflies," Clover declares, her sea eyes wide. "And Nat did. Every single one of them." Clover's words hover in the air, like she's written them out in the sand.

"We have to wait anyway. The tide," Nat adds, gesturing helplessly at the water. The grey expanse of sea, and the arms of the bay around us, not quite letting us go.

I nod. "A funeral then. So we can say goodbye."

THIRTY-THREE
Pearl

Clover picks dandelion flowers and makes a carpet of yellow in an old toy boat. Dad carved it once out of driftwood. It was our favourite plaything, until we got older.

Clover's brow puckers. She adored that boat. I can still hear her peels of giggles, and one day wails – genuine grief – because she wanted to fit into the boat and sail away, and knew she'd never be small enough. It was a year or so after Mum died.

"Dad wouldn't mind us using it," I offer. "You're right, the butterflies should have the right send-off."

"Like Mum…" Clover's voice breaks.

Mum was going to be cremated like a regular compounder, but Dad couldn't stand it. He didn't want her on land a moment longer. He broke Mum out of the hospital morgue with George and they brought her back to our platform together. They put her in our best rowing boat and we laid her out with flowers from her greenhouse and cast her off.

Mum was the best thing we ever gave to the sea.

When she was far enough away, Dad threw in burning rags. We hadn't expected that, Clover and me.

Water.

Fire.

Air.

Spirit.

"Can I do it?" Nat asks gingerly, standing to the side as Clover bends down to pick up the butterflies.

"I don't mind," Clover says, almost eagerly.

I pull her back gently.

"Nat should. He brought them," I say.

"Don't start that!" Clover says.

I shake my head again. "He found them. He grew them. Even last night, we'd have lost all of them if he hadn't jumped in when he did."

Clover nods quickly, understanding, and puts the boat with the yellow flowers down in front of him.

"They've lost some of their colour," Nat says, as he picks up the butterflies.

"They shed scales in the storm," I say.

"Scales?" Clover looks puzzled. "Like a fish?"

"Butterflies are called lepidopterans, from Ancient Greek. *Lepis* is scaled, *pteron* means wing." I don't know why I'm saying this now. Somehow I feel I need to, like it's important for the dead butterflies that someone knew what they were. Like when Dad said all those things about Mum, the day we said goodbye to her.

That she was the best mother in the world.

That we were her best invention.

That we would miss her forever.

Nat looks at me curiously. "Insects of the order lepidoptera," he says.

"Yes," I say, meeting his gaze. "Their wings wear out over time. If they're touched or…"

"Thrown about in a storm," Nat finishes miserably, laying the delicate bodies in a double row in the little sailing boat.

Clover squeezes his arm. "You weren't to know. You don't normally get storms like that in summer."

"I found them by Billy Crier's windmill. I knew about summer storms," he says. "I should never have brought them to sea."

Clover won't let us launch the boat until she's had chance to change. I know exactly what she'll pick. She comes back from our cabin in her white dress, with an appropriately sad look fixed on her face.

"Farewell, butterfly friends," she says, as Nat places the

boat in the water and gives it a little push. "You've got your angel wings now."

"They barely lived at all, did they?" Nat says sorrowfully.

"They still mattered," I say fervidly. "We won't ever forget them."

Nat looks across at me strangely, and I wipe away the tears that have fallen down my face in rivulets of sadness. There's a last flash of dandelion-yellow in the grey sea, and the tiny boat disappears into the waves.

THIRTY-FOUR
Nat

"Shouldn't we be going?" I say to Clover, once we've sent the dead butterflies off into the sea. "To check on your dad? Tide's almost in."

Yesterday we had to manhandle Clover back from setting out on her own, today she's stalling.

"Yeah," Clover says, watching Pearl, who's sweeping the platform with a broom. Returning some of the seaweed and washed-up shellfish to the water.

"Are you OK?" I ask her.

Clover's eyes are fixed on the land. "Sometimes I see why Pearl wants to stay here forever," she says heavily. "If we never went to land, we wouldn't find out anything bad, would we? The whole of the rest of the world could die, and we wouldn't even need to know."

"I know some of the compounders who work in the

hospital, Clover. They're good people. Good, clever people. I think your dad will be fine."

Clover looks at me nervously. "You're not just saying that to make me feel better?"

"No," I say, swallowing. "I wouldn't do that. We're friends, aren't we? We don't lie to each other."

Clover stands abruptly. Her eyes dart to Pearl, who's stopped sweeping and is standing tall, alert on the edge of the platform. We both look to the water to see what's stopped her.

A boat.

"It's George," Clover says, going to stand next to her sister. "Good old George. He'll be coming to check we're OK after the storm, won't he?"

Pearl glances across to me nervously. "He's got someone with him."

"Is it Mum?" I say, but even as the words leave my mouth, I see it isn't. The person with the old boatman is taller, thicker. They're not standing as straight. A lump forms in my throat.

Clover and Pearl are side by side now.

"You should hide!" I cry. "Quickly."

Pearl shakes her head. "It's too late. They've got binoculars. They've already seen us. All of us."

There's a finality to Pearl's voice that cuts into me. Clover's white dress blows up and around her. Could she still pass as a ghost now?

"Maybe George brought someone to help with the storm damage," Clover says, uncertainly.

Pearl shakes her head. "He wouldn't. He'd know Dad wouldn't want that."

"Then why has he brought someone? You don't think…" Clover stumbles over her words. "You don't think he'd have said anything? About the butterflies?"

"He said he wouldn't," Pearl whispers.

"He's kept quiet about us all these years. Surely he wouldn't have betrayed us now?" Clover says.

We look at each other helplessly.

"We could try and catch them," Clover starts.

"There isn't time," I say. "We've just got to keep whoever it is away from the greenhouse."

I edge out of line. We wouldn't normally be standing in a row waiting to greet new arrivals, especially while the end of a storm is still raging.

I recognize the extra person as a peacekeeper in her smart, tailored suit. I wonder if Pearl and Clover even know that. Peacekeepers don't come here, they said.

George is red-faced and his eyes are flitting about at ground level – he's not looking at us, not even at Pearl, who takes in their ropes and is wrapping them tight round the tether posts.

The peacekeeper is watching Pearl and Clover, her eyes

wide and hungry.

"Do you have news about Dad?" Pearl asks George directly. "We're about to go over."

George looks up then, surprised. "To land," he says to Pearl. "You?"

"Dad got worse," she says.

"You're not going anywhere. I have a warrant," the officer interrupts. "To search your farm. We've had reports of concealed pollinators."

I watch Pearl flinch for just a moment, and then straighten right away, composing herself.

The peacekeeper is looking agape at Pearl, at her ragged clothes, still damp from the storm. The seaweed in her hair. The shell necklace. The wildness in her eyes. I must have looked at her like that too, that first day. No wonder Pearl hated me.

I wait for Pearl to turn away or disappear and leave me to fill the silence that's hanging in the air. I wouldn't blame her.

"Butterflies," Pearl says brazenly. "They started as caterpillars, but now they're butterflies. We looked after them."

"Pearl!" Clover squeaks beside me. I put my hand on her shoulder, to calm her.

"It's OK," I say quietly.

"But it's se—" Clover starts to protest.

"It's OK," I say again.

Pearl turns to face me. The butterflies – they were too big a secret to keep. Pearl's expression says it all. They're flying in a transparent dome. How could we even think we could hide them? The peacekeeper knows already. That's why she's here. George told on us.

THIRTY-FIVE
Pearl

Nat leads the way. The ropes are limp and everything's slippery – the platform, the edges of the boats – and water laps up capriciously, still bursting with storm energy. Nat barely seems to notice. He's found his sea legs.

The woman notices. She's terrified and angry with it, like it's our fault, mine and Clover's most of all. She stumbles behind us, clinging wildly on to the ropes. I could go ahead with our wooden gangway – lay it out across the wider traverses of water – but why would I do that? Why would I make it easy for her when she looks at me and Clover the way she does?

"What will happen, Pearl?" Clover whispers beside me. "Will she take me away?"

"She's not here for you," I answer under my breath.

"But the way she looked at me, Pearl. She thinks

I'm an outrage!"

"Keep quiet. Don't draw attention to yourself!" I say.

'Peacekeeper', it reads on a badge sewn on the woman's sleeve. But I know enough from Nat to know a peacekeeper is never bothered about bringing peace. He catches my eyes, frightened.

It would have been better if the woman had come before the storm. Nat would have been prouder then, more confident. The butterflies were spectacular. The peacekeeper couldn't have failed to see how much he'd looked after them.

Today the greenhouse is battered and derelict. There's seaweed covering everything. The panels are dislodged and cracked. Plants have been pulled up and Mum's old pots are scattered everywhere. There are briny pools of water on the floor.

The officer steps inside nervously, clearly worried it's all going to fracture and come down on top of her. But she gulps, steeling herself, and walks into the middle of the space. It's Nat she turns to, softer now, like she's trusting him to help. She thinks he's her ally, I realize. Not Clover and I, who she sees as some kind of aberration, or George, who skulks between land and sea, blurring the district's neat edges. Nat is a compounder. A landlubber, just like she is.

Nat turns away from the officer and puts his hands in his

pockets aloofly, and there's a spark of warmth inside me. He's on our side now.

There are butterflies on the nettles and a couple in the corners of the ceiling, their wings beating gently.

The officer gazes around, bewildered. She's only seeing the damage and the water all around. How very far away she is from dry land. "Where are the pollinators? The…" the woman pauses and looks at me this time, "butterflies." She drums her right fingers against the knuckles of her left hand.

"They're up there, aren't they?" I say dispassionately. And then as I watch her frown, and the lost look in her eyes, "You do know what they look like, don't you?"

The woman is visibly flustered now – red-faced and embarrassed. "Show me," she says, losing her patience and resorting back to an order. She directs it at George, who gestures miserably to the top of the greenhouse, where one solitary butterfly is flying.

The woman steps backwards. Maybe she didn't believe any of it till this moment. I don't know what she thought she was doing out here, but I don't think she expected to find actual butterflies.

"I need to take them back to land. Central will want to see them," she says sharply, gathering herself back together. She takes out a yellow notebook and starts scrawling notes of some kind.

Nat gasps and I stare at him, disconcerted. I wonder what she's writing. Property of Central District? Pollinator? Or that something beautiful the world thought had been lost forever has come back. Butterflies in Blackwater Bay.

"Get on with it then. Catch them!" the peacekeeper says, breaking the stunned silence.

Clover draws her breath in. "But you can't take them! We've looked after them. They belong here! They're ours!"

"They can't be left here!" the woman exclaims indignantly. "Look at this place!"

"That's only after the storm!" Clover protests. "Tell them, Nat. Tell them how we mended everything. How we made it perfect for them." Clover tugs at his arm.

I hate seeing the woman's eyes on Clover. Hate seeing Clover looked at like she's a monster. Clover, who's so desperate to fit in on land.

"If you'd seen the greenhouse yesterday," Nat's saying. "It was safe for them, I promise. It only looks like this because the greenhouse broke away in the storm…"

"Nat even jumped into the sea to stop it floating away," Clover cuts in. "And Pearl did too." Her eyes flit to me. "The butterflies might all be dead without them, not just the ones we had the funeral for."

"A funeral?" the officer says in disbelief.

"Some of them died in the storm," Clover says dolefully.

"And where are those ones?" The peacekeeper is

250

incredulous now. "Where's the evidence?"

"Evidence?" Nat asks, not understanding.

"We let the sea take them," Clover says. "The dead ones."

The woman swipes her hand in front of her face. "Enough! I am taking the remaining pollinators back with me. Their presence here contravenes siege state laws."

"We aren't doing any harm. We're going to set them free," Nat protests.

"Free?" the woman baulks. "They're Central's property. They're priceless."

Anger seethes up inside me, like the worst of the waves last night, and the cracks of lightning. I imagine the butterflies back in Central – flying in a sealed cell or pinned to the wall by someone in gloved hands and a white suit. Exhibit A. Pollinators.

"They didn't go back to Central, though, did they?" I say in a simmering voice. "They came to Blackwater Bay! That's where Nat found them."

"Blackwater Bay is no place for pollinators," the peacekeeper says. "These creatures are far too important to leave to a bunch of unkempt children."

Clover and Nat crumple under her insult but, in the pit of my stomach, something breaks loose.

"Catch them then," I say, my voice loud and clear.

The officer looks at me uncertainly. "Pardon?"

"Catch them," I repeat, my eyes blazing. "Take them

back with you. To Central District."

The woman's taken aback. She obviously hasn't thought any of this through. "I'll need one of those cages we passed. Errr, you," she says, indicating George. "Bring one for me."

I glance at Clover and she starts moving silently through the thistles, wafting her hand at the settled butterflies. Her motion's almost inconspicuous, but not to the butterflies. They start swooping around and the woman shrinks back.

"A cage!" she says again to George, her voice louder now to contain its tremble. "This minute!" She waves the notebook in the air.

George shuffles glumly to the door.

"I'll get it," Nat offers miserably, striding out in front of him.

George backs away sheepishly. "No, I will!"

"I'll need you to catch them," the woman instructs, nodding her head at me now, expecting me to do her bidding.

"Me?" I exclaim loudly. I put my hands out with a little flourish, like Clover might when I reprimand her for not doing one of her chores.

Clover looks over at me, surprised.

"I can't catch them!" I say.

"You must," the woman says, annoyed. "You and your … sister." She places the last word awkwardly, glancing at Clover. "Which is another transgression that will need looking at. But the butterflies certainly are Central's property and as such I am confiscating them. Here. Now. Don't you see? It's what has to be done!"

"Yes, of course," I say, mimicking Clover at her sweetest. "Confiscate them. But you'll have to do it. We couldn't possibly catch them. We're just unkempt children. Look how fast the butterflies move."

"And they're delicate too," Clover chips in quickly, as the woman puts her hand out nervously. "You wouldn't want to damage them. Not if they're priceless. We saw last night in the storm how easy they are to injure."

"Every time you touch them their wings shed more scales," I say brightly.

"How did you bring them here?" the woman asks Nat, determined to regain control of the situation.

"They were caterpillars then, like we told you. They were easier to manage." A smile escapes from Nat's lips.

"This is not a laughing matter," the woman says.

"I'm not laughing!" he says.

"We wouldn't dare!" I say, as Clover moves again through the thistles, and the butterflies fly their own tornado round our heads.

The woman launches the oyster cage into the air and traps a cloud of empty sea air.

Clover lets out a stream of giggles and suddenly we're

all laughing – the three of us – at the incredulity in the peacekeeper's face.

"I will report you all for non-cooperation with district rules and enforcement," the woman's saying, backing out into the doorway of the greenhouse to get away from the fluttering wings. "And I'll come back with support to seize the pollinators. Everyone is to remain on the farm, on my orders."

"What about our dad?" Clover pipes up.

"It's a direct command," the woman shouts, clearly keen just to get back to land.

"Tell him," a voice says gruffly. George. "Tell the boy what you've done."

THIRTY-SIX
Nat

The atmosphere shifts in the greenhouse. Clover stops giggling. Pearl clutches the shells round her neck.

"Tell me what," I say. The greenhouse rocks at a bigger than usual wave and the peacekeeper clings to one of the vertical supports that holds up the ceiling.

"Go on," George urges her. "The boy deserves to know what you people have done."

"What you've done?" I ask, my voice getting shriller. Clover and Pearl gravitate closer to me.

The woman's face clouds over and she regains her balance. "We had to act on the reports we heard of stolen pollinators. Siege state laws demand it."

I nod, to press her on.

"As a compounder you'll be aware that under the age of fourteen, penalties count against your parents?

Or, in your case, parent."

I snatch a breath. My one parent. Mum.

The woman looks uncomfortable but her voice comes out fixed and hard. "We haven't had a pollinator crime in years. We have to make an example of it. Pollinators are essential to district recovery plans. To the whole world's recovery. You all know that." She puts the oyster cage down at her feet.

A butterfly sails in front of the woman's face and she flinches away from it. "None of you remember the Hunger Years. None of you know what it was like—"

"Your mother's on the ship, boy," George interrupts miserably. "I took her there myself. Under district orders." He glares at the woman as he says the last bit.

"The boat we saw," Clover says beside me.

"The boat," I repeat back slowly. George's boat, with the prisoner in it, looking right at us.

We were scared they had come for the butterflies. I never thought for a moment it was Mum that was in danger.

"But it's nothing to do with my mum!" I yell, my voice rising louder. "*I* took those caterpillars. *I* did. *Me!* Why are you punishing my mum?"

"You admit it then. You stole them off district land?" the woman looks at me, hungrily now, her fingers on her yellow notebook.

"I wasn't stealing!" I cry. "It wasn't like that!"

"Those butterflies are migrants," Pearl says. "Their parents probably flew thousands of miles to lay eggs."

"Migrants!" the woman says.

"It's true! I read it in a book," Pearl says, glancing sideways at me. "They're called Painted Ladies. They can fly thousands and thousands of miles. They're free as a bird. They're not property of the district, or anyone. They might have come from Africa."

"Africa? That sounds unlikely," the peacekeeper says scathingly.

"You can see the book!" Pearl cries. "It's on the ship. I can go now and get it."

"Pearl!?" Clover says. "Why didn't you tell us you found them in a book?"

Pearl's eyes flit to me remorsefully. "I was angry with you for being here, Nat."

"It's OK," I say. "I'm a landlubber, I get it."

"No!" Pearl cries desolately. "I don't think that. Not any more."

"It's too late," Clover says dramatically.

"No, it's not too late. I'll get the book," Pearl says. "We can go now, can't we, George? You too." She indicates the peacekeeper. "And you can get Sora released. Benjamin Price might not have signed her in yet. She shouldn't be there. She didn't break any rules."

The woman shakes her head, bewildered.

"Price signed her in," George says heavily. "He signed her in in front of me. I watched him, Pearl."

The woman gives a brisk smile. "It's not in my hands any more. Once people get taken to the ship, it's a new chain of command. The governor decides."

I shiver, like a cool draft is blowing down my spine.

"Sora doesn't deserve that. It's not fair!" Pearl says bitterly and looks at George for help.

"I'm sorry, Pearl, Clover… I didn't mean to say anything. It was never meant for the authorities. I was just so amazed to see the little creatures, I told a couple of folk at the Tavern. I wasn't blabbing. It wasn't like that."

The girls stare at him in horror.

"But Sora's good!" Clover wails hysterically. "She's good!"

"I'll go to the ship," Pearl's saying. "I'll go in our boat. Sem'll show me to Benjamin Price if I ask him. I'll talk to the governor myself. I'll go now. I will!" She's making towards the door.

"Dad!" Clover interjects, giving me a guilty side look. "*Dad*, Pearl!" She snivels loudly. "We have to go to Dad!"

The woman tuts impatiently. "As I have said, no one is going anywhere. You'll need to stay here while I go back for reinforcements."

Back on the main platform, the woman opens up her report book. The girls stare at it blankly. The yellow book clearly doesn't mean anything to them, but she's giving them their first civil disobedience point.

Pearl's next to George, standing by the table with the open pages of her ledger. He's taken her pencil and is writing straight on to one of the pages. Pearl steps in front of him, to shield him from view of the peacekeeper. I raise my eyebrows quizzically and she gives a slight shake of her head. Clover's crying loudly in the corner.

The woman finishes writing the form and tears it out with a flourish. She gives it to Pearl.

"You mustn't lose it," the woman says. "It needs to be given directly to your guardian."

"Our dad?" Pearl says. "He's sick, in hospital. We told you."

"Your mother then."

"We don't have a mother," Pearl says, her voice unwavering.

The woman flushes and changes the position of her feet on the seaweed-strewn floor. She almost slips. "Well, keep it safe until he's home."

Clover sobs loudly again and the woman pushes forward on to the motorboat. "Remember, none of you are to leave. Or let those pollinators go. It's an official order now." She waves the report book in her hand, like it's all the authority she needs.

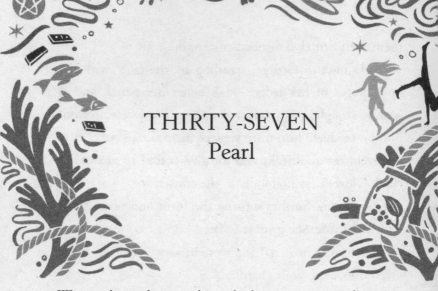

THIRTY-SEVEN
Pearl

We stand together watching the boat move away, listening to the fading throb of the engine. Clover's still crying, but quieter now. I put my arm round her

"Clover," I say. I want to find more words, to make things better, but they don't come.

And I can't say I'm sorry, not truthfully. Not when I was the one that made it happen. I made it all happen. Dad. Sora. The storm. The dead butterflies.

"You should go to your dad," Nat says to us both.

"She said we shouldn't," Clover says. A torrent of despair rushes out of her. "Will I be sent to the Communal Families, like Barnaby was?"

"No!" I say forcefully. I push Barnaby out of my head. I wish Nat had never told us that story.

"You should go," Nat repeats, looking at me now.

"To the hospital. Your dad will want to know you're OK after last night."

Sora will be worried too – shut in her room on *Aurora*, worrying about her landlubber son at sea in a storm. Guilt colours my cheeks like scarlet paint.

"Nat's right," I say to Clover. "We need to go and see Dad."

"You'll go?" she asks surprised.

I never wanted to go and visit Mum in hospital. In her bare, lit room that stank of bleach. Your visits make her better, Dad said every day, for weeks and weeks. But Mum rarely smiled when she saw me. I don't think she wanted me there. I think she'd rather I had stayed with Clover and George back on the platform.

"You'll come with us, won't you?" I say to Nat.

Nat shakes his head. "I can't risk more points. Those yellow forms, they're serious."

"You're not coming?" I ask, feeling my stomach drop.

"I'm trying to do the right thing. For my mum. Civil disobedience points … they're a big deal for compounders. I've let Mum down enough already." Nat's eyes flick wretchedly to *Aurora*.

"What did George write down for you?" he asks suddenly, striding over to the table. My ledger is still splayed open on the table. I was sketching a butterfly wing, close up, to get all the detail in. I did two separate sketches – one top, one bottom. You only need one side, because butterflies are symmetrical. Each side is a mirror image of the other.

George's writing on the bottom of the page is small and scratchy and all in capitals, like Clover out on the flats. *GO TO EZRA.*

Nat reads it out loud, his forehead furrowed pensively. "Why does George think Ezra will help my mum? Ezra can't intervene just because she works for him, can he? It'd undermine his position!"

"It's guilt speaking," I say. "George blabbed about the butterflies. He wants to think he can fix it but he can't."

Nat's frown deepens. "But why would he suggest going to Ezra if he didn't think it would help?"

I shrug my shoulders.

"Unless you know him?" Nat asks, staring at me now. "Unless George means that Ezra will help *you*."

"We've never even met Ezra," I say swiftly.

"What if George does mean us though, Pearl?" Clover says, turning to me. "There's that photo of Ezra and Mum I found when I was clearing out Mum's office."

"That was from ages ago," I mutter. I made Clover shove it straight in the big storm trunk along with the letters. I didn't want to upset Dad further. "They worked together once, that was all. That's what got Mum sick, remember! Setting up that place with Ezra was the biggest mistake of her life. Look what it did to her! And have you forgotten that he's behind those horrible rules?"

Nat shakes his head. "Siege state laws? Ezra didn't have a choice about them. Mum says he used to try and resist Central, when we first came to the bay. But it's like the fight went out of him, it must have got too hard."

I glare at him. "He's put your mum in prison, Nat! He's trying to take over our farm."

"Is he?" Nat asks. "Would he really send me and Mum if he was planning to seize control of your farm? We're hardly threatening."

"He sent the peacekeeper to take the butterflies," I say, my voice high and tight.

Nat shrugs again. "How do we know it was Ezra? And I don't think that woman even knew what she was looking for until she saw them. Did you see the look on her face? The rules don't mean anything any more."

"Exactly!" I say. "The rules are meaningless but he still upholds them, doesn't he? Ezra Heart! He's like Central's puppet!"

Nat scratches his head. "When Tally's mum died, it was Ezra who petitioned Central to ask if they could keep Barnaby. Even though he was practically a recluse by then, Ezra still tried to save Barnaby."

"So you're defending him? The man who signed off on your mum's prison papers?"

Nat shrinks back from me. "He's not all bad, is what

I'm saying. We shouldn't dismiss him if he might be able to help us."

"You go to him then," I say. "If Ezra's so good, you go to him and get him to get your mum off the ship."

Nat's face hardens. "I can't break the order. You're not a landlubber. I know you don't get it, but for us it's important."

Landlubber. He looks right at me as he says it. I'd thought he wasn't bothered by that word, but he is.

"But you could go to Ezra, couldn't you?" he continues. "The two of you could go. Since he knows about you already."

I stare back at Nat. Does he have any idea what he's asking us to do? Ezra's been enemy number one our entire lives. But I can see *Aurora* as a dark spot in the corner of my eye. Of course Nat would risk anything to save his mum. Sora doesn't deserve any of this.

"Where would we find him?" I sigh, non-committedly.

"I could draw you a map," Nat says eagerly now. "He's not in the compound. He moved to one of the old streets a few years ago. Just about the only one that's left. It's easy to find. Even for a sea girl."

His eyes stay fixed on me. They're dark and frightened and he's asking for our help.

THIRTY-EIGHT
Nat

Pearl and Clover have taken the motorboat to land, but the little rowing boat they use to circle the oyster farm, that's still here.

I have to do something. I have to explain that it was me who took the caterpillars. If I can get the butterfly book Pearl talked about and find the section about Painted Ladies and them being migrants… Maybe if I could show that to Ezra Heart he'd take it all seriously. Or Benjamin Price even. Someone's got to listen to the truth.

The boat's small and low in the water. It bounces around like a cork. I fight to keep the oars in my hands as the waves pull at them. I wish I'd paid more attention to Clover's technique when she was rowing.

Up close, the ship is bigger than you'd imagine. *She*, Clover insisted. Ships were always female, she said.

She towers over me – a giant, floating city. Vertical walls of fibreglass, a strange mix of orange and brown that, up close, you see are all blistering bubbles of rust. She looks like she'd be happy to give up now, to sink down to the bottom of the sea and find her resting place.

Pearl talked about a supply hatch. There are windows but they're all much higher than the level of the water. The bottom of the ship looks impenetrable – a shell, clasped tight. I try and manoeuvre the rowing boat round, looking for signs of a way in, while trying to keep enough distance away so I'm not smashed up against her.

I get flashbacks to last night. Saltwater in my eyes and nose and throat.

The waves could take me under the ship. *Currents.* *Riptides.* Clover drilled these things into me in her swimming lessons. Would *Aurora* have her own currents? Mum would never know how close I'd got to her if one took me now.

I imagine dark shapes underneath the water. Sharks, whales. Moby Dick come back to get me. *Do you know what your people did?*

Then suddenly the little boat's pushed towards the ship by a wave, and I spot the tarnished metal of a rusty old chain that's stained a different shade of orange against the side of the ship. High above it is a big brass bell. I lean out and pull the chain.

THIRTY-NINE
Pearl

"We should land out of sight," Clover says quietly, as we approach the shore.

I turn the engine off and we pick up the oars to do the last bit by hand.

We row just round the headland, then we drag the boat up through the mud. There are rows of abandoned boats, stranded above the tideline in the marram grass, rotting away, and a hundred different signs each saying the same thing. That no one's welcome.

NO LANDING IN BLACKWATER BAY. MIGRANTS WILL BE INTERNED. ACCESS FORBIDDEN. NO ENTRY. ARMED PATROLLERS.

"Is that true?" I ask Clover nervously. "An armed patrol?"

Clover shrugs. "Maybe there was one once. I don't think anyone comes here any more."

I nod.

"You have to put the shoes on," Clover says.

She indicates Mum's old brown shoes in the bottom of the boat. Footwear is important, Clover says, or else we'll stand out.

Clover watches impatiently as I squeeze my toes into the blunt points of the stiff shoes. I squirm. I don't remember Mum in shoes at all. She was barefoot on the flats or in the water, or had her feet tucked out of sight under hospital sheets.

I remember Nat's feet the first day after he walked on the flats. His soles cut and bleeding.

Clover's eyes move up and down me slowly as I teeter to my feet. "You should take off your shell necklace," she says. "And here..." She pulls an orange hair tie from her head and hands it to me. "Tie your hair back."

"Why do I need to tie my hair back if you don't?"

"Because..." she says awkwardly, her cheeks flushed. "Because you stand out more." She spreads her silky blondeness over her shoulders. Even after the storm, Clover looks pristine.

I slip my necklace in my pocket – the shells clacking dully.

"We ought to get away from the boat," Clover says.

"Which way do we go?" I ask.

Clover points towards the town as we climb over

the concrete sea defences. "Let's stay close to the shore. That way we can hide against the wall if anyone comes."

Before the town there are salt ponds and someone's there, raking out the salt crystals. It's a boy, not much older than Nat. He's singing to himself softly. Clover soundlessly gestures for me to follow as she slips landside of some ramshackle waterfront buildings.

"Will it really be that bad if someone sees us?" I ask. The boy at the salt ponds looks harmless, carefree. Would it really be so bad if he saw two girls he didn't recognize, walking by the sea?

"Less so me," Clover says, squinting. "You've got to blend in more. Stop looking at everything like that. Like you never saw it before."

I blush and fall into step behind her. We're single file on a tiny track behind the old warehouses that were built long ago to store things brought in on big container ships.

It's land here, but it still feels like the sea, or some in-between zone. The mud path has shells and seaweed and marram grass, and there are dunlins – the birds methodically pecking for insects and worms with their black beaks.

"The hospital's past the compound, up Drylands Road," Clover says, scrutinizing Nat's map. She's taken charge because she knows I can't. I'm out of my depth, struggling to pick up my feet as the ground gets more solid.

I don't need the map anyhow. I still remember the way.

The slight incline of the road, away from the sea. The compound on one side, Edible Uplands on the other. The green cross on top of the hospital building.

"Do you think they'll let us in, if we say he's our dad?" Clover asks.

We're on a pavement now. Cracked concrete, with circles of yellow lichen. The earth rising up, reclaiming its surface.

"He *is* our dad," I say.

My eyes are blurring and my heart's pounding too fast. The incline's slight, but in the flatness of everything it makes a difference, and we've gained enough height that we can see our farm now, back over the sea defences. It looks so tiny. And in the distance beyond, there's the prison ship.

"What if Ezra Heart will help Sora?" I blurt out.

Clover falters. "Dad," she says. "*Dad*, Pearl."

I gulp, steeling myself. "I've been thinking, I should go and see Ezra first."

Clover's face furrows into a frown. "We need to see Dad!" she repeats. "You promised!"

"Sora's on the ship, Clover! I have to help her."

I've got Nat's face in my head, when I mentioned the butterfly book. He couldn't believe I hadn't told him about it. He's simple and good, where I'm twisted inside, with sharp edges.

"I have to help Sora," I say again, my eyes fixed on the ship. "Because I wished it, Clover. I wished all of it."

Clover stiffens and walks on but I catch up with her. I'm certain now what I need to do.

"I wished Sora away, Clover. I offered up Nat's butterflies in exchange for Dad. I brought the storm and I brought that peacekeeper too. It's all my fault."

Clover stops and shakes her head. When she speaks, her voice is a whisper. "The wishings are just a game, Pearl. You didn't do this. You couldn't!" She looks almost frightened of me.

"I did," I say. "I did, Clover. That's why I saw the storm way before anyone else could. Because I conjured it. I brought it to the bay."

"We have to see Dad," Clover says simply, her eyes wet and her poise slipping. She doesn't want to listen to any more of what I did.

"You go to Dad," I say. Clover starts to cut in but I stop her. The way ahead is clear. "I stand out more than you. You said it and it's true. I don't even know how to walk properly in shoes."

"No!" Clover says. "Pearl!"

"It's true," I say, putting my hands either side of her, holding her up together and taller. I try to smile. "Dad's OK. I know he is. I wished it and the sea answered. So I know he's OK. And that's why it's OK for you to go to the hospital on your own."

"I want you to come," she says, crying now. "I want you

with me, Pearl. I need you!"

"No," I say. "Two of us together, and me looking like this, like I walked straight out of the sea. They'll stop us. But you on your own – you could easily pass as a landlubber!"

"Do you think?" she sniffs, surveying herself.

I smile. "Yes, I do."

I point to the cross in the road. "Ezra's house is that way. Nat says if you go down far enough, at the end, there's an old row of houses, facing the sea. Bedrock Terrace."

Clover nods slowly. "And then I'll see you back at the boat, when I've checked on Dad?"

"Exactly. I'll help Sora. You check on Dad."

Clover squeezes my hand. "Are you scared?" she asks.

I nod. All these years of blaming and hating Ezra. All these years of hating land too.

But last night a landlubber boy jumped into the ocean to save butterflies. Now it's my turn.

FORTY
Nat

The clanging of the bell is out of place in the middle of the sea and there's no answer. I pull at the chain more desperately.

Suddenly the hatch opens up above me and a man's face leans out. His mouth opens in surprise when he sees me and he starts shouting. The bell sounds through the wind yet his words are snatched away by it. I can't work out whether he's barking out instructions or telling me to move on.

The waves lash against the prison ship, surging me forward. My situation seems more precarious than ever, but I can't do anything except go with the pull of the water.

The man's shouting something about ropes. He mimes a throwing action and suddenly I realize what he means.

I grab one of the coils of rope from the floor of the rowing boat and fling it through the air to him. As soon as it's left my hands I know I misjudged it. The rope drops down into the sea.

My face reddens and I clumsily start hauling the sodden twine back in.

"Another!" the man shouts in a dip of wind. "Use another."

I take the remaining dry rope and get ready to throw it. I picture Pearl's overhand throws in the storm as she sent the greenhouse ropes to Clover. Every single throw strong, on target.

The man catches the rope and starts to reel me in, and I go back to pulling up the first wet rope and coiling it round again so he can catch this one too.

Once I'm close enough to reach, the man urges me out of the boat impatiently, up the narrow, frayed ladder. "I'll tie you in," he says gruffly.

"Will the boat get smashed up?" I ask breathlessly. "By the waves?"

The man shakes his head. "The fenders will take the impact. The storm's on her way out."

I nod weakly and haul myself up the ladder into the ship, before the man closes the hatch behind me. We're in a kind of service area – a narrow space with buckets, mops, ropes and crates.

"I need to see the prison governor," I say weakly. "I need to get someone released."

The man tuts crossly and pushes me up more steps. I can tell from the metal shelves stacked with plates and the heat coming off the oven that I've come into the kitchen. An old woman in a blue apron stands against the wall, staring at me.

"You were almost smashed against the hull," the man says, coming up the steps after me. He's rubbing his hands where he must have burned them pulling on the ropes. "That tiny boat in water like this! What were you thinking?"

"I'm sorry," I pant, my heart still racing. "I thought the storm had passed."

"I bet you can't even swim, can you?" the man exclaims.

"I can," I assert. "I can, a little. Do you know who I am?"

The man laughs gruffly. "We don't get many children ringing that bell! Are all compound kids this stupid? What was Pearl thinking, letting you come here?"

"Pearl didn't let me come," I say fiercely. "She doesn't know. She's gone to land."

"Pearl? To land?" the man asks in surprise.

"She had to," I say miserably. "Atticus got worse. My mum called from the hospital a couple of days ago but we didn't see the message, and then the storm started and a peacekeeper came and found the butterflies."

There's a faint gasp from the old lady, who's still watching me silently.

"Did they see the girls?" the man demands straight away. "The peacekeeper. Did they see the girls? Both of them together?"

"She saw them," I say, deliberately not meeting his eyes but still garbling on, letting the words spill out of me, relieved to tell someone. "George said my mum was brought here because they think she stole pollinators, only she never stole a thing. She never would. *I* took them."

I look over at the woman. Her hands are wrinkled, fingernails bitten down to the quick. She doesn't meet my eyes when I look at her. I wish she would. I'm desperate for someone to look at me like they don't blame me for everything that's happened.

"You're Olive, aren't you?" I say, moving towards her. "Pearl talked about you. There was a book you showed her about butterflies. I need to see it."

Olive draws back into the wall.

"I need to see Benjamin Price too," I say desperately, to the man this time. Sem, Pearl called him.

He laughs quietly. "You're a fool if you think talking to Price is going to do your mum any good. Or them girls." He puts his head in his hands for a moment, like he's thinking.

"I have to!" I cry. "Someone has to tell Price the truth.

Mum didn't take the butterflies. I did!"

Sem laughs coldly. "Is that your sworn confession? You want to be here instead, do you? You want to swap places with her?"

"No," I say, looking around nervously. "Course not. But the butterflies weren't anyone's to steal in the first place, and they weren't even from our district really. Pearl says they're migrants."

"Migrants?! Pearl says that, does she?" Sem splutters, a faint smile appearing on his face.

"She read it in the book. She says the butterflies might have flown here from thousands of miles away. If someone in power could listen to that, they'd realize how ridiculous it is to have locked Mum up. Mum's a scientist. She wants to help people! She's wants to help the district so we don't have to worry about food all the time. So everyone can have more freedom!"

"Freedom?" Sem says, looking at Olive, who's still cowering against the wall. "Everyone? Wouldn't that be nice?"

"Where is the governor?" I ask meekly.

Sem shakes his head incredulously. He steps towards me so his face is directly opposite mine. His breath smells of fish. But there's water in his eyes, like he's sad not angry. "You can't reason with Price. The governor isn't going to be charmed with a few flying insects. If he finds you, you'll be a new name on my feeding list, and your mum's sentence will be doubled."

"No!" I cry. "That's not fair! Mum didn't do anything wrong!"

Sem gestures to Olive. "You think she did anything wrong? You think I did?"

I look down the steps towards the landing hatch. I can hear the waves beating against it. Any bravado I was feeling before about coming to the ship alone has evaporated. My back and shoulders ache from the rowing and my stomach contorts with hunger. I shiver, cold and miserable.

"Look," Sem says, sighing. "You're worn out. None of us got much sleep last night in that storm. I've got lunch to make for the prisoners. I bet you've not eaten today?"

I shake my head. Our morning all seems like a dream. A nightmare.

"I can feed you," the man says, softer now. "It'll give you the energy to get back to the oyster farm, and the storm time to finish making its way out."

"Thank you," I say gratefully, grabbing at the chance of food and more time to be near Mum, even if I can't see her.

"The butterfly book," Olive says in a quiet voice. Her eyes are fixed on me, though her eyelids flutter shyly. "I'll show him."

Sem looks unsure. "In the library?"

"Please!" I clutch hold of Sem's arm. "If Benjamin Price

won't listen, maybe someone else will. Maybe Ezra Heart, if I can get the book to him."

"Ezra won't do anything. Not out here," Sem says, darkly bitter.

"But if people don't try, things won't ever change, will they?" I say, exasperated now. "Not ever. You'll grow old and die here, and my mum will too. If the butterflies think Blackwater Bay's worth coming back to, maybe it's a sign. Maybe they really are what everyone's been waiting for, like it says there, in the statutes."

I point to the wall where the laws are written out in a gold frame. Faded now, and water damaged from storms even worse than last night, but still there.

"Go and find this precious book then," Sem says reluctantly. "But keep out of sight. You'll get me and Olive in a load of trouble if you're seen."

FORTY-ONE
Pearl

I walk in the shadow of Edible Upland's grey concrete tower. It's got its own defences – twisted razor wire on top of high metal fences, chained together, endlessly.

There's a strange hum coming from inside the tower and I imagine it as Sora described it. The pinkish light, the people in white suits, and rows and rows of salad and vegetable plants, fed with liquid nutrients.

Here, behind the metal barriers, there are plants too. Nettles and flowering thistles at the sides of the road, and crimson-red flowers. Poppies – the name comes back to me suddenly. Mum grew them and for a second I bend down to touch one, till I hear Dad's voice in my head. The land here is contaminated, radioactive, toxic, deadly.

The flowers bloom anyway – upright, blood-red.

I see the road sign before my eyes can make out the

words, but I know what it says. The sea took the other roads. It rose up, angry, and swept them all away.

But Bedrock Terrace stands steady. It's at the end of the vast space taken up with Edible Uplands, before the land becomes a desolate nothing. Just the pylons stretching out into the distance, taking electricity inland from the solar fields.

I expected some gated, stilted building for the District Controller's house. Gilded, like the butterfly cocoons.

It's almost the opposite. It's like the past. The world Mum would talk about occasionally. The world that got flooded and starved.

There's an old yellow door, the paint cracked and peeling. I bang on it again and again, but no one comes, and the house starts to seem empty and left behind.

I'm about to give up when a man appears on the other side of the door – his face against the pane of glass, staring at me, appalled.

"What are you doing here?" he spurts out, as the door opens.

My hands automatically go to my hair, to pull it over my face, but it's still gathered back with Clover's hair tie. "I need your help," I say. "I'm from the oyster farm, out in the bay."

The man continues to stare, and I think he's not understanding me. I worry my words aren't sounding properly. That my voice can't be heard on land. I open my mouth to try again.

"Pearl! I know who you are," the man says.

I gulp, unsure if this is a good sign or not. "We're in trouble," I start, but then I pause, unsure how to carry on, and what's most important anyway. Sora, on the prison ship, for stealing pollinators she doesn't even know exist. Nat, alone on our sea farm after a storm. Dad in hospital, and Clover making her own way in to see him. How could I make her do that journey on her own?

"Are you Ezra Heart?" I ask, because he could actually be anyone. He looks like he's only just woken up, and his eyes are red and his cheeks saggy.

The man nods. "One of my officers was here yesterday with some nonsense about stolen pollinators on your farm. I sent them away."

"A peacekeeper came," I say sharply. "They've taken Sora to the ship."

Ezra tenses and looks at me anew. He holds out his hands. "Sora, on the ship? A peacekeeper? I told my officer to ignore it. That it was nonsense!"

Anger dislodges inside me and rises up to the surface. Ezra didn't even bother investigating and yet one of his zealots got a peacekeeper to come anyway. The rules and procedures here are out of control.

"There are pollinators then?" Ezra says astonished. "Out there on your farm?"

"Yes," I say bitterly. "And they're not stolen. They're butterflies."

"Butterflies? Where on earth did you get them from?" he asks, like he can't believe we're having this conversation.

I shut my eyes. Just for a couple of seconds. To think it all through and put my words in order so no one gets in any more trouble.

Ezra dashes forward and I open my eyes in alarm.

"I thought you were going to faint," he says, his breath fast and shallow.

"No," I say abruptly. "I was thinking." I step back because he's too close, and his eyes are too intense.

They'll never have seen anything like you, Clover said.

And that day on the flats when she told me she wanted to go to school. *I'm not a sea girl*, she said, like that was the biggest insult there was. Is that what Ezra is seeing now? Do I stink of fish and saltwater?

Halfway girls, Mum called us, but that was just a story. A homespun fairy tale to keep us happy. I haven't set foot on solid land for five years and I've forgotten how to walk in shoes.

"You don't know who I am, do you?" Ezra says sadly.

"Of course I do," I say sharply. "You're the District Controller. That's why I came to you. This was done in your name. Sora's on the prison ship!"

He shakes his head slowly. "That's not what I meant.

Your mum, Vita..." He sighs sadly. "Vita," he says again, like the name hurts him.

I glower at him for saying Mum's name in this place. Vita. It means life, but Mum died years ago. The land killed her.

"Vita," he says again, more urgently now. "She was my sister."

"Sister?" I repeat uncertainly, my mind catapulting on, unable to make sense of what he's saying. "Sister." The word spins round my head. "She couldn't have been."

"Sister," he repeats. "You and Clover. You're my nieces."

"No. We can't be," I stammer, stepping back further. This is the man who outlaws sisters. And brothers too. Nat's friend's little brother was sent away inland. Barnaby. He was just a baby. "We can't be..." I say. "No one is allowed."

Ezra shakes his head sadly. "No. We were a secret too. Vita was raised by a neighbour, by our mum's best friend. No one could ever know what she was to us. We had to limit the time we all spent together as children, so no one got suspicious. Vita never even seemed to mind that I was the one that got to live with our parents. She was so generous. Good." He has tears in his eyes. "I lost her too, Pearl."

"No!" I cry, turning away from the sourness of his breath. My legs are buckling under me and I feel exposed without the ring of shells round my neck. I look for the sea, to get strength from it, but it's obscured behind the grey buildings of the Uplands.

"You don't believe me?" Ezra says, impatiently now.

"We can't be related to you!" I cry.

"Why not?"

"Because you live here. And we live out there," I fling at him. Dad, Clover and I, we're sea people. We don't belong anywhere but on that oyster farm, and scavenging out on the flats where no one goes, digging up treasure from long ago.

Ezra looks wounded and nods his head slowly. "So Atticus never told you?" he says.

"Dad knew?" I ask.

Ezra nods.

"I don't believe it," I stammer. "I don't believe any of it."

"I'll prove it," Ezra says intently. "Come in."

"No!" I gasp. Here on the doorstep I'm still in sight of the sea. Here I can run if I need to. I could take off the shoes and run, like we do on the flats.

"Wait, then," Ezra says reluctantly. He pauses. "You will wait, won't you? You promise?"

"I'll wait," I say.

He brings out a photo in a frame. Two children playing on the shoreline. Clover and me.

"How did you get a picture of us?" I snatch it from him.

"Look closer," he says.

I glance at him strangely, and then back to the picture, drawn in by it. Two children, one blonde, one dark. The sea defences high behind them, without all the lichen and cracks they have now.

I look back at Ezra before me – how his dark eyebrows are furrowed and underneath them he's staring at me with green eyes. Sea-green. Witch-green.

The picture's not of Clover and me at all. It's Ezra. And Mum.

"People thought we were best friends," he says. "But we were more than that. I miss her too, Pearl."

I touch Mum's face in the photo.

"I know it's not what you wanted," Ezra continues painfully. "I know what your dad thinks about me. All the bad things he's told you."

"He says the Uplands killed her," I say bluntly. "He blames you."

Ezra winces and gestures towards his growing empire. "We worked on it together. It was so difficult to get new materials. It was Vita's brainwave to use the old cooling tower and grow vertically… Maybe something dangerous in there did get into her system. We'll never know. But I do know that people would still be hungry round here if it wasn't for your mum, Pearl."

"Why didn't you ever come to see us?" I ask.

Ezra scratches his head, his face screwed up with sadness. "It was too raw in the beginning. For your dad. For me too. I thought you were all better off without me. But lately it all just seems so absurd, that you're both so close, and so far away... I've been sending letters."

"Dad never opened them," I say. "Not one of them." I hadn't opened them either. I put them straight in the storm trunk, along with all the other things we don't look at any more. Like father, like daughter. "Is this why you think you can take our oyster farm?" I say. "Because Mum was your sister?"

"No," Ezra says angrily. "I don't want control of your blasted oyster farm. We should be working together. We should be on the same side. And I wanted you, Pearl! You and Clover. You're the reason I sent Sora. I needed a way back to you both."

"But we're impossible!" I cry. "Illegal! The peacekeeper you sent saw us."

"I didn't send them. I never would," he says, angry. "Central might think they own the pollinators, but they don't own you. They can't take you two."

"They took Barnaby," I say.

"They did," Ezra says sadly. "I tried to save him but—"

"And they've taken Sora to the ship," I cut in.

Ezra shakes his head slowly, like he's got the entire world on his shoulders and it's crushing him to the ground.

But I don't have any room left in me for sympathy. All I can think about is Clover.

"I want to go to the hospital now, to see my dad," I say. "You have to get me in."

FORTY-TWO
Nat

I follow Olive through the windowless corridors of the ship. The walls have an unnerving sheen to them, which flickers under orange strip lighting. They're closing in on me, and my heart thumps erratically. "Wait!!" I cry, snatching for air that's stale and hot.

Olive turns back, surprised.

"We're not going down?" I gasp. "I can't…" If we go down, it feels like I'll never come back up.

"There's a window, in the library," Olive offers.

I nod gratefully and force myself to scuttle after her.

When we reach the library, I stand in the doorway, my mouth wide open, before Olive motions anxiously for me to move into the room so she can shut the door behind me. The compound library is mostly desks, and what books there are, the bound pamphlets of stories, are all different versions of the same one. Stories to make ourselves feel better about our life in the compound. That's why Tally won't touch them.

These books aren't pamphlets. They're thick, solid, and they're here in their hundreds, on steeped wooden shelving and piled up in towers by the door. Others are still scattered on the floor. The prison ship must have been thrown about too last night. I can feel it rocking now, and the seasickness from the first couple of days on the oyster farm comes back tenfold.

What would Mr Rose say if he could see this place? All this knowledge kept for one man.

"Windows," Olive says, seeing my green face and pointing to thick panels of glass.

I walk up the steps and stare back at the oyster farm and then the land beyond it. Seeing everything back to front, and further away, is disorientating.

For a moment I forget what I'm even doing here, among all these books. There will be whole worlds here for me to explore... Lighthouses, forests, whales, unicorns. Manor houses with turrets. Man-made canals with narrowboats travelling to different places.

Olive thrusts a book into my hands. It's not thick or heavy. *Pocket-sized*, it says on the front. My hands tremble as I open it. It's got all the pictures the computer's encyclopaedia had lost, or someone had removed.

I scan past some of the butterfly names Lucas had called out. Meadow Brown, Brimstone, Swallowtail, Gatekeeper. Until I get to the one I'm looking for.

"Painted Ladies," I read aloud. I recognize them immediately.

Olive leans closer, her dark eyes glistening.

"We grew them, on the sea farm," I say, pointing down at the page.

"Pearl?" she asks.

"It was me," I say fast, greedy, even though the butterflies are what brought Mum here.

"Could you get my mum?" I ask Olive suddenly. "Without anyone seeing?"

Olive shakes her head in alarm.

"Or take me to her? Just for a moment. Just so I know she's OK. She still won't know what any of this is about," I plead. "She's innocent!"

"No." Olive shakes her head again and looks frightened. "Price," she says.

She hesitates for a moment and then goes to the bookcase nearest the door. It's full of thick, bound volumes. She opens one to a page of ruled lines.

Mum's name is in the last row. *Sora Okamoto of South-East District*. The crime is written in black ink. *Pollinator theft*.

I stare at the words in horror, and then flick back

through the book desperately, at all the names over the years. I recognize some from the compound. And the meaningless crimes – food theft, disrupting social order, breaking border restrictions, endangering national security, non-compliance with compound protocol. What do those things even mean?

Olive takes another book down from the same shelf and lets it fall open. The dates are earlier here – they go back to the start of the Hunger Years, soon after siege state laws were first brought in.

Her fingers point to an inconspicuous row and a name leaps out at me. *Olive Crier.*

"Olive Crier," I read out heavily, aghast. "Crier? That's you?"

I'm back in the windmill, my finger on the carved letters. Billy's mates. Except Olive wasn't his mate. Olive was his sister.

Her crime is stamped in capitals. *SURPLUS CHILD.* And her age is there too. Ten years old. The same age as Clover.

Olive's eyes, bright despite all the years she's been here, plead with me for recognition. "Billy Crier," I say quietly. "We tell his story, back in the compound. He was your brother?"

Olive groans very slightly. A quiet, guttural sound from deep within her.

"I saw your name, Olive," I say. "It was carved in the windmill, next to Billy's. With your friends' names. Jones, Yusuf, Mara."

Light flickers in Olive's eyes like sun on water.

You know Crier wasn't his real name? Tally said. She was obsessed with Billy's story because she thought it was real. But the story was wrong. Details had been left out and forgotten. Crier *was* Billy's surname, and there was someone else. A whole other person. Another half to the tragedy. *Surplus child.*

Was Olive taken before or after Billy died? Did their parents have anyone left to love?

There's the sudden sound of footsteps outside in the corridor and Olive startles, gazing at me in terror. She pushes over a teetering pile of books and they topple down the stairs. She shoves me in the direction of the tallest shelving, just as the door opens.

A man has come into the library. From between the shelves of books, I see Olive's legs tremble. "What's happened to my books?" he's asking, his voice deep and dragging.

Olive stays silent. I wish she'd speak up and defend herself.

The man's getting closer to her.

All Olive needs to say is it was the storm, and she shouldn't even need to say that. The governor was here too last night. How could the books possibly have stayed on the shelves?

Benjamin Price's voice winds on cruelly. "I give you this privilege and you don't even keep them safe."

He's right up close to her now and Olive's shrinking back, like she's worried he'll strike her. I want to shut my eyes and block up my ears, or scream out loud and put a stop to it. The governor's attention would turn off Olive pretty quickly if I did that.

Benjamin Price laughs horribly and he plucks his right fingers into the air, as if on a whim he's decided on a different course. "I wanted a book," he announces. "Deserts, I think, with all this rain. Find me a book about deserts."

My heart pounds in my chest and my eyes dart to the titles above me. Dust-covered books on forest, grassland, wetland, tundra. I don't know what all these things are, but the word on the next spine sucks the breath from my mouth. Desert.

"Well," Price is saying angrily. "Where would that be?"

"I... I..." Olive stammers, knowing very well where I'm hiding.

Then there's another clatter, bigger this time, like the rolls of thunder last night. The tallest tower of books by the doorway has toppled over, and others are coming down around it, like dominoes.

The governor swings back towards Olive. "You did that on purpose. How dare you!"

I don't stick around to see what happens. It won't do Olive any favours if I'm discovered here too. I steal behind the next set of shelves while Price is turned away from the door, and I slip out into the corridor and run.

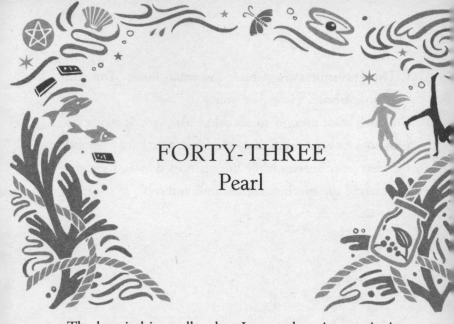

FORTY-THREE
Pearl

The hospital is smaller than I remember. A man sits in a blue uniform behind a desk. He looks at me oddly and opens his mouth to say something – to protest against my dishevelment maybe – but then he sees Ezra Heart and shuts it again.

It's hard not to feel like I'm eight years old again, coming to see Mum under the bright lights and behind the oxygen mask.

After speaking with the man, Ezra beckons for me to come forward. "Atticus is on the top floor, Pearl. I'll take you." He sounds tentative.

"You don't have to," I say, turning left for the stairs, just as I remember. "Dad won't want…"

But I stop talking as memories uncover themselves in front of me. Mum was on the top floor. Three floors up.

There are no windows in the stairwell. I hated that feeling, that lack of sky.

She'll get better, Pearl. Dad said it every visit, until the last.

Ezra follows in my wake. Despite his authoritative voice at the desk, he's nervous.

"Turn left here. Your dad's at the end of the corridor," Ezra says at the top, even though I'm already running. I feel I'm being led with a magic thread to Dad and Clover.

"Pearl!" Dad's sat up in bed, looking straight at the door. My dad, in hospital sheets, with tubes in his arm, but sitting up, breathing. Alive. He squeezes me tight when I go over. Tighter than he has in months. "My big one, you made it."

"You're OK?" I ask, patting his arms and his face and his chest, checking he's solid. "Your foot? Your foot's OK?"

The sheets move slightly as Dad wriggles his leg. "They saved it. Saved me," he says sombrely.

"So you'll be all right now?" I gasp.

"I'm getting there," he says. "Slowly. I've been waiting for you. I knew you were coming. I felt it." He puts two fingers up against his heart.

Clover's curled in a chair next to the bed, sleeping. She must be exhausted after last night's storm.

"Clover said you went to see Ezra Heart about some butterflies? Butterflies, Pearl?!" Dad says. I can't read his face, whether it's anger or astonishment.

"Yes," I say, going over to the window where you can see rows and rows of shining panels. The solar fields Nat talked about. That's where Nat wanted to spend his summer, not out at sea.

Every so often there's a wind pump, to suck saltwater back out of the land. Without the pumps this whole area would be marshland. One windmill stands out in the distance – darker than the others, broken. That must be where Nat found the caterpillars. Billy Crier's windmill.

"Ezra told you, didn't he?" Dad says quietly.

"Of course he did," I say sharply, looking right back at him. "You don't not say things like that. We had a right to know."

"Pearl," Dad whispers plaintively. "My precious Pearl!"

"You should have told us!" I cry.

"Told us what? Pearl!" Clover says, my raised voice waking her. She jumps up and wraps her arms round me, almost pushing me off my feet. "Dad's better. He's better, Pearl! The nurse says he can come home in a few days." Her voice babbles with happiness.

"They let you in OK?" I ask.

Clover laughs. "I turned on my biggest smile, like you said."

I smile back at her. "I knew they would. No one can turn you down, Clover."

"What did Ezra Heart say, Pearl?" Clover asks. "Will he get Sora off the prison ship?"

"I don't know," I say truthfully, the hugeness of everything coming back to me. "Prison-ship rules aren't up to him. He doesn't have the authority, not when people have already been taken there. Only Benjamin Price does."

"Likely story," Clover says angrily.

"No," I cut in, glancing fretfully to the door. "It's true, Clover. Unless..." I pause.

"He's out there, is he?" Dad says, observing me and pointing to the door. "You brought him?"

I shake my head. "He brought me. He got me in here."

Dad stares for a moment into mid-air and then starts shouting. "Ezra! Ezra! Show yourself! Your nieces want you!"

"Pearl! What's he talking about?" Clover looks at Dad like he's delirious.

"Ezra! Ezra!" he's calling. "You better go and find him," he says to me. "He was never very good at sticking around in a crisis."

Clover runs to the door and puts her head out into the corridor. "There's no one there," she says confused. And then indignantly, "What do you mean, *nieces*? What are you both talking about? You've got a secret, haven't you? What are you keeping from me?"

Dad shifts miserably in his bed.

"Pearl!" Clover demands loudly. "What's going on? Why did Dad say nieces?"

"You tell her," I say, looking at Dad. "Tell me too. Why we never knew."

Dad turns to Clover reluctantly. "Ezra Heart is your mum's brother, Clover. Your uncle." He sighs heavily at the word.

"An uncle!" Clover shrieks at the revelation. "We have a secret uncle! Pearl?" She looks to me for an explanation, but I keep my eyes on Dad.

"Why did we never see him?" I press. "Why did we never know?"

"Siblings are illegal, aren't they?" Dad shrugs.

"No!" I rage. He doesn't get off that easily, even if he did just almost die. "You know Clover and I can keep secrets. It's our secret too!"

Dad exhales again loudly, looking to the window. "You saw him the odd time, when you were small, Pearl. But things changed when your mum and I took on the oyster farm. Everyone in the bay thought we were mad to return to the sea, including Ezra. Ezra more than most! He wouldn't give us any backing, and demanded we still do our shifts on land." Dad laughs snidely. "But we showed him. We made it work. Vita was always the one with the ideas!"

"Ezra said it was Mum's idea to use the growing tower?" I say.

Dad swallows. "I tried to persuade her against it, but she couldn't let the idea go. All that space to grow food. She worked so many hours on that site, clearing it. He was the one getting the glory, but it was your mum putting in the hours, on poisoned land, making it all work. She'd seen what hunger could do and she was fixing it. Vita!"

Dad stops talking, and makes this awful sound, like he's in pain all through his body.

I perch on the edge of the bed.

He takes my hand. "When we found out Clover was on the way, we moored further out in the bay. We thought we could escape everything. Do you remember how happy we were, Pearl?" Dad stops to sigh. His hand is shaking. "But it was too late for your mum. The land and that place had done its worst and she must have brought the sickness with her. I thought I'd got her away in time, but I hadn't. I hadn't! Your uncle cut us off completely," he finishes, savagely now.

"He says he had to," I say quietly. I stare back at Dad miserably. "He had to. Because of Clover. Ezra would have had to enforce Central's rules. Send her off to the Communal Families. It was better to ignore us, he said. Better for him to pretend we didn't even exist."

Clover screws her eyes shut and wraps her arms around her knees. I put my hand on her shoulder to comfort her.

"Ezra tried a few years ago to get permission for a second

child, for one of Nat's friends, after their mum had died," I tell Dad.

"Barnaby!" Clover interjects.

I nod. "But he didn't get permission. He couldn't. Central refused and the child was sent away. Maybe if that had worked out differently."

Dad shakes his head wretchedly.

"Did Sora know?" I ask him suddenly. "About Ezra being our uncle?"

Dad bites his lip. "No. No one knew except George."

Clover draws an angry breath. "George is the reason Sora's on the ship. He blabbed about our butterflies."

Dad puts his hand out. "You can't blame George. He wouldn't have thought through what he was saying. Butterflies shouldn't be a bad thing. I might have shouted about them myself."

"I wish you could see them, Dad," Clover says, her eyes bright now.

"I'd like to see them," a voice says.

Ezra Heart is standing in the entrance to the room.

"Uncle?!" Clover says melodramatically.

"Clover!" Ezra smiles gently back at her even as he looks apprehensively for Dad's reaction.

"You know who I am?" Clover asks.

"You're the spitting image of your mum. And Pearl…" Ezra's eyes turn to me.

"I'm like my dad," I say loyally, worried Ezra will claim me as his.

Ezra laughs. "Indeed you are." He turns to Dad. "Atticus. I only just heard you were sick, or I would have gone over to the farm myself to check on the girls."

"We didn't need checking on," I cut in. "We can run the farm ourselves, Clover and me, especially now we have Nat to help."

"Why did you send Sora in the first place?" Dad asks Ezra angrily. "Why couldn't you leave us alone?"

Ezra's face clouds over with frustration. "They're my nieces, Atticus! My blood. My family. I can't go on ignoring that."

Dad huffs. "We've been all right all these years without you, haven't we, girls?"

I nod my head. Even Clover does, though she's gawping at Ezra, sizing him up for all the ways he might be like Mum.

Ezra takes another step into the room. "There's the district too. It's not safe being so reliant on the growing tower. Sora's been telling me for years now. We're growing too much, too close together. It would just take one crop disease and people would starve. Again! Surely you can see that, Atticus? Vita always thought we should use the sea too. I thought she was foolhardy all those years ago, but you've proven she was right. You feed the whole ship, for goodness' sake. Isn't it time we put all Vita's work together now, like she'd have wanted?"

Dad shakes his head slowly. "You want us to work together? After what you did to her!"

"And what was that?" Ezra cries. "You think I wanted her to die? My sister." His voice breaks as he says it. "I was clearing that tower too. Lots of people were. No one else got sick like Vita did. All these years I've blamed myself, because that's what you wanted me to do, and my loss was nothing compared to yours, but has it never occurred to you that maybe Vita was just unlucky? That we were all just spectacularly unlucky, to lose her like that?"

"Unlucky?" Dad spits. "Unlucky her brother turned against her and is stealing her legacy now."

"Stealing? Is that really what you think I'm trying to do?" Ezra exhales loudly. He raps his foot against the floor. "Listen to yourself. It's not a war, Atticus! I'm not suggesting we take over the farm; I want us to work together. If you'd opened a single one of my letters you'd know that!" Ezra looks at me for help, but I turn away.

I saw George bring the letters on the supply runs. I saw him hand them over and Dad's face go dark. *From the District Controller.* I never wanted them opened either. We didn't want the world to touch us.

Clover would have opened them if she'd seen them. Clover would have brought everything out into the open.

Dad's scowling like he's wishing he was anywhere but here.

"Dad!" Clover exclaims, tugging at his arm. "Ezra is our family! Mine and Pearl's!"

Ezra looks at her gratefully. "I thought Sora would be able to do what I couldn't," he continues, his eyes back on Dad. "You wouldn't listen to me, but I thought you might listen to Sora and see it was time to put the past behind us."

"What about her?" Dad says, looking down at Clover's hand on his arm. My beautiful illegal sister.

Ezra waves his hand in the air dismissively. "Sora wouldn't say a thing about them, nor would the boy. They've lived here long enough to know the consequences."

"And now?" Dad says. "My two girls, here on land. Two of them, clear as day. The nieces you claim to care so much about. They've been seen by a peacekeeper, Ezra!"

Clover's eyes dart across to me helplessly. "We should go back, Pearl," she says, frightened. "We should go back and never come to land again."

I shake my head slowly. I've had enough of Dad and Ezra battling about old feuds and resentments and competing over who's lost the most. None of that matters now. "No," I say loudly. "That's not fair, is it? That's not how it should be. There are butterflies in Blackwater Bay. Butterflies!"

Clover gazes at me, surprised.

"You knew there were caterpillars and you let Central take them away," I say to Ezra. "Why didn't you stop them?"

Ezra sighs heavily. "I didn't think they'd survive here. The land. The saltwater and the toxins."

I shake my head. "Don't you see? The ocean was poisoned too, but if you look at the seaweed out in the bay now it's like a whole forest! The oysters, and the fish, and the porpoises…"

"Porpoises?" Ezra interrupts. "In the bay?"

"Yes!" I say. "And all kinds of seabirds. Nat saw moths, round the lights on our platform. You're missing all of it because you're not bothering to look! None of you are!"

I'm trembling and screaming with rage at both of them. Ezra and Dad.

I hear voices out in the corridor, but no one dares come in while Ezra is here. He has all this authority and yet he's letting Central dictate the things that matter most.

I'd go back to sea and never come here again, but what about Clover and her dreams? What about Nat's friend Tally and the brother she wasn't allowed to keep?

Ezra's voice wavers. "You're just like her. Vita."

I glower. "*You* should be like her too! You're her brother! And you're District Controller. You uphold the rules and this is in the rules, isn't it? The return of pollinators? It's not just words. It has to mean something! We have to make it mean something!"

FORTY-FOUR
Pearl

The storm's completely gone now. The sea's flat and mirror-like. It's done its worst for a while and sparkles enticingly.

Clover and I lead Ezra to the boat. He's coming back with us to our farm, to see the butterflies. I thought Clover would bumble on like she did when Sora and Nat first arrived, but instead she's quiet, thoughtful.

It feels strange that Ezra – District Controller for this whole area – is the one following us down the gravel path. I notice him looking around at the shells and seaweed, the odd bits of driftwood that have washed over the storm surge barrier. Sometimes he'll open his mouth as though he wants to say something, but then he'll shut it again.

"Do you walk here often? By the sea?" I ask.

"No," he says shortly. "I should. I should have done."

I feel sad for him. Shut up in that house all these years,

missing Mum. We missed her too but we all still had each other. What must it be like to live all those years without anyone? Blaming yourself for someone's death. Hating yourself.

Maybe he's right and the land didn't poison Mum at all. Ezra survived. Plenty of people did. Sora has worked maximum shifts for years and she's alive, healthy.

Clover suddenly reaches for Ezra's hand and he looks down, surprised, and then smiles gratefully. She takes my hand as well.

"You too, Pearl," Clover says, nodding her head. "Take our uncle's hand."

I stare at her, my arms hanging limply by my side.

"Pearl!" she commands. "Hold hands. We're bound by the same tragedy. We should acknowledge it. Say a blessing for our reunion."

"Clover!" I squirm.

Ezra's eyes pass over her strangely amused, but he takes my hand anyway. His is warm and rough.

"You say the words, Pearl," Clover says.

"No, Clover!" I say, annoyed with her now, a blush of pink on my cheeks.

"But you're the best at it. Please, Pearl," she says.

I pull my hands back from them both, breaking the circle. "The wishings don't make sense out here. You need the tide. And we have to get back, to Nat,"

I say to Clover pointedly.

"Yes, Nat. Sora," Ezra says, like he's waking up from an old dream. "They don't deserve what's happened. I need to see these butterflies of yours. Gather evidence for Central District. They've been playing us long enough."

Then he glances around and back towards the salt pond, where that boy is still raking out the crystals. "But another time, we'll come here – to land again, together. I'll show you round the Uplands. So much of it was your mum's doing." His eyes are wet.

Clover looks towards me warily, waiting for me to refuse. I look at the growing tower, looming above us, and I nod at Ezra. I've hated that place for years but it was Mum's work. She was a pioneer, Sora said, and Blackwater Bay lost her just like we did. Would things have been different here too, if Mum hadn't died? Maybe Ezra would have had the strength to push back against the cruel rules from Central District. Maybe Nat and his friends would have grown up playing on the flats with me and Clover.

FORTY-FIVE
Nat

Sem sets me off on course, the butterfly book wrapped tightly in a piece of oilcloth.

"Will Olive be OK?" I ask, just before he casts me away. I can't get the sight of her out of my head, cowering under Price's threatening hand.

Sem nods his head grimly. "She's been through worse. He'll still want her for the books."

"She never even did anything wrong!" I say furiously. "And she's been here since she was younger than me, without anyone to take care of her. How can anyone think that's right?"

Sem shakes his head heavily. "None of it's been right. Ever since it started, none of it's been right."

There's an angry current rippling through him – his hatred for Benjamin Price runs deep – but there's a kind of helplessness too.

"Why don't you leave?" I ask. Sem's not like the other prisoners. He's not locked in a cell. He opens the hatch for deliveries, and with a boat he could leave this place. Slip away in the dead of night and leave Blackwater Bay far behind. It's not like there are armed guards patrolling the decks. He could have taken my boat if he'd been so inclined.

Sem indicates back over sloped shoulders to the dank interior of the ship. "Too many people want feeding," he says roughly. "And where would I go? My old home's underwater now."

"Where did you come from?" I ask.

A faraway look dances into Sem's eyes. "A town in the Netherlands. Just a small one. We were known for our windmills!" There's a glimmer of pride in his voice as he gestures vaguely over the grey water, remembering his hometown. "The sea came in the end. It rose too fast."

I blink, not wanting to hear any more of it. Seeing Benjamin Price with Olive, it feels I've seen the rotten heart of Blackwater Bay. I can't listen to more devastation.

"I should go. The girls might be back soon. Thank you for the food, and for hiding me." I pause. "If you see my mum," I say, the words coming out fast, "could you tell her? That I came for her?"

Sem puts his hand up to stop me speaking. "Things

like that, they don't do anyone any good out here. No one wants more reasons to be in trouble. That applies to those two girls too," he says deliberately, his brow furrowed, and some of his anger directed at me now. "Life for them is difficult enough."

I hear Pearl's voice in my head, dripping with anger. *A regular landlubber wouldn't get it.*

"I'm sorry," I say inadequately. "Can you tell Olive I'm sorry too? And thank her for finding me the book?"

Sem pushes me off, leaning over the water to give a hard shove, to get me as far as possible from the ship.

I row backwards for a while, through the dark water of the ship's shadow. The hundreds of tiny windows, like eyes. Tears roll down my cheeks as I move into clearer water, closer to the oyster farm. I wish I'd never even seen those caterpillars.

A shape emerges from the sea, blurred through my tears. My stomach lurches momentarily, but then a triangular fin arcs out of the water beside me. "Grey?!" I cry happily. "You came back!"

The porpoise swims away, disappointed, or scared.

Was it Grey? I don't even know.

"Clover! Pearl!" I call, stepping on to the platform and wrapping the rope around the tether pole.

My heart sinks as I realize the motorboat isn't back yet. What if they've been detained by Customs and Immigration? Or that peacekeeper got them, if she's still lurking around the bay.

I walk the length of the platform. The ropes criss-crossing the different boats are slippery with seaweed and slack. It all needs pulling back together.

The door's hanging off mine and Mum's narrowboat. The guest quarters that Clover prepared so lovingly. It feels like the storm came for me and Mum most of all. The ceiling's come in a bit and the mattresses are sodden. There are shells floating on the floor.

I won't be able to sleep in there for a while. Not that it matters, the girls won't want me here after what's happened. I wish I could stay. I've no idea what will happen to me now. You can't live at the compound without a working grown-up to do shifts for your rations and be assigned your disobedience points. Will I be sent inland, to the Communal Families? Or to the ship? I declared my crime to that peacekeeper after all. Will she come for me next?

I push past more damaged sections of the farm, to the greenhouse at the end. The remaining butterflies are at the top, settled on the panes, soaking up the sunshine. I breathe a sigh of relief. They're safe at least. If I took away one of the panels now and let them go, like Pearl said we should, the proof would fly away.

They might fly a thousand miles across the sea, to wherever they first came from.

"Nat!" a voice calls out through the farm, loud and excited. "Nat! Where are you? We came back! Nat!"

Clover flies into the room and throws her arms round me, like we've known each other for years and years, not less than the lifecycle of a butterfly.

"Clover!" I say, squeezing her tight with relief. "How's your dad?"

"He's OK! He's OK!" she says breathlessly.

"And Pearl?"

"She's right behind me. She did it, Nat! She walked on land!" Clover's voice vibrates with pride.

Pearl walks into the greenhouse, her shell necklace clacking. She's lit up in the sunlight but not like a ghost or a witch. Solid. Alive.

"You survived the land?" I say.

Pearl tosses her hair back and her eyes seek mine furtively, like she wants to communicate something. "We brought someone…" she starts to say. "There's something—"

"We have a surprise for you," Clover interrupts, clinging on to my arm excitedly. "Our own long-lost secret! Wait 'til you hear!"

"Hear what? What do you mean?" I ask, puzzled, laughing slightly at the way Clover says *secret*. Like it's fizzing up inside her.

A man steps into the greenhouse and the laughter dies on my lips. I run up to him and beat my fists against his chest. I pound my fury into him. All of it. Mum. Tally. Barnaby. Olive.

"No! Nat!" I can hear Clover saying faintly. "It's not what you think! Stop it!" She's yelling at me. "Stop! You've got to stop!"

I don't listen. I can't listen to anything except the rage inside me that's finally found its way out.

The man, Ezra, doesn't even try and defend himself. He stands and lets me pound him. Heavy punches across his chest, until finally Pearl comes up behind me and pulls me back.

"Enough, Nat," she says calmly. "Enough. He's come to see your butterflies."

FORTY-SIX
Nat

Pearl's lying on her back in the greenhouse, eyes up at the sky. The butterflies are swooping around above us. Zinging with solar energy.

Clover's hanging out of the crow's nest, our appointed lookout. Ezra's bringing Mum back from the ship. To hell with protocol, he says, he's District Controller. He said he'd fight his way in if he needed to. He took backup too. George's boat, loaded with a couple of compounders. Tally's dad volunteered to go with them, and I would have gone too, if they hadn't insisted they drop me off here on the way.

I've been back on land for a couple of days, hanging out with Lucas and Tally, cycling in the day and sleeping on Lucas's sofa at night. It was great to be with them again, but I was surprised how much I missed being at

316

sea, and the butterflies.

I should be watching with Clover in the crow's nest, but we won't have the butterflies for much longer. Once Mum's seen them, we're letting them go. The peacekeeper's report is filed, but Ezra's is too. The butterflies are captured on film and paperwork is already on its way to Central District, asking for a repeal of siege state laws in Blackwater Bay.

"What do you think Central will do?" I ask Pearl. "About the butterflies?"

"They should stick to the rules. They wrote them."

"But if they don't…" I start.

Pearl shrugs. "I don't know. Things can't go back to how they were, can they? Not now."

I shake my head firmly. "Everyone in the compound is talking about the butterflies. Even the grown-ups are tramping across the solar fields to look for more caterpillars. They're calling it a miracle."

I catch a smile shimmering on Pearl's cheeks.

"I know it wasn't a miracle really," I say.

Pearl laughs softly. "The butterflies are their own miracle." She pauses. "You always knew you had to let them go, didn't you?" Her eyes are still on the clouds, following them as they shape and reshape themselves.

"Where do you think they'll go?" I ask thoughtfully.

"Who knows? Probably just back to your windmill.

Somewhere inside them, they'll remember where they're from. It's the place their mum picked out for them to be safe. That means something."

I glance across at her. She's different since she came back from land. Taller, straighter. Her black hair is shining so hard it's almost blue, like the mussels.

She and Clover have dug out the old photos of their mum from the storm trunk and fixed them around the cabin, next to the jars of sea glass and Pearl's mermaids. There's a framed photo of Ezra too. A boy, playing on the seashore with his sister, in the shadow of the sea defences.

"Did you speak to your dad this morning?" I ask.

Pearl nods. "There was a radio call first thing." She laughs. "He never got up that early here! He wants to come home. The nurses say a couple more days. I suppose... I suppose they know what they're doing. He stayed alive."

"Your wishings worked," I say.

Pearl rolls over on to her side to face me. "It wasn't the wishings, I know that."

"I think they did something," I say. "I think everything we've done this whole time did something." I pause, thinking back to the days since I stepped off George's boat and how much has changed. It feels like I stepped from the dark into the light, almost. Or like the horizons expanded. The world opened up. Would Pearl understand any of this? I smile sideways at her. "It's like I was a different person when I came here."

"Landlubber," Pearl says quietly, smiling at me. "Your face, when you first saw me! Like you'd seen a ghost!"

"I thought I had for a moment!" I laugh, remembering that day. Most of all I remember showing Pearl and Clover the chrysalises. How I thought they were dead and I'd killed them, but then they trembled when Clover touched them.

"Your uncle says it took a child to see it. That this will be a whole new age. After the Decline and the Hunger Years, this will be new. The Recovery. Now they've got the butterflies as proof, and your ledger too. Central can't ignore all that, surely?"

Pearl grunts dismissively. "Central can ignore anything if they choose to."

I shake my head, sitting up now. "Ezra says Blackwater Bay will refuse to comply. They'll go rogue. One of the northern districts have done that."

"Ezra said that to you?" Pearl says to me, surprised. She frowns. "I think he's shy of me. I think he feels guilty."

"He should," I say fervidly. "Ignoring you all those years. Ignoring everything except those stupid rules. He'd given up, after he lost your mum. But he's changing now, isn't he? The butterflies are just part of it. Now he's got you and Clover back, and he's seen the things you're doing out here. With Mum to help him—"

Pearl shuts her eyes and puts her fingers up to her hair, holding them against her temples like she's holding her head still.

"I'm sorry," I say quickly, annoyed with myself for getting carried away. "I didn't mean to upset you…"

"I just get scared," Pearl says. "I wanted things to stay the same forever – me, Dad, Clover, the porpoises. Now everything's going to change."

I stare out at the porpoises, diving in and out of the shining water. Grey, Salt, Snort, Smile. I don't know how the girls tell them apart.

"I bet you wish we'd never come," I say gloomily. "Mum and I."

"No, I don't," Pearl says earnestly. "I did, in the beginning. I was furious at you both then. At you most of all, with your jars of creatures. But not now."

"You're not just saying that to be nice?"

"I don't care about being nice, do I?" Pearl laughs. "I was so scared of things changing, I didn't see that some things needed to change. Because Clover was lonely and Dad wasn't happy." She pauses. "Dad might have died out here, without your mum making him go to hospital. I thought the sea would save him, but maybe it wouldn't have. It didn't save my mum."

I nod quietly.

Pearl traces her fingers on the cracks of the panels.

She and Clover repaired it while I was back on land, Ezra helped them. It can be a proper greenhouse again. Clover insists she'll be able to get her hardware man to order new seeds in, like Vita did all those years ago. I bet she will too. Clover can charm anyone.

"It would have been different if Mum had lived," Pearl says. "Maybe we'd have gone to your school, tides allowing."

I smile, thinking of Pearl and Clover at our school on the mainland. I wonder who they'd have flagged with? Clover could have her pick, I bet. She'd have a flock of admirers. She could be top flagger in her year, if she wanted.

I don't know about Pearl. She'd fit in with me, Lucas and Tal. I reckon Tally would like another girl to hang out with. Someone who wouldn't pity her.

"Will you go in September?" I ask her. "To school?"

Pearl shakes her head and looks away from me. "Nah. Too much to do here." She hesitates. "But I won't mind Clover going. She's wanted it long enough."

"And I can still come here, for larking and to help with the oysters?" I ask.

Pearl pushes me gently on the arm. "Course! You've still got to learn to dive, remember? Clover won't forget that."

There's an excited shout from the crow's nest. "Nat! I can see them! Your mum! Come quickly!"

I jump to my feet and leap out of the greenhouse, flying across the ropes towards the main platform.

FORTY-SEVEN
Pearl

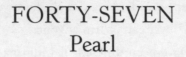

7th August
Pip and Magwitch are parents to two baby cormorants!
The babies are lighter than their parents. Brown and grey,
with a white underside. They can already dive!

"I feel nervous," Clover says. "What if they don't like me?"
She's hopping from side to side in the moonlight, her feet
barely touching the sand. An apparition in her white dress.

I roll my eyes. "Everyone likes you, Clover. *Everyone.*
You don't need to worry."

"You promise?" Clover smiles and turns three cartwheels
in a row.

"They'd better be here soon," I say fretfully. "The tide
will be coming in."

I glance down at our burning stash of driftwood.

Each piece brought in from somewhere else. Old sea defences, lost forests, collapsed houses or sunken ships. It's all lived countless lives already. I hope Nat's friends appreciate it.

Ezra says the cogs of the Communal Families system are already turning. Barnaby's been located. It's optimistic, he says. A wishing probably isn't necessary, but we decided to do one anyway, Nat, Clover and me. Clover says she believes in the wishings again. I reckon she just wants to do it with an audience since it gives her a chance to perform.

Three figures emerge from behind the storm defences. Nat in the middle, slightly ahead, with Tally on one side, taller than him, purposeful, and Lucas trailing behind, looking either side of him warily. They've all removed their shoes. Three pairs of trainers left out in a row under coils of razor wire.

"You came!" Clover cries. "You all came!"

"Course we did," Nat says, blushing slightly.

"Are you going to do the introductions then?" Tally says eagerly, poking him. "Have you gone shy?"

Clover giggles.

"I know who you are," Tally says, smiling at her. "I've seen you on your supply runs. Clover, right?"

Clover nods happily and pushes me forward proudly. "This is Pearl, my sister."

Tally smiles easily. "I'm Tally. Well, Tallulah, but you can call me Tally, or just Tal. This is Lucas," she says, pointing to the boy beside her.

"Nice to meet you both," Lucas says politely, smiling. "We've been looking forward to meeting you."

Clover does a sudden, delighted leap. Tally's stepped right up to the fire and is putting her hands out to feel its heat. "When does the magic begin?" Tally asks, turning back to us. "You've kept us up late!" Her toes curl into the sand as she speaks, her face flushing red in the firelight.

"It's better at night," Clover insists. "The magic is stronger."

Tally nods. "We need it strong. 'Cause I need him back."

Nat looks across at me nervously, as if he's worried our ceremony won't live up to how he's imagined it. Or how Tally wants it to be. Needs it to be.

I point my arms out around me. Surely Nat knows not to worry. The flats exude magic. I mean they always do, every single day, but on a night like tonight it hovers over them. You can touch it. Starlight brought right back down to earth.

Nat grins at me.

"We have to draw out a star," I say. "A pentangle."

"A five-pointed star," Lucas says knowingly.

I nod back at him as Clover starts marking it out with her foot. "It's got to be one continuous line," she says importantly. "So the magic isn't broken."

Clover's eyes keep flicking to Tally. She wants to impress her as much as Nat does.

"Did you bring the offerings?" I ask. It felt like we should use land things since the wishing is for them. Clover made sure Nat was well versed in the separate elements.

"I've got them." Tally steps forward and starts to take things out of a green bag she carries over her shoulder.

"Did you get garlands of wild flowers," Clover asks feverishly. "Bluebells and foxgloves and mallow?"

Nat rolls his eyes. "Clover! Those things don't exist any more. Not in the bay."

Clover sniffs defensively. "That's what they used in the book I'm reading!"

Tally laughs. "Nat says thistle flowers would do, and dandelions. And we found gull feathers out at Billy Crier's."

She's tied them up with orange ribbon. Two little bouquets of grey and white, and yellow and purple. She lays them down on the sand.

"Thank you," I say.

"This was from the fields," Lucas says shyly, handing a stone to me.

It's cold in my hands. Weighty. I can feel the earth on it. "It's perfect," I say.

"And this was Barn's." Tally thrusts out a spoon-shaped piece of wood. "My dad carved it for him. I thought you could burn it, for fire."

I take the wooden object from her carefully. It's got leaves engraved on the side and must have things inside. Tiny things, as it jangles softly as you shake it.

Clover sucks in a loud breath. "We can't burn your brother's rattle!"

"We don't need to burn it," I say assuredly, giving it back to Tally. "Having the fire's good enough. Keep that with you. It'll help focus your energy. You have to have your brother in your thoughts."

I don't give Tally time to react. I start sorting the different objects, to get the right placing before the sea comes in. "The stone and the flowers, they're earth," I say, moving them to the right spot. "The feathers are easy, that's air. And they can be spirit too." I pluck a single white feather out of the little bouquet.

"For Billy Crier," Nat says.

I gaze at him, surprised. "For Billy," I say.

"For Billy Crier," the others repeat together, and I think how I'll tell Olive about this tomorrow, when I go the ship. I'm going to get Nat to take me to that windmill and show me Olive's name carved out above her brother's. Maybe Olive can come too, one day.

"Do you have the sea glass?" I ask Clover, checking again over my shoulder for the tide.

Clover nods solemnly and pours the pieces on to

the sand. Seven of them. They glint like gemstones. "Water," she pronounces.

"And we have fire already," I say, dragging one of the burning pieces of driftwood to the final point of the pentangle.

When the objects are in place, I scatter a handful of salt crystals. They burn yellow when they hit the fire and we stand in a circle round the pentangle, listening to the crackle.

"Ready, yes?" Clover says, looking at me for direction.

I nod at her, and she starts walking around the fire and the pentangle, arms in the air, turning looping, flowing motions that travel through her entire body. I see Nat and Lucas gawp at each other but Tally joins in straight away, mimicking Clover's every turn. I join in too, so the boys don't have any excuse not to follow.

We could be pagans. Back way before everything. Before the Decline and the Greedy Years and everything that led up to it. There could be trees right up to the shoreline, and so many creatures swimming in the sea – whales, sharks, octopuses, squid. If I shut my eyes, I can picture it. I can almost be there.

When I feel the water on my toes, I stop. "One last thing," I say, shyly now. "I brought this. For the centre." I place the mermaid down in the pentangle. Miranda. She's painted ready. I finished her yesterday – hair, eyes, nose, mouth. Her face glows orange in the firelight.

Tally gasps. "But you can't! She's too beautiful!"

I shrug. "I'm giving her back to the sea. She's going to a new life."

"Are you sure, Pearl?" Nat asks.

I smile. "That's what the mermaids are for. A new life somewhere else."

"Can we start the chant now?" Clover says impatiently, squirming beside me. "Is it time?"

I nod, and Clover gives me the biggest, happiest grin.

"Say it with me, Pearl," she says. And we begin, as the water washes around our ankles and licks at the burning wood.

"*Mother Sea,*
Sister of the Moon,
We are your children,
Our tears are proof of it."

Thanks

I've been so lucky with the reception for *Where the World Turns Wild*, launched into the world just as COVID-19 was starting to do its worst. Huge, eternal thanks to the readers it's found so far, including the teachers, librarians, bloggers and fellow writers who have shouted about it, and sent quiet kind messages telling me how much they enjoyed it. Special mention for my Book Penpals 2019-20: Lucy Georgeson and Year 7 Book Club at The Carlton Academy, Nottingham; Andrea Brimelow and Year 5 and 6 at Dean CE School, West Cumbria; Liz Alston and Year 6 at Fosse Way Academy, Lincoln. Apart from this, I'm not listing names but only because I don't want to miss anyone out! Honestly, I've got the best readers. Thanks for taking Juniper and Bear into your hearts.

Between Sea and Sky had two first-class editors. Katie Jennings helped me dig this book up from the mud –

thanks, Katie, for your patience, insight and illumination. Then Mattie Whitehead seamlessly stepped in when Katie moved on to Oneworld. Mattie – thanks for bringing fresh light and helping make my world watertight.

Little Tiger Press have done so much to support *Where the World Turns Wild* and get a second book afloat in a pandemic. Thank you Charlie Morris, Lauren Ace, George Hanratty, Kate Newcombe, Nicola O'Connell, Sarah Shaffi and Elle Brenton-Rounding. Thank you Susila Baybars, for thoughtful and meticulous copyediting, and Leena Lane for painstaking proofreading. For this beautiful and perfectly balanced cover, thank you Kate Forrester, for once again illustrating my strange story world so exquisitely, and Pip Johnson for your clever and spirited design. I'm deeply grateful to you both.

Gillie Russell, thanks for support, kindness and weather forecasts from the Isle of Wight!

What a year 2020 was. I missed my family in Doncaster – thanks for staying in touch and always being positive. All the friends I walked with and chatted to in the street, in gardens and online – thank you. I must mention regular walking chums, Anja, Fiona, Nemone and Sarah M. Also, Roisin and Sarah T, for allotment champagne and coffee under the trees. You all helped keep me buoyant!

Bryony, Lizzy, Nabila, Nicky and Stella – thanks for being yourselves and for being my friends. Thank you Amanda, for always being so kind about my writing. My amazing book club — thanks for intelligent ideas about what makes a book work. Thank you, Swaggers, for being a continual source of wisdom, laughter and sisterhood.

To my household! Matilda, Daisy, Freddie and Beatrice — because of you I was never lonely, never without hugs, never without a reason to smile. Thank you Dom, for always being around and being my best friend. Pearl and Polly, thanks for relentless purring and cuddles. You're all my absolutely favourite company. Thank goodness!

Much gratitude to the c2c trainline for taking me to the Essex coast, for longed for horizons, sea and swims. Thanks to the Diamond Gem for a week on water with the Norfolk swans, and to all the green, and blue, spaces of my home borough of Haringey. Thank you, the books I read, the box sets I devoured, the films I escaped into.

Lastly, my thanks is always to you, reader. You're who it's all been for. I hope this takes you far out on to the mudflats, on the sunniest of days. May you find the best treasure there is.

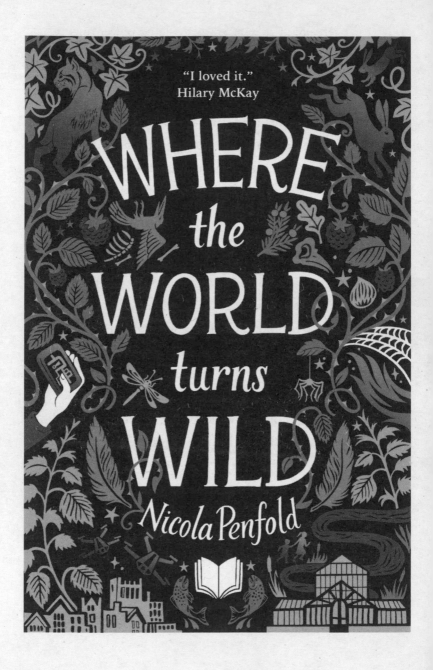

WHERE
the
WORLD
turns
WILD

Nicola Penfold

PART

I

City

1

Once upon a time, almost fifty years ago, climate change and deforestation and humans ransacking everything good and beautiful, had driven our planet to breaking point. Nature was dying – plants and trees, animals, birds, insects – new species disappeared every day. But then the ReWilders created the disease.

It was grown in a lab by their best scientists and let loose in a population of ticks – eight-legged little creatures that hide in the undergrowth.

The beauty of the disease was no animal or bird ever got sick, only humans did. Humans got so sick they died. Lots of them. And the disease was so complex, so shifting, it was impossible to treat and impossible to vaccinate against. The only way for humans to survive was to live enclosed in cities, shut away from all other living things. And that, of course, had been the ReWilders' plan all along. For in the abandoned wastelands outside the cities, nature could regrow, and it grew wilder and wilder. Wilder than ever.

It was humans or the Wild and the ReWilders chose the Wild. I would have chosen it too.

* ✱ ✱ ✱ *

The glass tank is slippery in my hands and my cheeks burn red as I walk down the corridor from Ms Endo's room. Stick insects. One of the city's few concessions. Therapy for wayward kids. For us to concentrate on, to control our out-of-control imaginations. The Sticks are the last remedy in this place.

Before you're sent to the Institute. That's the next step. The cliff edge. There's no going back from that.

There's a whisper around me. Kids in my year and Etienne too, though he's calling my real name – "Juniper! Juniper!"

They're not going to forget this in a hurry. Juniper Green, getting the Sticks. But if I concentrate hard enough I can shut them out. I can shut them all out.

I grab my bag and storm past everyone – through the door and the playground, and across the road that separates Secondary from Primary. Bear will be glad of the insects at least.

But my brother's not in the surge of bodies rushing out of his Year Two classroom. I catch the teacher's eye quizzically and she beckons me over. "I'm sorry, Juniper. He's in with Mr Abbott. You'll need to go and collect him."

I gulp and my eyes sting with held-back tears. Not Bear too.

Ms Jester looks at the tank. "Your turn for the stick insects, huh?"

She puts a hand on my shoulder. She was my teacher once. One of the good ones.

I nod vacantly and make my way down the corridor, keeping my gaze straight ahead. There are fractals on the walls either side – repeating patterns that are meant to be good for your brain. Soothing or something. Usually the fractals are OK, but today the grey geometric patterns leading to Abbott's room make my eyes hurt.

The head teacher's room is right at the top of the school – a glass observatory from where he can survey not just Primary and Secondary but the whole of the city almost. I take a deep breath, but even before I knock Abbott's voice rings out from behind the door. "Enter!"

I go in, leaving the stick insects outside so he doesn't have another reason to gloat. The Sticks are Ms Endo's thing. Abbott wouldn't allow them if he had his way. They're not meant as punishment – Ms Endo's our pastoral support worker and she's not like that – but still everyone knows. I'm on my final warning. One more slip up and I'll be sent to the Institute.

Bear's curled in a plastic chair – his eyes rimmed red, his cheeks blotchy and swollen. I rush over. "Bear! What's happened?"

"Your family is surpassing itself, June. Twice in one day," Abbott chimes, signalling an empty chair. But Bear's not going to let me disentangle myself now, so I sit on the same chair and Bear folds himself into me, his head pressed against my chest. He's shaking.

"I'm afraid it was another disruptive day for your brother," Abbott says, frowning at Bear, who's completely turned away from him, his hands over his ears.

"OK," I say, wary, stroking Bear's long dark locks. The curls the other kids rib him for.

"I've made several attempts to contact your grandmother."

"She'll be in the glasshouse. She never hears the phone in there."

Abbott glares at me – his porcelain face cracked, like the vases you get in the Emporium, the old junk store just around the corner from our block. "Then make sure she checks her messages. We have to come up with a plan. Your brother's becoming increasingly difficult to control."

Use his name, I shout silently at Abbott. It's because he hates it, the same way he hates mine. Animals, trees, flowers – our city forbids them all, so I'm always June to Abbott. Plain, ordinary June.

"What happened?" I ask instead.

"Your brother threw a chair. It could have hit another child."

"It didn't?"

"That's not the point. He's wild." Abbott leans in closer and I can smell the carbolic. It's coming right out of his pores.

"He'd like to be," I say, nervous, wishing Annie Rose was here. She wouldn't hold back. Not when it comes to Bear. Well, of course he won't sit at a table all day and be quiet. He's a child. He needs to be outside more!

Abbott looks astonished. To him any defence is just impertinence. "I think we've heard enough on that subject for one day!"

The whispered hiss of the other kids comes back to me.

It's coming up to fifty years since the city declared itself tick free and our citizenship class had been asked for essays. 'Reasons to be proud.' The best ones were to be read out before the whole of Secondary. I should have known Abbott would get involved. Get involved and twist everything around.

What was I even thinking? 'The beauty of the disease.' 'Choosing the Wild.' I gave Abbott a plate of gold when I handed in that essay.

"Bear wouldn't want to hurt anyone," I go on, quieter now. If you knew him, I think. If you could see him with the plants in our glasshouse.

"Perhaps you'd care to see a clip of him this afternoon."

"No," I say quickly. "I don't need to."

But it's already playing. On the white screen Abbott has waiting on his desk for the ritual shaming, the humiliating rerun of misdemeanours.

Bear's a different person on that screen. Like a caged animal, if we even knew what that looked like any more.

"I'd really rather not watch," I say. I can feel Bear's heart racing – fast, fast, too fast. His fingers are pale from holding them against his ears so tightly that not one decibel goes in. I want to pick him up and carry him away, but I've had enough warnings today about where rebellions lead.

I wish I could shut my eyes, like Bear has, but Abbott's gaze doesn't leave my face. He's watching my reaction. He's enjoying this.

On screen, Bear's thrown a pot of crayons across the floor – scattered them, like a broken rainbow. Ms Jester's come over, smiling, but cautiously. The other children have formed an arc. Leering around him, they're laughing, expectant.

"Why did he do that?" I ask. "Bear loves drawing. Something must have upset him."

Abbott remains silent. I can hear the chant through the speakers.

"Through the city storms an angry bear."

The on-screen Bear is bristling. If he was a bear, all the

hairs on his body would be raised.

"Shall we pick these up?" Ms Jester's saying. She's kneeling down to help him, but the chant's getting louder.

"*An angry bear*
With his long brown hair.
Send him back! Send him back!
Send him back to the forest!"

"Class, please! Quiet!" Ms Jester's begging them but Bear's already starting to shriek. Hands over his ears, he's opened his mouth as wide as he can and he's screaming.

The children explode into laughter – they're pointing and coming closer. It's not an arc any more, it's a circle and Bear's in the middle of it – screaming, lashing out.

"Please turn it off," I say to Abbott. My tears are coming now.

"This is the part, here," he says dispassionately.

That's when Bear breaks free of me. He runs out of the room and down the stairs, and I go after him, I have to, only just remembering to pick up the Sticks on my way. So I never see Bear picking up that chair. I never see whether he meant to hurt anyone. I wouldn't blame him if he had.

About the Author

Nicola Penfold was born in Billinge and grew up in Doncaster. She studied English at Cambridge University. Nicola has worked in a reference library and for a health charity, but being a writer was always the job she wanted most. *Where the World Turns Wild* was chosen as a Future Classic for the BookTrust School Library Pack, and shortlisted for several regional awards. Nicola writes in the coffee shops and green spaces of North London, where she lives with her husband, four children and two cats, and escapes when she can to wilder corners of the UK for adventures.